His gaze, uncompromising and intent, settled heavily on hers. There was something so powerful in that look—an energy that flowed into her.

Victoria shuddered with a mingling of fear and awe. Indomitable pride, intelligence and hard-bitten strength were etched into every feature of his face. His mouth was firm, with a hint of cruelty in it, there was determination in the jut of his chin and arrogance in his square jaw. It was a face that said its owner cared nothing for fools. His compelling purple-blue eyes were watchful and mocking, as though he found the world an entertaining place to be providing it did not interfere with *him*. His expression was set and she suspected he did not often smile readily.

Victoria forgot her manners and stared back for as long as she was able. She felt her cheeks grow pink, sure he'd somehow read her mind. He wasn't handsome in the classical sense, but with his shock of unruly hair as black as pitch he had the look of a pirate or a highwayman about him—or even the devil himself.

AUTHOR NOTE

I've always been a history buff, which is why I love writing Mills & Boon® Historical Romance—be it the pageantry of Elizabethan, Tudor and Stuart periods, the glittering Regency, or Victorian and Edwardian times.

MASTER OF STONEGRAVE HALL is set in my beloved home county of Yorkshire—the north Yorkshire moors, to be exact—which proved to be an interesting setting to work with.

Laurence and Victoria's journey is beset with equal measures of joy and heartache, but in the end the power of love is too strong to deny.

THE MASTER OF STONEGRAVE HALL

Helen Dickson

First published in Great Britain 2013
by Mills & Boon, an imprint of Harlequin (UK) Limited.
Harlequin (UK) Limited, Eton House, 18-24 Paradise Road,
Richmond, Surrey TW9 1SR

© Helen Dickson 2013

ISBN: 978 0 263 89854 5

Harlequin (UK) policy is to use papers that are natural, renewable and recyclable products and made from wood grown in sustainable forests. The logging and manufacturing process conform to the legal environmental regulations of the country of origin.

Printed and bound in Spain
by Blackprint CPI, Barcelona

Helen Dickson was born and lives in South Yorkshire, with her retired farm manager husband. Having moved out of the busy farmhouse where she raised their two sons, she has more time to indulge in her favourite pastimes. She enjoys being outdoors, travelling, reading and music. An incurable romantic, she writes for pleasure. It was a love of history that drove her to writing historical fiction.

Previous novels by Helen Dickson:

THE DEFIANT DEBUTANTE
ROGUE'S WIDOW, GENTLEMAN'S WIFE
TRAITOR OR TEMPTRESS
WICKED PLEASURES
  (part of *Christmas By Candlelight*)
A SCOUNDREL OF CONSEQUENCE
FORBIDDEN LORD
SCANDALOUS SECRET, DEFIANT BRIDE
FROM GOVERNESS TO SOCIETY BRIDE
MISTRESS BELOW DECK
THE BRIDE WORE SCANDAL
DESTITUTE ON HIS DOORSTEP
SEDUCING MISS LOCKWOOD
MARRYING MISS MONKTON
DIAMONDS, DECEPTION AND THE DEBUTANTE
BEAUTY IN BREECHES
MISS CAMERON'S FALL FROM GRACE
THE HOUSEMAID'S SCANDALOUS SECRET*
WHEN MARRYING A DUKE…
THE DEVIL CLAIMS A WIFE

Castonbury Park Regency mini-series

And in Mills & Boon® Historical *Undone!* eBooks:

ONE RECKLESS NIGHT

Did you know that some of these novels are also available as eBooks? Visit www.millsandboon.co.uk

Chapter One

❧∽◦∾❧

1820—Late spring

The stagecoach clattered to a halt in the inn yard in the market town of Malton in the North Riding of Yorkshire, some twenty miles equidistant from both York and Scarborough. The first of the passengers to alight, Victoria looked around for a post boy to assist her with her baggage. She would have liked to go inside the inn to partake of some refreshment, but she had another journey ahead of her and was impatient to be on her way before nightfall.

Attired in a cinnamon dress and a matching bonnet, the crisp wind flirted with the cluster of soft ringlets cascading over Victoria's shoulders and played with the hem of her skirts, while it brought a fresh flush to her cheeks.

Trim and bandbox polished, she was a most fetching sight for any man, many of whom paused after passing and openly glanced back for a second taste of her beauty.

The inn was thronged with an assortment of people going about their business and travellers, some sitting about waiting for stagecoaches to take them to their destinations. She was glad it wasn't Saturday, which was market day, being largely attended by families and farmers from the surrounding countryside, causing congestion both inside the town and the nearby roads. She managed to secure the attention of a young post boy who was hauling luggage from the back of the coach.

'Excuse me,' she said as he placed her trunks on the ground, 'I want to get to Ashcomb tonight. Is there anything going that way?'

He shook his head. 'Not today, miss. You'll have to go tomorrow—unless,' he said, glancing over his shoulder to where a horse and piled-up cart stood beneath a dusty old clock, 'you don't mind going by carrier. Tom Smith goes that way three times a week. He's to set off for Cranbeck within the next half-hour. He might give you a lift.'

'I would be most grateful. Would you see that my trunks are transferred?' she said, slipping him a coin and almost jumping out of her skin when a tinny horn blew, announcing the arrival of another stagecoach.

The lad grinned at her, slipping the coin into his pocket. 'Glad to, miss. I'll go and have a word with old Tom first.'

She was about to follow him when the arriving stagecoach was drawn to a halt. Suddenly, the door was flung open. Too late to take evasive action, it hit her and knocked her back. Stunned by the force of the blow, it was only by some miracle that she managed to remain upright. A slender young man smartly dressed in whipcord breeches and jacket accompanied by a woman stepped down. The man, fair-haired and with a lean, sunburnt face that spoke of warmer climes, clearly agitated, glanced round the door and glowered crossly at her.

'Good Lord, young lady! Have you no more sense than to walk in the path of the stage!'

'I—I realise that, but it was not all my fault,' Victoria protested, setting her bonnet straight with trembling hands.

'It most certainly was not,' the elegant young lady attired in silver grey said, coming to Victoria's aid, a deeply concerned look on her lovely face. 'Are you hurt? Can I be of assistance?'

'Thank you, but I am not hurt. The gentleman—'

'My husband.'

'Yes—he was quite right. I should not have been walking so close to the coach. But as you see the inn yard is a throng. I have just arrived in Malton myself.'

'Well, you do not appear to be hurt,' the young man said, clamping his tall hat on his head. Somewhat agitated and clearly wanting to be on his way, he peered at her intently. 'You *are* all right?' he asked impatiently.

Despite the sharp pain in her arm, which she realised she must have hurt when she had bumped into the side of the coach, and not wishing to make a fuss, she replied that she was.

'That's all right then.' He gave Victoria one final brief glance before turning his attention to his wife. 'Come along, Diana. We must get on. I see Bartlet is here with the carriage.'

'Yes, I can see he is, but you go on, I'll be along in a moment.'

Unconcerned, he strode off and did not turn to look at Victoria again.

'I'm so very sorry. Are you quite sure you are all right?' the woman called Diana asked, distraught on behalf of her husband's rudeness. 'We've been abroad and my husband is eager to get home. He—he…'

'Please, do not concern yourself,' Victoria

was quick to assure her. 'I really am quite all right—albeit a little winded.'

The lady looked anxiously at her husband's retreating figure.

Victoria smiled at her. 'You'd better go. Your husband is leaving you behind.'

'If you're sure—but can I not assist you in any way?'

Victoria saw in her eyes nothing but kindness and concern. She shook her head. 'You are very kind, but I am not hurt.'

'Well, if you're sure.'

'Perfectly, and thank you for your concern.'

Victoria watched her run across the yard in the wake of her husband. Still feeling a little shaken despite what she had told the lady, and her arm now beginning to throb, she made her way to the carrier cart, which was about to set off for the coastal town of Cranbeck.

'I'll be glad of the company,' Tom Smith the carrier said, hoisting a sack into the back. 'Mind you, I won't have time to take you all the way to Ashcomb. I have to be in Cranbeck at my sister's place by dark and not up on the moor. All kinds of miscreants travel the coast road at night. I can drop your trunks off in the morning on my way back.'

'You're quite right, Mr Smith, and I agree. It's a brave man who ventures across the moor after dark. You can drop me off at Ashcomb lane end. I can perfectly well walk to the village.'

'That's settled then,' he said handing her up onto the cart without more ado.

The arable farmland which was a feature of the Yorkshire lowland slowly gave way to moorland as the carrier's cart climbed higher. They passed through sun-filtered woods, up grassy banks and down sheltered valleys, until they reached a narrow lane that veered off to the left and the small village of Ashcomb.

'Will you be all right, miss?' Tom asked as Victoria jumped down from his cart.

Adjusting her bonnet, she smiled up at him. 'Of course I will and thank you for bringing me this far. You will bring my baggage to the cottage tomorrow on your way back, won't you, Mr Smith?'

'Aye, I'll see to it. I'd take you all the way, but I'll have to get a move on as it is.'

'I understand. I shall enjoy the walk.'

Tom tipped his cap and urged his horse on. 'Have a care how you go now.'

When he'd driven off Victoria stood for a moment to take in the view. The charm and tranquillity of the sweep of moorland, with rolling hills, folded valleys and the muted greens and browns of scrub and earth, wrapped itself around her in an endless vista and seeped into her bones. She breathed deep of the fresh tang of the sea beyond the moors. Combined with the warmth of late spring and the first petals of the season, it made a heady fragrance. Soon the heather would spring to life and, come July, these hills would be cloaked in glorious pinks and purple.

Two miles in the distance and nestling in the shelter of the surrounding hills was the sprawling village of Ashcomb. It was a quiet village in an obscure setting of moorland and fast-flowing streams, uneven red-roofed cottages and smoking chimney pots. Victoria was alive with that tingling thrill that surged through her whenever she came home. She drew in a deep breath, her heart soaring at the welcome sight, and the more she gazed, the more she wanted to avail herself of such joyous abandon and run. There was no disguising her love of this wild open land. The kind of satisfaction it gave her was not given by another but achieved from within, and with the fresh breeze on her face, she moved forwards, savouring every moment.

Ashcomb was home and she'd been away far too long. Her life at the Academy in York and the minor society events she'd attended with her friend Amelia and Mrs Fenwick, Amelia's mother, had been exciting and fun, but Ashcomb and her mother remained the loves of her life, the fiery beacon on a faraway hill that beckoned her home. Here she would settle back into the leisurely rhythm of country life.

A flash of scarlet caught her eye. Pausing a moment, she focused on it. A woman was galloping along the side of the beck that ran along the valley bottom. A gentleman mounted on a chestnut horse was way behind her, and the way he was riding he was clearly in hot pursuit. The clothes they were wearing and their splendid horses told her they were gentry—they also rode the moors with the God-given right of those whose family owned them, and rode the lower slopes with authority and arrogance.

Eager to see her mother, whose health was giving her cause for concern, with a spring in her step and carrying a small satchel, Victoria started on her way, smiling happily at the sheep that nipped the short moorland grass on the side of the road. A narrow ditch ran alongside and, nearing a part of the road where it narrowed and turned sharply, she was snatched from her preoccupation on seeing a horse and rider in scarlet habit hurtling towards her. Too late the horse was almost on top of her when with a cry and a diving action she went headlong into the ditch.

There had been rain the previous day and

the silt and grass at the bottom had become soggy. *Oh, no*, she thought in perfect horror. Momentarily paralysed and stunned, she lay there gasping. She knew she wasn't hurt—although her arm had taken another knock—but she also knew she was angry. In fact, she was furious.

Retrieving her satchel and clawing her way out of the ditch, with her bonnet hanging down her back by its ribbons, her hair in disarray and her skirts muddied, she stood at the side of the road and stared open-mouthed at the woman who had pulled her horse to a standstill. The woman gave Victoria an imperious look down her long nose and when she spoke her voice was high pitched and haughty.

'Why didn't you look where you were going?' And then on a more concerned note, she asked, 'Are you all right?'

Victoria Lewis—the product of eighteen years of careful upbringing and the product of five years at Miss Carver's Academy for young ladies in York which had, until now, produced a charming and dignified young lady—looked up at the stranger and regarded her with scathing animosity. The woman's tone—condescending, authoritative and at the same time lightly contemptuous—made Victoria's hackles rise.

'I've almost been run over by your horse,'

she fumed, quite beside herself. 'Of course I'm not all right. It is *you* who should have looked where you were going. You might have killed me.'

The girl's boldness and forceful attack infuriated the woman on the horse. Her initial concern that she might be hurt vanished. 'How dare you speak to me so!' The words were shrill, like those that might have come from a shrew.

'I dare and I do. And look at your poor horse.' Victoria pointed to the restless mount which was all a-lather. 'And look at me.' She held out her soiled skirts.

'It's your own fault. If you hadn't been wandering in the middle of the road, you wouldn't have fallen into the ditch.'

Victoria stared up into the beautiful, arrogant face above her, seeing angry grey eyes blazing in a soft-skinned face, topped by a feather-adorned high scarlet hat to match the velvet habit that had a white ruffle at the neck. The snug waist and fitted bodice enhanced the woman's voluptuous body and the abundance of her light brown hair was secured in a net at her nape. Clearly she was a woman of note, but after Victoria's run-in with the gentleman at the station and now this, she was in no mood to be browbeaten by anyone.

'Me? If you hadn't been racing your horse to death, I should not have fallen!' she retorted before she could stop herself. 'You shouldn't be allowed on the road. Do you always ride like a lunatic?'

Her face a mask of blazing indignation, the woman could scarcely believe what she was hearing. 'What? What did you say? Why, you impertinent little baggage! You will do well to watch your tongue. I swear you will pay for this insolence.' Like a flash the woman's arm went up, the riding whip with it, as she cried indignantly, 'You dare to say such things to me—to *me*!'

At this point another horse and rider appeared on the scene, a gentleman, and he couldn't believe his eyes at what followed, for he saw the girl standing in the road reach up, grab Clara's arm and wrench the whip from her grasp. Then in one swift movement she snapped it in two and flung it into the ditch.

'There, that's where it belongs. How dare you raise your hand to me! Do you make a habit of going around beating people?'

'What's going on here?' a deep, throaty voice broke in. 'Clara? What's all this about? It looks like a minor riot to me.'

The moment was brought to a halt by his mount. Restless at being pulled up when it had been in full stride, it tried to move on. Before the horse was brought under control it had made a full turn and moved closer to Victoria, who, always nervous around horses, eyed the beast warily and stepped out of the way of its hooves.

Distracted by the arrival of her companion, when Clara turned her head towards him a flush rose to her cheeks. Victoria saw her expression soften visibly and her eyes light up. Why, she thought, it was as if the gentleman had lit a candle inside her. The woman's affection for her companion was more than obvious.

'This—this girl was in the middle of the road and when I came round the corner she lost her balance and fell into the ditch,' Clara explained on a gentler note than the one she had used on Victoria, her gaze reluctant to leave her companion.

'Must you and your animal claim the whole road while lesser mortals take to the grass?' Victoria retorted, feeling that she had to remind the woman of her presence.

Clara looked at her, but addressed her companion. 'Never have I been so insulted! When I asked if she was all right the insolent girl accused me of being an idiot and a lunatic. Really! The audacity!'

'Which you are,' Victoria flared. 'I'm not

sorry for calling you those things. I could have been trampled to death, or terribly crippled.'

'I don't know who you are, but you should mind your manners, girl, if you know what's good for you. And who might you be? Well?' Clara demanded, her voice unnecessarily loud in the quiet of the countryside. 'Where do you live?'

'In Ashcomb,' Victoria replied, lifting her chin proudly and looking directly into the narrowed grey eyes. 'And there is no need to shout since my hearing is perfectly sound.'

Fixing the gentleman with her gaze, her eyes restless and pensive—the very essence of tempestuous youth—she was rendered momentarily speechless by the appearance of this scowling, masculine presence. An indescribable awe—or fascination—came over her as she stared at him. She had made a study of animals in her lessons to be able to pick out in an instant the dominant male and there was no question whatsoever that he was it.

He sat tall and lean in the saddle with strong shoulders straining at the seams of his well-cut olive-green jacket. Snuff-coloured breeches were fitted snugly about his muscular legs, which gripped the horse. His boots were brown and highly polished, and he wore no hat. There was a certain insolence in the lift of his head and in the casual way his body lounged upon his horse. Even his shadow, which stretched along the ground and almost touched her feet, seemed solid.

His gaze, uncompromising and intent, settled heavily on hers. There was something so powerful in that look, an energy that flowed into her. She shuddered with a mingling of fear and awe. Indomitable pride, intelligence and hard-bitten strength were etched into every feature of his face. He was clean shaven, his skin dark, slashed with eyebrows more accustomed to frowning than smiling. His mouth was firm with a hint of cruelty in it, determination in the jut of his chin and arrogance in his square jaw. It was a face that said its owner cared nothing for fools and in the purple-blue of his compelling eyes—the purple-blue of amethyst—silver flecks stirred dangerously like small warning lights. They were watchful and mocking as though he found the world an entertaining place to be providing it did not interfere with *him*. His expression was set with determination and she suspected he did not often smile readily.

Victoria forgot her manners and stared back for as long as she was able, suspecting he was a man diverse and complex, hard-edged and fine-tuned, with many shades to his character and much of it hidden. She felt her cheeks grow pink, sure he'd somehow read her mind. He wasn't handsome in the classical sense, but with his shock of unruly hair as black as pitch, he had the look of a pirate or a highwayman about him, or even the devil himself.

Yes, she thought, feeling her stomach roll over, she sensed a wildness about him that would surely terrify the most experienced of women. He bothered her, bothered her senses. She tried to put that thought aside.

'I see you've got yourself into a spot of trouble. Then thank God you are unharmed,' the man said. 'You *are* unhurt?'

'Yes—but look at my clothes,' Victoria said, upset that her mother would have to see her looking like this when she had so wanted to arrive home looking perfect. 'They are quite ruined.'

The man, Laurence Rockford, looked down at her with interest and a furrowed brow. Her self-possessed response startled him. She wore a knee-length pelisse which matched the dress beneath. The expression on her face was interesting—wary, challenging, confident, all at the same time. It was familiar to him, that face, but he couldn't for the life of him remember where he might have seen it before.

When she tilted her head back, his stare

homed in on her slender neck and white fichu tucked into her neckline. He was struck by a jolt of unexpected lust Victoria little realised. Her dark-brown hair with shades of mahogany, caught in a mass of ringlets, cascaded over her shoulders. It was rich and luxuriant—and in disarray, having come loose from the pins that had tried to keep them tamed, due to her tumble into the ditch. Golden strands lightened by the sun shimmered among the carefree curls. He felt an absurd temptation to get off his horse and caress the bountiful silken mane and the delicate cheekbones blooming with colour. Her features were perfect, her eyes a warm shade of amber against the thick fringe of jet-black lashes. The soft pink lips were tantalising and he could imagine them curved in laughter, but just now they were turned down and her eyes were bright, fuelled with the same fire as his haughty companion's.

Laurence's eyes passed briefly over her muddied skirts and upwards, lingering a while longer on the swell of her bosom heaving beneath her pelisse. She glared at him like a slender pillar of indignation. Two rosy flags of resentment sprung to her cheeks, for had she not suffered enough indignity for one day?

'That is unfortunate, but I am sure the mud can be washed out.' As if to dismiss her—

although he thought it would be impossible for any man to dismiss such a fetching creature as this—he looked at his companion. 'You must have gone hell for leather and taken a shortcut to get ahead of me, Clara. In my book that's cheating.'

'I'm beginning to wish I hadn't,' Clara waspishly replied, 'then I wouldn't have had the misfortune to encounter this girl.'

Victoria glowered at her in righteous indignation while the gentleman held back, one eyebrow cocked mockingly, as if he found the whole situation an amusing turn of events. But my goodness, if the woman wasn't taking the offensive by accusing her of being in the wrong! She threw back her shoulders and lifted her head, the action saying quite clearly that she was not going to be put on the defensive. 'I am no girl,' she flared. 'Have you not the decency at least to apologise to me?'

Clara's cold eyes settled on her. 'Certainly not. I wouldn't dream of it. I have nothing to apologise for.'

'Come now, ladies, the way I see it it was no one's fault—an accident, surely.' Laurence looked down at Victoria slightly disapprovingly. 'You have a temper on you, young lady. It could get you into trouble if you don't learn to curb it.'

'And she is very rude,' Clara quipped.

Rather than inspiring her silence, these words caused a fresh surge of anger to course through Victoria. 'I wouldn't call it rudeness, more like retaliation justly deserved. I don't take kindly to people raising a whip to me.' She looked directly at the gentleman. 'Sir, you should have more control over your wife.'

Clara turned to Laurence and raised one elegant and faintly satirical brow. 'Wife,' she murmured softly, her expression softening as her eyes caressed her companion's face. 'Now there's a thought.'

In a bored drawl and carefully avoiding his companion's eyes, the gentleman said, 'You are mistaken. The lady is not my wife.' And nor will she ever be, his tone seemed to imply.

And not through want of trying, Victoria thought when she saw the flash of angry frustration that leapt into the woman's eyes. She sensed the gentleman was distracted and not as caught up in the spirit of discussing marriage as the woman was. Realising her mistake, had the circumstances been different Victoria would have been mortified by her blunder, but as it was she really didn't care. When the woman's horse nudged its nose towards her she sprang back.

Amused by her nervousness, Clara laughed,

her beautiful brows rising slightly. 'Don't worry. She doesn't bite,' she said with insulting solicitude.

Victoria seethed inwardly. 'I have only your word for that. If she is anything like her mistress, I have reason to be wary. Excuse me. I must get on.'

'Are you sure you're unhurt?' the gentleman asked. He trailed a leisurely stare over her and slid her a rakish smile that caused the woman to flash him an angry glare.

Remembering that this was the second time today that a gentleman had asked her that question, Victoria held his gaze. His brilliant blue eyes were fixed on her with immense interest, as if she was worthy of close and careful study, and, at the same time, with great appreciation. Every moment seemed to shrink her further.

'Yes, perfectly all right,' she replied, briskly detaching herself from his gaze.'

'Are you heading for Ashcomb?'

'Yes—not that it's any of your affair.'

'Oh, but it is,' he said silkily.

'How is that?'

'You're on my land.'

The silence after this quiet statement was deafening.

'I see,' she said in a small, tight voice, beginning to realise who he was and feeling trapped, but trying none the less not to show it. 'You are Lord Rockford!'

If he had been astonished before, he was now thrown a little off kilter. 'You have heard of me?'

'Who in these parts has not?' Afraid that her nerve would fail her, excusing herself with a toss of her head, she walked on.

Clara watched her go before turning on Laurence. Her heart leapt in dismay on seeing the warm glow in his eyes as they followed the girl down the lane. Resentful and hurt and wishing he would look at her that way, she took refuge in anger, a fierce glint lighting her eyes. 'Why didn't you do something? I can't believe that chit broke my whip. I don't know who she is, but I swear she'll pay for it. She's an uncouth, insolent chit and wants putting in her place.'

Without moving his gaze from the figure of the girl striding along the road—her spine ramrod straight, her chin tilted high with indignation and her bonnet bouncing against her back—he said, 'For what? The whip or the damage to your pride? Don't be silly, Clara. You were about to strike her. She was only defending herself.'

Clara faced him, her face convulsed with fury as she tried to hide the anguish that rippled through her caused by his obvious interest in the girl. 'How dare you take that chit's side against me! She is nothing but an upstart.'

'Don't be foolish. Calm yourself. Don't let your temper get the better of you. You'd already run her into the ditch. I'm surprised you retaliated the way you did. Normally you would not have lowered yourself even to address such a person, let alone acknowledge her existence by attacking her.'

'On any other occasion I would have snubbed her for her boldness, but I could hardly ignore her when she fell into the ditch.'

'If you'd brought that whip down on her, you could have found yourself in grave trouble. Come—I'll ride with you to the Grange.'

Angered and hurt by his nonchalant manner, pulling hard on the bit, Clara brought the horse round and galloped off, dashing away a rogue tear that ran down her cheek.

Clara's sister Diana was married to Laurence's younger brother, Nathan, and it was Clara's burning ambition to marry Laurence Rockford now he'd returned from his travels abroad. But he treated her with little more genuine warmth than he did his servants. Nevertheless, she always eyed him with unveiled longing whenever he called at the Grange to see his brother, for, despite his cynical attitude, there was an unmistakable aura of virility about Laurence Rockford, something that was as dangerously attractive as sin, and just as wicked, that made her heart beat faster—for anyone who looked into those cynical blue eyes of his could tell there wasn't an innocent or naïve fibre in his superb, muscular body. Whether he was riding a horse or dancing at a ball, he stood out among his fellow men like a magnificent panther surrounded by harmless kittens.

It crossed Laurence's mind as Clara rode ahead of him that he hadn't asked the girl her name—one of the village girls, no doubt—and then he shrugged and went on his way.

As soon as Lord Rockford and his companion were out of sight, Victoria slowed her pace. Her nerves felt raw, her anger all-consuming. Gradually the initial shock and outrage at being spoken down to and almost beaten with a whip began to wear off. She was mortified that she had just behaved in a manner no respectable young lady should in the presence of Lord Rockford of Stonegrave Hall.

The woman, whoever she was, was a savage, stuffed full of pride. But her manner and attitude and Victoria's own volatile reaction reminded her that despite her time at the Academy and being taught that she must conduct herself with dignity, grace and refinement at all times, it was as if she'd never learnt anything at all.

Nothing had changed. She was still the daughter of a village schoolmaster and people like that woman would never let her forget it. She didn't expect to see either of them again. People like them dwelled in a world far beyond her reach and would therefore vanish from her life for ever.

Victoria entered the village and walked across the vast expanse of green covered with moorland grass. Sheep grazed freely and several villagers were going about their business. At the far end of the green was the Drover's Inn and Mr Price's blacksmith's shop. A swinging board with a trademark on it above the property next door distinguished the wheelwright's shop, and further on was Mr Waller's baker's shop and next to that the butcher's and then the village shop, which sold everything necessary for village life.

Victoria's gaze went to the building that stood back from the village, up a cobbled lane across from the church. A lump clogged the back of her throat. This was the schoolhouse where her father had taught. Upon his death,

Victoria and her mother had moved out of the schoolhouse into a cottage behind the church.

On reaching the cottage she opened the gate and walked up the short path to the door, noticing that the flower garden was overgrown and badly needed tending. She tried the door, only to find it was locked. Going to the window, she peered inside. There was no sign of her mother and there was no fire in the hearth. In fact, she was unable to see the familiar table and fireside chairs. She frowned, standing back. Perhaps Mrs Knowles across the way would know where she could find her mother.

Mrs Knowles was a widow who had always been kindly disposed to her and her mother. She was a busy, house-proud little woman who lived with her son Ned. Ned worked up at the Hall looking after the master's horses. Her mouth fell open with astonishment when she saw Victoria standing on her doorstep. Delighted to see her, she drew her inside.

'Why, just look at you. A right bonny lass you've turned out to be. Your mother will be right proud of you.'

The cottage was warm and above the smell of baking Victoria could detect the fragrance of beeswax. The wooden floor was covered with pegged rugs and two comfortable chairs were drawn up to the log fire, while a pile of neatly folded laundry and bunch of spring flowers in a copper jug stood on a gate-legged table under the window.

'I expect you want to know where your mother's gone,' Mrs Knowles said, offering her a chair by the fire and a cup of tea, which Victoria declined.

'Yes, Mrs Knowles. I thought I'd surprise her. I—I know she hasn't been well of late and I've been most anxious about her, which was why I left the Academy. I couldn't stay any longer knowing she was ill.'

'Aye, well, you're right about that. She's been right poorly ever since you went back to that Academy. I told her to write and tell you to come home to look after her, but she wouldn't hear of it.'

Victoria was mortified. Her mother had begun coughing a lot over the last twelve months. In fact, she'd had what she referred to as a ticklish cough for a number of years, but she had refused to find out the cause. Last summer it had become more persistent and she had finally succumbed to Victoria's pleading and allowed the doctor to examine her. He had confirmed that she had consumption. Resigned to the fact that the time she had left was limited, she had insisted that Victoria return to the Academy until the time when she took to her bed.

'My mother needed me. I should have been here.'

'When you went away I told you that I would look after her. I did what I could, mind, but she needed more care than I could give her.'

A feeling of sick dread began to take root in Victoria. She stared at Mrs Knowles, seeing the anguished expression in her eyes. This was serious. Her blood seemed to chill in her veins. 'She is very ill, isn't she?'

'Aye, lass, she is.'

'Then where is she? Where has she gone?'

'The master came and took her to the Hall.'

Victoria stared at her. 'The master? Lord Rockford? How extraordinary! But—I don't understand. Why would he do that?'

'Lord Rockford heard how poorly she was and thought she would be best taken care of up at the Hall. I suppose it's something to do with her being his mother's maid.'

'But that was years ago—before she married my father.'

'Be that as it may, Victoria, I reckon that when the master came up from London and heard how ill she was, he felt obliged. Nobody could have been more solicitous in seeing she was conveyed to the Hall in comfort.'

'And the cottage? When I looked in at the window it seemed empty.'

'That's because it's been made ready for the next tenant.'

The colour slowly drained from Victoria's face. 'The next tenant? Are you saying that Lord Rockford has turned us out?'

'Well—not exactly.'

'Then where are our things—our furniture?'

'They've been packed up and taken to the Hall.'

'But he can't do that. The cottage is our home.'

'Can you afford to keep it?' Mrs Knowles said gently.

'Of course. Father left us well provided for. How else could Mother have been able to afford to send me to the Academy?'

Mrs Knowles clamped her jaw shut and turned away to stir a pot on the hob. How Betty had managed to send her daughter away to be educated was her business, but Mrs Knowles knew, she had always known, that there was more to it than that. 'Well, you can see about the cottage later—when you've spoken to your mother. She's the one you should be concerned about just now.'

Victoria was silent as she absorbed what Mrs Knowles had told her, unable to believe this was happening. She thought of Lord Rockford. The details of his face remained strongly etched in her mind, along with the conviction that this man would mean something, impinge on her life in some vital way.

'You are right. I must go to her,' she said, fighting to control the wrenching anguish that was strangling her breath in her chest. She refused to think about her home just now. Her mother would explain everything. But the thought of having to face Lord Rockford again was abhorrent to her.

'It'll soon be dark and it's a long trek over the moor to the Hall. You don't want to be going up there at this time. There's no telling what might happen to a lass all by herself.'

'I have to, Mrs Knowles. If I leave now and get a move on I'll be there just after dark.'

'Nay, lass, I won't hear of it. Ned's out the back. I'll get him to take you in the trap.'

'Thank you. I'm most grateful, Mrs Knowles. It is heartening to know my mother had you. I can't thank you enough.'

'Get along with you. What are friends for if they can't help each other out in times of need? Now I'll go and get Ned. The sooner you start out the better.'

Ned didn't mind taking her to the Hall. Victoria had known him all her life and he'd never been one to indulge in idle chatter. She was content with this for she was happy to keep to her own thoughts on the journey to the Hall. She had never been inside, nor had she seen the master until today. As a child her playground had been the moors and she had often stood at the closed gates and looked at the house, never imagining that one day she would step inside and certainly not in circumstances such as these.

The old Lord Rockford had been well respected. His youngest son, Nathan, was a fun-loving man who preferred his horses and country pleasures, while the oldest son, Laurence, was reputed to be a surly, arrogant individual.

According to tales, following a broken romance some years ago, Laurence had left England and gone abroad to seek out fresh enterprises. By all accounts he had succeeded on a grand scale. It was said he owned large tracts of land in America and had a fleet of ships, with warehouses in both America and London filled with silks and spices from the east, furs from Canada and industrial machines which he sold to the woollen mills in Lancashire. His company, Rockford Enterprises, was headquartered in London. Immensely wealthy, Laurence

Rockford had become one of the most powerful men in the north of England.

When Victoria had been a small child her mother had regaled her with stories of her time at Stonegrave Hall as lady's maid to Laurence Rockford's mother, and often told her of the grand events that had been held there during the late master's time. Victoria had absorbed the stories in wide-eyed wonder, reliving the fantasies in her dreams. She didn't know what to expect when she got there, or how Lord Rockford would react when he saw her.

The sky was darkening by the time they reached the high moor, and the upper part of the Hall set behind high walls came into view. Dark and sombre and set amid acres of gardens and lawns, it was a large, forbidding structure, a gentleman's manor house, three storeys high, with Gothic turrets rising up into the sky.

Passing through the tall wrought-iron gates, Ned drove the cart up the long, straight, gravel drive, but there was no sign of life. Victoria's trepidation increased a thousandfold by the sheer size of the building. It made her feel even smaller and more insignificant than she already did. The door was opened by Mrs Hughs, the housekeeper. Victoria informed her of her identity and Mrs Hughs let her in. Once inside the Hall the warmth struck her immediately, causing her to glance towards the roaring fire set in the deep stone fireplace.

Mrs Hughs gave a sad shake of her head. As soon as the master had heard of Betty's illness, he had set the whole household agog by going to the extraordinary lengths of having her brought to the Hall.

'The master has spared neither trouble nor expense to see that your mother is taken care of. He has been goodness itself.'

'I'm sure he has and I am grateful.'

'Your mother is very ill, Miss Lewis. Indeed, she cannot rise from her bed,' she told Victoria in a quiet, sombre voice. 'I'm very sorry.'

'Please will you take me to her?'

'Of course. Come with me.'

Victoria followed her up the wide, oak staircase on to a long gallery. Everything was very stately and imposing to her. She was aware of gilt-framed pictures on the walls, graceful marble statues in niches and the richness of the Persian carpet beneath her feet, but unaccustomed to such grandeur and with her mind set on reaching her mother, she did not give them much further attention.

She was ushered along a corridor that led to the domestic quarters. After several twists and turns they entered her mother's room. It was small yet comfortable, offering a splendid view of the moors. A vase of flowers and a bowl of fruit stood on a dresser by the window.

Her mother was in bed. Her face was still beautiful. Age had faded the intensity and colours of her beauty, but not the structure. Her grey hair was long and braided and draped over her shoulder, her skin so pale it was almost translucent. Once so tall and fine, she was now all bones and her lips were blue.

Victoria knew that over the years her mother had tried her best, but she had never loved her as deeply as her father had. Her mother had rarely held her, and Victoria could not remember her coming to her room to kiss her goodnight except on the rare occasions in her childhood when she had been ill. Often when she had tried to hug her mother, she had been gently put away from her, with the words: 'Not now, Victoria, Mother is tired',' whereas her father had been more affectionate, sitting her on his knee while he read her stories and giving her bear hugs when she hurt herself. Victoria had always assumed that she was too much trouble for her mother, which was probably why she had been happy for her to go away to school.

Without her father to turn to, Victoria had taken the pain and turned it inwards and for a while she had been adrift. But now, seeing how ill her mother was, she decided to cling to those things that were wonderful about her and to ignore the insecurity, instability and anxiety that had beset her all her young life.

On opening her eyes and seeing Victoria, Betty offered a weak smile. 'Why, Victoria! Is it really you? What a lovely surprise. I was not expecting you for several weeks.'

Victoria had not cried in a long while, not since the death of her beloved father when she had been a girl. Now tears threatened and she struggled to keep them at bay. Approaching the bed, she reached out and took her mother's hand, bending over to kiss her mother's brow.

'I did not know you were so ill, Mother. Truly I didn't. Why was I not told? I would have come home immediately to take care of you.'

'I didn't want to worry you. Your time at the Academy was almost over and I knew you would soon be home. Don't look so worried, my dear,' she said, seeing her daughter's eyes bright with tears. After an awkward moment she reached up and with a slender thumb she wiped away a tear. Her eyes were soft and unafraid. 'Don't be concerned.'

'But of course I'm concerned. I don't understand why you are here—at the Hall.'

'Because I was lady's maid to the old mistress.' She smiled. 'Lord Rockford has been very kind to me. When he heard I was ill and alone in my cottage, he had me brought here where I can be looked after properly.'

Full of remorse and resentful that she was to be denied taking care of her mother when, for the first time in her life, she needed her—for was it not a daughter's duty to look after her mother?—Victoria took her hand, relieved that she did not pull away. As poorly as her mother was, she had decided not to mention the cottage. But she wanted answers and only one man could give them to her. 'I should have been here to look after you—and I would have been had you not sent me away.'

'I have told you over and over again that it was for your own good, Victoria,' she whispered, coughing. She closed her eyes, drawing a deep breath and expelling it slowly before continuing. 'You know how important your education was to your father. It was what he wanted.'

Victoria gave her a tender smile. 'While you always wanted me to be a lady.'

'Which is exactly as you've turned out. Why, look at you—a proper young lady. You make me so proud. And you've done well at the Academy. Whatever you decide to do, you have a bright future ahead of you, Victoria.'

Victoria remembered the time when she had been taken out of the village school where her father had been the headmaster and sent to the Academy in York to be shaped. *Into what?* she had asked. *A young lady*, her mother had replied.

'You cannot remain here. Will you come home now I am here to take care of you?'

'Lord Rockford is most adamant that I remain at the Hall. I am well looked after and my every need is taken care of.'

'But—Lord Rockford! I have heard he is most fearsome.'

'Do not judge the master too harshly, Victoria. There is good in everyone. Always remember that. And there's a great deal of good in him. He has shown it with his kindness to me.'

Victoria had almost forgotten her father's words as he lay dying, telling her mother not to worry, that the master would take care of her. Until today she had never given Lord Rockford a moment's thought, a man with whom she had never come into contact. She'd been too young and stricken with grief to realise that one day he'd be something more.

'You must speak to him,' Betty said. 'I know he has been looking forward to meeting you. I—would like you to stay here with me, Victoria. Lord Rockford will suggest it.'

'I see.' Victoria didn't see, not really, and she would do everything within her power to take her home. But her mother was becoming visibly weaker and her eyes were closing so she let the matter rest. She sat by her, the person who had remained the one constant throughout her life, and she told herself that if anyone deserved God on their side, it was she.

Chapter Two

It was dark when Laurence arrived home, having ridden with Clara Ellingham to the Grange, where she lived with his brother Nathan and his new wife Diana, Clara's sister. Six weeks ago they had left for France on their honeymoon. They were expected back at any time.

He crossed the hall and went into his study. After a few moments Jenkins, the butler at Stonegrave Hall, entered. He carried a salver with some correspondence that had been delivered in the master's absence and a glass of brandy, which the master always insisted on before dinner.

'Some correspondence and your brandy, sir,' he murmured diffidently as he placed both beside him on the desk.

Wordlessly, Laurence picked up the glass and took a drink.

All this was executed with the precision of a minuet, for Lord Rockford was an exacting master who demanded his estate and other business affairs ran as smoothly as a well-oiled machine. There was an authoritative, brisk, no-nonsense air about him. His sharp, distinguished good looks and bearing always demanded a second look—and, indeed, with his reputation for being an astute businessman with an inbred iron toughness, he was not a man who could be ignored.

He had always measured his own worth by how hard he worked, how many successful business transactions he could complete from the time the sun came up until it went down. His diligence was his calling card and the foundation of his fine reputation. He had built his sense of worth one step at a time.

The servants were in awe of him, regarding him as a harsh, sometimes frighteningly un-approachable deity whom they strove desperately to please.

Jenkins knew he'd been riding with Miss Ellingham, a young lady who had ambitions to be the mistress of Stonegrave Hall. But the master was having none of it. After being jilted at the altar some years earlier by a young woman in favour of a suitor with a loftier title, Lord Rockford had good reason to be cynical where women were concerned. However, he was still regarded as a tremendous matrimonial prize in high social circles.

'How is Mrs Lewis?' Laurence enquired without lifting his head.

'The same, I believe, sir. Her daughter arrived a short while ago. She is with Mrs Lewis as we speak.'

'I see.' Laurence's voice was without expression. 'Have her brought to me, will you, as soon as I have eaten.'

Victoria sat with her mother until Mrs Hughs popped her head round the door half an hour later.

'The master's home and asking to see you. He's down in the hall.'

Somewhat nervous, not wishing to keep Lord Rockford waiting, Victoria went immediately. On reaching the bottom of the stairs she stopped. A man stood in front of the fire. Within the circle of firelight he looked to her to be tall and dark. There was something else she could not put a name to. It wasn't frightening, yet it was unsettling. His dark head was slightly bent, his expression brooding as he gazed into the fire, his booted foot on the steel fender.

He'd taken off his jacket, and beneath the soft lawn shirt his muscles flexed as he raised his hand and shoved it through the side of his hair.

Power, danger and bold vitality emanated from every line of his towering physique. Thinking back to her earlier behaviour when they had met on the moor, mortified, she was contemplating fleeing back to her mother's room, but he must have sensed her presence because he turned his head and looked directly at her. Her eyes collided with his. They were focused, intently, on her, the expression she could not fathom.

'Well, well,' he said, noting that her eyes held a gravity that matched his own. The devil in him stirred and stretched, then settled to contemplate this latest challenge. 'So you are Victoria Lewis. I should have known, although you were not expected back just now.'

'I knew my mother was ill, which is why I left the Academy at the end of the Easter term. I was deeply concerned about her. I also hoped to surprise her.'

'Come and join me. I would like to take a closer look at the young woman I met earlier, who played such havoc with my companion's temper.'

Victoria complied, albeit hesitantly, and walked towards him, yet there was something in the impatient, yet formal tone which gave her a slight feeling of nervousness. Lord Rockford's dark face, stern features and gathered eyebrows gave his face a grim look. She could see there was something purposeful and inaccessible about him, and those blue eyes, which penetrated her own, were as cold and hard as newly forged steel. There was no warmth in them, no humour to soften those granite features.

Yet she felt no fear of him, only a little shyness now. A not unpleasant aroma reached her nose, a mixture of sweat, tobacco fumes and leather mixed with a distinctive smell of horseflesh.

When she stood before him he took a step towards her and before she knew what he was about to do, he put a strangely gentle finger under her chin, tilting her face so that he could see it better. He looked at it hard, seeming to scrutinise every detail, probing her eyes with his own, searching—for what? she wondered. He nodded slightly, as if he had found what he was looking for. Victoria pulled away from his hand, almost tripping in her eagerness to get free, suddenly aware of the intimacy of the moment, the nearness of his searching eyes, the touch of his hand on her skin, his strong chin, the lovely deep blue of his eyes and the warmth of his breath on her face. She moved further away from him, her cheeks touched with colour.

'Do you always subject people to such close scrutiny when you meet them, Lord Rockford?' she asked directly. 'I am not used to being looked at like that and find it extremely unsettling. Is there something wrong with my face that makes you examine it so thoroughly?'

A faint smile tugged at his lips. 'I assure you, Miss Lewis, there is nothing wrong with your face.'

'That's all right, then.'

Laurence saw no trace of the girl he had met on the moors earlier. This young woman was the personification of elegance, refinement and grace. Her loveliness was at once wild and delicate. As fine as sculptured porcelain, her face expressed a frank, lively mind and a mercurial nature, full of caprice—the sort of girl who would play her way or not at all. But as he gazed at her he was most keenly aware of her innocence. He felt the touch of her eyes, felt the hunter within him rise in response to that artless glance. Though her wide amber eyes hinted at an untapped wantonness, he could sense the youthful freshness of her spirit, a tangible force that simultaneously made him want to cast her away from him or bare his soul.

He would do neither, but he did nothing to

stem the rakish twist of his lips. 'Don't disappoint me, Miss Lewis, by acting sensibly now,' he said, his eyes agleam with a very personal challenge.

Victoria stiffened at his silken taunting, but could hardly take offence after her unacceptable behaviour earlier.

'Don't be nervous. You're not afraid of me, are you? Where is the girl whose pluck to stand up to my companion earlier won my admiration?'

Victoria mentally took a deep breath to barricade herself against the nervous jitters.

Laurence gestured to a chair by the hearth, indicating that she be seated. She did so, her every movement graceful and ladylike, even the way she crossed her ankles and tucked her dainty feet under the chair. Looking down at her, he searched the delicate features, yearning to see some evidence of the fire he had seen in the girl earlier.

'That's quite a temper you have, Miss Lewis. Miss Ellingham was still seething when I left her.'

Victoria dropped her gaze, feeling her cheeks burn with embarrassment, wishing he'd do her a favour and just forget that excruciating incident, but she seriously doubted he would.

When she looked up she found her gaze ensnared by the glittering sheen of his blue eyes.

'I would appreciate not being reminded of the incident, sir. You must think I'm the most ill-behaved female alive,' she murmured dejectedly.

'No, but I think you are undeniably the *bravest* one.'

Victoria was surprised. 'You do? Why is that, pray?'

'Because you aren't afraid of Miss Ellingham.'

'That's because I was too angry to think straight.' Her confidence began to return on being able to speak freely. 'Perhaps if I were to meet her in different circumstances, it would be a different matter.'

'Ah, but you didn't show fear, you see, and that is not a bad thing, because once Miss Ellingham realises another female is frightened of her, she uses that knowledge against her.'

Victoria's lips twitched with amusement. 'Really? You make her sound like an ogre. But you must consider I was returning home to see my mother after a considerable absence. Looking my best, I wanted to surprise her.' Standing up, she looked down and spread her arms out in a gesture to indicate her soiled skirts and sighed with dismay. 'As you see, my carefully

arranged elegance has turned into the dishevelled disarray of any village girl let loose on
the moor for the day. You saw what happened,
so I will not go into it again—only to say that
your companion lacked the manners of a lady.
I will not be browbeaten.'

'So, it is a matter of pride as well,' Laurence
observed.

'I suppose it is my greatest sin,' she confessed.

'Mine, too,' he said with a slight smile. 'It
breeds stubbornness. But it also gives us the
will to endure adversity. Did you enjoy being
at the Academy?'

'Yes, very much—although until today I
would have said they had done a very good
job on me, filing down my rough edges. Yet
when I encountered your companion, I realised
it was all wishful thinking on my part.'

'I wouldn't say that. You were provoked by
her horse toppling you into the ditch—either
that or you bewitched the beast.'

'I did no such thing and nor was Miss Ellingham's horse to blame. The reins were in
her hands. She was in control and, in my opinion, she was riding in an irresponsible manner.
Through her thoughtlessness I could have been
badly hurt.'

'You may be right. Miss Ellingham is somewhat reckless when on horseback. So, I think you were justified in anything you said. I am sorry it happened, but relieved that there was no real damage done.'

'Thank you. It is most kind of you to say so. I'm sorry it happened, too—but not for what I said to her. Miss Ellingham was arrogant and very impolite.'

Laurence chuckled softly, finding it a refreshing change to find someone who was prepared to stand up to the formidable Clara Ellingham. 'Forbearance, patience and understanding never were on the list of Miss Ellingham's strong points.'

'I am sorry if I appeared rude. I really must learn to control my temper.'

Laurence thought for a moment. So many young ladies were turned out by their mothers and governesses to a pattern—you couldn't tell one from the other. But Miss Lewis was of a turn of character that he doubted would ever conform to type.

'So, Miss Lewis, you have left the Academy for good.'

'As to that I cannot say for certain. I actually finished my education last year, but knowing my heart was set on teaching, Miss Carver, who is the head of the Academy, suggested I stayed on.'

'Is that what you want to do? Teach—like your father before you?'

'Yes. He instilled in me the importance of education, that it is only through learning that you will get that which will make you get on in the world. He taught me in my early years and was very proud of my success in class and that I inherited his interest in mathematics.'

'And you are not concerned that with all this learning you are in danger of being accused of being a bluestocking?'

'Not at all. I am not ignorant of the meaning and would not be insulted of being named as such. I have enjoyed my time at the Academy, but unlike some of the pupils, who come from wealthy families and will marry gentlemen who will be delighted to marry a clever woman, as an independent woman who will have to make her own way in the world, education is important and necessary to my future.'

'Your father would have been proud of you.'

'I would like to think so.' Victoria wondered what Lord Rockford would say if she were to tell him that her father's dedication to his profession and to making sure his only child would be able to take care of herself when the time came, was due to his wife's impassiveness and lack of involvement in both their lives, caused by her clear devotion to his own mother, her previous employer.

'I have always had the idea of following in my father's footsteps,' she went on. 'Not, of course, to go to university because ladies are not admitted, but staying on at the Academy would fit me out to be a teacher. I have my future to consider and there are few occupations appropriate for young women.'

'I suppose a position as a governess may offer intelligent young ladies a roof over their heads.'

'Exactly, and many gracious families prefer to employ a resident governess for the education of their daughters and younger sons than send them away to school.'

'I suppose it is an occupation which will keep you occupied from morn till night without a moment to be spared for frivolous pastimes with which some ladies fill their days.'

'I do not spend my days light-mindedly, sir, though I do leave myself time to do as I please.'

'Indeed? The picture I have of you is that you do not employ yourself with useless activities.'

Victoria bristled. Was he implying that he found her uninteresting and plain? 'We have only just met, sir. I cannot imagine that you have any picture of me in your mind. In fact, I fail to see how you have had the time to form any picture at all.'

'I recognise an intelligent female when I see one, Miss Lewis, and I can only extend my sincerest admiration when I do.'

'You do?' Victoria wasn't convinced.

'Indeed. My mother involved herself in improving the education of young ladies—and other charitable works. She was quite the saint, in fact.'

'I am no saint, sir. Far from it.' The mere thought of it brought a smile to her lips.

The unexpectedness of it sent a jolt through Laurence that stole his breath and robbed him momentarily of his common sense. He, Laurence Rockford, who had stared down thieves and cut-throats on the meanest streets from Europe to America, who snapped his fingers at death, found himself mesmerised and weakened in the presence of this pretty girl. How utterly absurd!

'And you are confident that you are competent in your subjects and able to impart your knowledge to others, are you, Miss Lewis?'

'I hope to achieve a certificate of qualification in further education very soon. Miss Carver has encouraged my ideas—and my mother supports my ambition.'

Drawing a deep breath, Laurence regarded

her with a steady gaze. At last they had got down to the reason why she was here at Stonegrave Hall. 'You have seen your mother?'

'Yes. She is very ill. I am grateful to you for bringing her here. I would very much like to take her home where I can take care of her myself, but I have been told the cottage has been taken from us. Is there some mistake in this?'

'No mistake. I would say your information is entirely accurate.'

'Forgive me if I appear confused and more than a little concerned, but I really do not understand what is happening. I return home to find I no longer have a home and my mother has been brought to live at the Hall. You must see that it is all most unusual and unsettling for me.'

The answer came, swift, decisive, and in distinctly harsher tones. 'It must seem that way and I realise how alarmed and upset you must have been at the time.' He gave her a narrow look. 'Do you have an aversion to staying here?'

She searched his eyes, then looked away. The anger she had felt when Mrs Knowles had told her that the cottage was being made ready for a new tenant was beginning to reassert itself. 'No—it's just…'

Laurence caught the flame that ignited in

her eyes before she turned away. His own narrowed. 'Careful, Miss Lewis. Your temper is about to resurrect itself.'

'Maybe that's because I have a streak to my nature that fiercely rebels against being ordered what to do.'

'I have a formidable temper myself,' he told her with icy calm.

Spinning her head round to look at him once more, she swallowed hard as his cold blue eyes bored into hers. It had not taken her long to throw good judgement aside and flare up at him. She must learn to control her feelings better, but with her emotions roiling all over the place it was proving difficult.

'When anything happens to my mother, do you mind telling me what I am expected to do—where I will live now my home has been taken from me? Surely you must understand my concern.'

'Of course, and I am sure your mother has taken everything into consideration.'

'She has? Will you please explain it to me?'

'I am sure your mother will do that if you ask her. I have not been made privy to her plans—and if I had it would not be my place to discuss them with you without her permission.'

'No—of course not. I'm sorry. I should have known better than to ask.' Victoria loathed herself for apologising and for being a coward. Another woman might rant and rave at him for taking it upon himself to do what he had done—or go beyond good thinking and slap his arrogant face. But she couldn't feature herself doing such a thing.

'Much as I admire your spirit, you should take special care to bite your tongue sooner,' Laurence chided. 'You will grow tired of pleading for my pardon if you do not.'

She glared at him with accusation. 'It is difficult to be silent when I find my home has been taken from me. Not only have you taken that, but my liberty as well. You have left me with nothing.'

'I disagree. Are you not comfortable here?'

'How would I know that? I have only just arrived.'

'The staff will see that you want for nothing.'

After a second's pause, during which the defensive tension in her shoulders eased slightly, she said, 'I know and I don't mean to sound ungrateful—but I would prefer to nurse my mother myself in our own home.'

'I can understand that, but you weren't here to be consulted. The decision to let the cottage go was your mother's, no one else's. Betty's condition has become progressively worse since she came here,' he said, with the familiarity of long acquaintance. 'She is far too ill to be moved. Even if you still had the cottage, the doctor would advise you against taking her back there.'

'But—when she is better…' Her words faded when she caught his look and a lump appeared in her throat. 'She's not going to get better, is she?' she said quietly.

He shook his head. 'I'm afraid not, Miss Lewis. I'm sorry.'

She nodded. 'Yes—I am, too.'

'It is her wish—and mine—that you stay at the Hall so that you can be close to her.'

'Thank you. That is very kind of you.'

Laurence gazed at her with a cautious half-smile. Either she had not heard, isolated at that Academy of hers in York, that he was the Devil incarnate, or she was too starved of male company to care. As someone who had little use for the human race, he found himself strangely moved by her shy smile.

'Nonsense,' he said on a gentler note. 'Your mother was kind to me when I was a boy. I grew very fond of her. I owe her a debt. So, would you consider my offer and remain here? I believe a room has already been made ready for you close to your mother's.'

Victoria felt as if he had just backed her into a corner from whence she could find no escape.

Why did she have this feeling of unease, that there was something not quite right about all of this? It was most unusual for an employer to show such concern for someone who had worked for his family so long ago.

'Yes, I would like to stay here. But—my bags. Mr Smith, the carrier, is to deliver them to the cottage in the morning.'

'I'll instruct Jenkins to have them brought here.' His eyes passed over her soiled skirts. 'Meanwhile I am sure Mrs Hughs will provide you with anything you might need.'

Laurence noted that she seemed to be holding her arm. He frowned. 'Is there something wrong with your arm? Did you hurt it when you fell?'

'Oh, no—it was before that—when I arrived in Malton. A rather irate gentleman opened a coach door, knocking me back into the side of it. I'm afraid my arm took the brunt.'

'Does it give you much pain?'

Absurdly flattered by his courtesy and concern and his understanding of her situation, and relieved because he didn't seem to hold an aversion to her for invading his house, Victoria shook her head. 'It's nothing. Truly.'

'All in all you've had a rotten day, haven't you, Miss Lewis?' he said softly. 'Doctor Firth is coming to check on your mother in the morning. I'll get him to take a look at it.'

'Oh, no, there's no need, really. There are no broken bones, just bruises.'

'Nevertheless it's best to be sure.'

Sensing that the interview was over, Victoria moved towards the stairs where she paused and glanced back. He was watching her. He was very attractive, she decided, but it wasn't just his good looks that drew her eyes to his profile, it was something else, something elusive that she couldn't pinpoint. Unable to stop herself, she smiled. 'Thank you. Goodnight.'

Two things hit Laurence at once. Light-hearted banter with young ladies just out of the schoolroom was completely alien to him and Victoria Lewis had a breathtaking smile. It glowed in her eyes and lit up her entire face, transforming what was already pretty into something captivating. But she was so clearly a mass of pent-up emotion. There was a tension about her, a sense of agitation. He watched her walk to the stairs and was strangely disturbed by the way she moved—like a racehorse, he thought. He had a sudden desire to see her legs. She somehow seemed to glide on them—they propelled her forwards in one smooth, easy movement, rather than in a series of steps.

He couldn't remember ever seeing a woman's face transform the way hers had when she talked about her mother. He'd seen ambitious women light up at the possibility of getting a piece of jewellery from him and give convincing performances of passionate tenderness and caring, but until tonight he'd never, ever, witnessed the real thing.

Now, at thirty years old, when he was hardened beyond recall, he'd looked at Miss Lewis and succumbed to the temptation to wonder.

'Goodnight, Miss Lewis. Sleep well.'

And so Victoria sought out her room. Not until she was in bed did she allow her mind to wander and go over the events of the day. It would seem that Stonegrave Hall was to be her home until her mother… She bit her lip to stop it trembling and pushed the thought away. She couldn't bear to think of that or what would happen to her afterwards. It was too painful and made her feel helpless.

But it was not only her situation that had rendered her helpless, but this man, the master of Stonegrave Hall, the dark and devastating Laurence Rockford. She admitted to a certain thrill on first meeting him. There was an aloof strength, a powerful charisma about him that had nothing to do with his tall, broadshouldered frame. There was something else— a feeling Victoria got when she looked at him.

This man had done all there was to do and see and all those experiences were permanently locked away—beyond any woman's reach.

That was his appeal. Like every other woman he came into contact with, Victoria wondered what it would take to get past that barricade and find the man beneath.

Sunlight streamed in through the open curtains of Victoria's room. Somewhere below, a horse's hooves clattered across the cobbled yard, disturbing Victoria's slumber. Dimly aware that she was not in her bed at the Academy, she opened her eyes, remembering her mother.

Washed and dressed, she immediately went to check on her. She was asleep, her face almost as white as the pillows on which her head rested. Not wishing to wake her, leaving the nurse Lord Rockford had employed to take care of her sewing by the fire, she found her way to the kitchen to partake of some breakfast. The house was large and comfortable. Taking a peek into some of the rooms she passed, she noted that there were many lovely pieces of furniture: gilded chairs upholstered in rich damask, with elegant sofas and walls to match, carpets into which one's feet sank and marble fireplaces with shining steel fenders.

* * *

After eating her breakfast in the kitchen, she left the house by a back door, taking a short stroll around the gardens. The air was pure, the sun shining from a clear blue sky. Here everything was fresh and clean. The lawns were extensive and two gardeners were busy in the borders. A red squirrel ran across the grass and dashed up the rough trunk of an oak, cheekily flashing its bushy tail before disappearing.

There were coach houses and stables at the back of the house; the mixture of the grey and pale-honey colour of the stone from which they and the house were built mellowed into a timeless graciousness.

She did not see the man who propped his shoulder against the window of his study, a closed and brooding expression on his face as he watched her. As if sensing his presence, she turned and looked in his direction. He turned away.

Victoria was enjoying the calm and the pleasant fresh air, yet listening with delight to a trilling blackbird, when a carriage came speeding up the drive and came to a bone-jarring halt in front of the house. A groom ran forwards and the young gentlemen tossed the reins to him and jumped down, striding purposefully up the front steps to the house.

'Good day, Mr Rockford,' Jenkins intoned as he opened the door and stepped aside.

'Is my brother at home?' Nathan Rockford asked, handing him his hat and gloves, clearly agitated about something.

'Yes, sir. You'll find him in his study.'

Nathan stalked past him and down the hall, his quick strides eloquent of his turbulent wrath as he flung open the study door and confronted the older brother he had last seen in London two months earlier. Laurence was engrossed in his ledgers at his desk. He glanced up and, seeing his brother, shoved back his chair and stood up to greet him, taller than Nathan by a head.

'Nathan! Good to see you back. How was Paris—and how is Diana?'

'Well—she is well. But I haven't come here to talk about Diana or Paris. Laurence, I cannot believe what you have done! When I got your letter I don't think you need me to tell you that I was outraged. How could you bring that—that *woman* into this house! It is not to be borne! I take it she is still here?'

'If you mean Betty, then, yes, she is.'

'Then she must leave. At once.'

He gave Laurence that beguiling look that ever since their childhood could get nearly anything he wanted out of him, but this time Laurence was unmoved. 'No,' he stated implacably, undaunted by his brother's soaring fury. 'Betty stays, Nathan.'

Victoria was passing through the hall to the stairs. Hearing raised voices coming from behind the closed door, she paused, intending to walk on, but on hearing her mother's name mentioned she became rooted to the spot. She felt a coldness seep into every pore at the words that came next. She was stung by them, as sharply as if by a hornets' nest.

A pulse drummed in Nathan's temple as he fought to control his wrath. 'Have a care, Laurence. By raking over old coals you are in danger of exposing our sordid and most intimate family linen to the scrutiny of all.'

'That won't happen.'

'And you can be sure of that, can you? I am telling you that bringing that woman here will portend no good. To allow her to remain at Stonegrave Hall is detrimental to our own well-being. If we are to avoid a public and very unsavoury scandal, she must leave. For goodness' sake, Laurence, she shouldn't be here and I strongly resent what you have done. Did you not think to consult me? Did my opinions on a matter as important as this not count?'

'Of course they did, but you weren't here.'

'And if I had been I doubt very much you would have sought my feelings on the matter. I have always respected your judgement in the past, but not this time. What in God's name made you do it?'

'You know why. I promised our mother that Betty would be taken care of should the need arise—and it did.'

'Mother's dead and this woman hasn't been inside this house for over twenty years. And if taking her in isn't bad enough, I believe you have extended your hospitality to her daughter. It beggars belief, Laurence, it really does,' he thundered, combing his fingers through his hair and pacing the carpet in frustration.

'None of this is Miss Lewis's fault. You must understand that.'

'Really! Then she must be made to understand that I don't want her here and you know damned well why.'

'I do,' Laurence retorted fiercely, 'and I'm going to find it very difficult keeping it from her whilst she lives in this house. I wish you would just tell her, Nathan, or at the very least allow me to do so.'

Nathan paled and gave his brother a desperate, beseeching look, sudden fear clouding his eyes. 'No, Laurence, I implore you not to,' he said, his voice low and hoarse with tension. 'Diana and I have just returned from our honeymoon. To have this thrust on me now is intolerable. I could not bear it—the explanations… For my sake, I beg you to keep this to ourselves.'

Laurence was silent. Seeing the tortured look in his brother's eyes he nodded. 'Yes— yes, I will.'

'Thank you. It means a lot to me. I am sure Miss Lewis is capable of taking care of her mother in her own home, where she doesn't have to hang about the Hall like a beggar or some charity case.'

'No,' Laurence said sharply. He might have agreed to keep the secret within the family to protect Nathan, but he would not turn Betty and her daughter out of the house. 'Betty is too ill to be moved. Whatever your feelings on the matter, mother and daughter are staying, Nathan, so you'll just have to get used to the idea.'

Nathan reacted to his brother's statement with withering contempt. 'I don't want to get used to it! A girl who is on a par with the kitchen maids?'

'Stop it, Nathan. She'll never be on a par in any way with the maids in the kitchen and you damned well know it—no matter how hard you try to ignore the fact by pretending she doesn't exist. She is the daughter of a schoolmaster—an academic, whose own father was a high-ranking military man. Betty is from good stock—the Nesbitts of Cumbria. The family fell on hard times and her parents died, which was the reason why Betty became a lady's maid, but they were of the class.'

'Good Lord, Laurence! We have gone into their heredity, haven't we?' Nathan retorted, his voice heavily laden with sarcasm. 'I was already aware of it.'

'I want you to know that my actions in bringing Betty to this house did not stem from a flash in the pan. I thought deeply on it.'

'And did you not consider the effect it would have on her daughter?'

'I did, but Betty has consumption and needed taking care of. She was my primary concern. I expect you to accept it.'

'You don't know what you are asking of me. I will never accept it! I may not live in this house any longer, but this is still the family home and I want her and her daughter out of it.'

'Nathan, I know you are not as heartless and unfeeling as you sound right now. At least try to imagine how Miss Lewis must be feeling—in a strange house, her mother at death's door.' When his brother remained silent and unmoved, Laurence ran out of patience. 'Damn it, Nathan! Have you forgotten how you felt when our father died? How you went to pieces? Think how she will feel when her mother dies. You are not unacquainted with death and loss—or have you forgotten the pain?'

They were facing each other now over a distance and the older brother's countenance had darkened. His lips were drawn tight and his unblinking eyes were implacable. Looking at his brother, he could see in his eyes that which must not be spoken between them, not named, not defined, for fear it would become an active, swift, deadly danger, rather than something still contained, locked away, for as long as possible.

Struggling with his emotions, Nathan stared at him hard, then abruptly turned and strode to the door where he paused and looked back at his brother. 'I will not set foot in this house until Mrs Lewis and the girl have left.'

'If you wish to take it like that, Nathan, then it is up to you. You'll always be welcome here, you know that.'

Too angry to reply, Nathan went out, leaving his older brother glowering after him. Closing the door behind him, he almost bumped into the very person who was at the heart of his fury and frustration. For a moment he was taken by surprise and shock and bewilderment—or was it fear that clouded his eyes?—but he quickly recovered.

'I don't believe it! Aren't you the girl my wife and I met in Malton yesterday?'

'Yes,' she replied tightly, his words still hammering painfully in her brain. 'The same.' Having heard quite enough, with humiliation washing over her in sickening waves, Victoria had been about to flee to her room, but now she stood her ground and looked him directly in the eyes. Unlike his brother, he was only a little taller than she was and perhaps five years older. He did not resemble his brother, his hair being fair and his features more refined. He also lacked the aura of power and authority that seemed to surround Laurence.

'I take it you are Miss Lewis?' His angular face was etched with slowly deepening shock.

'I am.'

'And by the look on your face you must have overheard what my brother and I were discussing.'

'Yes—at least, most of it.'

'In which case I won't have to repeat myself, so before you go any further you should know where you stand,' he told her coldly. 'When anything happens to your mother you will leave here. Is that understood?'

'Don't be absurd! After what I have just

heard, why would I want to remain here a minute longer than is necessary? I make my own way in life,' she said, her tone sharpening as she showed him her determination. 'I won't starve.'

'You have cheek, I'll give you that.'

'I give as good as I get, that is all.'

'Your impudence is most unappealing!'

'Oh, don't worry. Your comments don't bother me. But next time have the decency to say them to my face.'

'My brother may be acting a little soft in the head where your mother is concerned, Miss Lewis,' he said coldly, 'but as far as I am concerned you would be wise not to outstay your welcome. It is a warning.'

Victoria arched her brows. 'Welcome? It is hardly that. And as far as issuing a warning— why, it sounds like a threat to me. However, it is what I intend,' Victoria told him, equally as cold.

'Good. Then we are in agreement.'

'Absolutely. And for your information,' she said, her voice low and shaking with anger, 'I am not a beggar nor am I a charity case. My mother did not ask to come here and I most certainly did not. I do not know why Lord Rockford insisted on bringing my mother to the Hall.

One thing is certain. Had I not been away it would not have happened.'

'As long as that is clear.' Grim faced, the look of hatred in his eyes was as potent as a spoken curse. Without another word Nathan Rockford strode across the hall and out the door—but not before Victoria had seen the tortured, fractured look in his eyes.

She stared after him. It was not his reaction to her presence at the Hall that unsettled her. It was his reaction to her, as a person. It was as if she meant something to him. She had surprised him—she had more than surprised him—seeing *her* had frightened him. There was something there. Something very strange—and she had to find out what it was. It was too important to ignore.

'I'm sorry you had to hear that,' Laurence said, watching her closely, having followed his brother out of the room.

'I'm not,' she retorted, beside herself with fury. 'And before you say another word I was not eavesdropping. Your brother was assassinating my mother's character and my own in a voice that could be heard in Ashcomb. How dare he? He insulted my mother and I will not allow anyone to do that. She is the kindest, gentlest of women ever to draw breath, but that is something a man as conceited as your brother would never understand. It is your fault that this has happened. I *hate* being here and I do not stay where I am unwelcome.'

Turning on her heel, her arms rigid by her sides, her hands clasped into tight fists, she marched to the stairs and up to her room, where she began shoving things into her bags, which had been delivered to the Hall earlier. The thought of staying in this house a moment longer was anathema to her. Suddenly the door was pushed open.

Victoria glanced up. Lord Rockford's eyes touched hers—coolly arrogant, he raised his brows. Looking away, she carried on packing. 'Someone should have taught you that before entering a room you should knock.'

'Why, when the door was partly open?' Laurence said with dry mockery.

'Well-bred young ladies do not entertain gentlemen who are not their husbands in their bedchamber, but since I do not come into that category I don't suppose I count,' she retorted drily.

Laurence was aware of his own transgression in being there. He chose to ignore the issue in favour of speaking to her. He glanced at the bag and gave her an arched look. 'Going somewhere?'

'To Ashcomb,' she replied, stuffing her hairbrush into the bag.

Chapter Three

Laurence crossed to the window and perched his hip on the ledge, crossing his arms with a casualness that aggravated Victoria's temper still further. 'Why?'

'I will not stay where I am made to feel uncomfortable. I will stay with Mrs Knowles. I do not want to be here.'

'And your mother? Are you about to abandon her? Because she is certainly not well enough to be moved.'

Victoria stopped what she was doing and glowered at him. Tears pricked the backs of her eyes. Furiously she blinked them away. If she broke down and cried, he would have the mastery over her. She would not grant him that.

'Don't you *dare* try to make me feel guilty.

I would *never* abandon my mother. Can't you see that by bringing her here you have placed me in an impossible position? If you were so concerned about her, you should have sent for me. Until then Mrs Knowles would have taken care of her. As it is, your interfering has made the situation worse.'

Laurence's black brows snapped together and his eyes narrowed, but his voice was carefully controlled when he spoke. 'Interfering? You are mistaken, and before you accuse me of abducting your mother, perhaps you should take a look at yourself. You seem to forget that your education at the Academy finished last summer. Your mother has been ill for some time. Had you not returned to further your education you would have been at home to take care of her yourself instead of leaving it to others. As it was, her condition deteriorated rapidly. I had her brought to the Hall where I took full control of her care.'

His words were insulting and their meaning cut Victoria like a knife. 'Control?' she repeated acidly. She should have withered beneath his icy glare, but she was too enraged to be intimidated by him. 'My mother does not come under the category of property, Lord Rockford.'

'Now you insult me, Miss Lewis.' His words

were like a whiplash, his eyes glacial. 'I have taken your mother in and I do not need to justify my actions for doing so, not even to you—even though you are her daughter. What matters is that she is in this house under the care of my staff and I—and you, now that you have finally turned up.'

Victoria glared at him, two bright spots of colour burning on her cheeks. She refused to look away, but there was little she could say in her defence. To a certain extent he was right. Last autumn there had been signs that her mother's consumption was getting worse and she should not have left her. But her mother had encouraged her in her ambition to become a teacher, insisting she return to further her education, which she hoped would increase her prospects of eventually making a good marriage.

'Have you nothing to say for yourself?'

'What's the point? You seem to have said it all.'

'You are still going to Ashcomb?'

'Yes, not that it is any of your business. You are rude, dictatorial and I cannot abide your superior male attitude. I shall not stay here a minute longer than I have to.'

Laurence arched his brows, faint amusement

and a stirring of respect in the depths of his eyes. 'That bad?'

'Worse. You are also insufferably arrogant.'

He looked at her with condescending amusement. 'And you, Miss Lewis, with a tongue on you that would put a viper to shame, can hardly be called a paragon of perfection.'

Victoria raised her head and gave him a haughty look. 'Then that makes two of us, Lord Rockford.'

'I realise that you have been inconvenienced by all this, Miss Lewis, but taking everything into account, you must see that I have been more inconvenienced than you.'

'In which case I shall do us both a favour and remove myself from your house. I shall come here every day and sit with my mother—if that is agreeable to you—but I will not sleep under this roof another night. Not only is being under it abhorrent to me, I have no wish to be the cause of contention between you and your brother.'

'You're not.'

'You could have fooled me.'

Laurence's dark brows rose in sardonic amusement. 'And what will you tell the villagers of Ashcomb? That the master of Stonegrave Hall has turned you out?'

'No. I am not one to tittle-tattle.' She stopped

what she was doing and looked at him squarely. 'Your brother is clearly deeply upset about my mother being here. In fact, I would go so far as to say he is positively hostile towards her. Why is that?'

'It's of no consequence.'

'Not to you, maybe, but it is to me. What's the matter? Do you think it would tax my poor female brain too much to be told the truth? What aren't you telling me?'

Laurence's eyes gave nothing away. Guilt and fear made him turn away from her questing look. Cursing silently, he realised that no matter what he told her now, she was going to feel duped if—when—the truth came out. Between that and the fact that he'd kept it from her because of his promise to Nathan not to reveal the true facts that had led to Betty leaving Stonegrave Hall, she was going to hate him thoroughly when this was over.

But not as much as he hated himself.

'Nathan cannot understand why a woman who once worked for my mother has been brought here to be taken care of in her final days. The explanation is simple. My mother was extremely fond of Betty and left clear instructions that she should be taken care of should she find herself in the situation she is now in.'

'I don't believe you. It is more than that. I know it. Your brother's bitterness—and I would even go so far as to say hatred of my mother—was evident. I heard him tell you that he will not set foot in this house until she has left—which gives me reason to believe it is a serious matter indeed. He said something about exposing your sordid and most intimate family linen to scrutiny and that to avoid a public scandal my mother must leave this house. Which leads me to ask how a woman who is knocking on death's door can possibly pose such a dire threat to your family.'

'My brother was angry. He exaggerates.'

'I don't think so. I know there is something you are not telling me and I swear to you, Lord Rockford, that I will find out. Now, if you don't mind, I would like you to leave so I can finish packing my bag.'

'Forget it,' he said coldly. 'You are going nowhere.'

'I do not remember asking your permission,' Victoria retorted defiantly.

Laurence stared hard at her. He was unaccustomed to being challenged by grown men, yet here was this slip of a girl doing exactly that. At any other time he would have laughed outright at her courage, but his annoyance and irritation caused by his encounter with his brother was still too raw.

Suppressing the unprecedented urge to gentle his words, he said curtly, 'It wouldn't make any difference. I refuse to give it.'

'Then please leave me alone. I wish I'd never come here and met you. I didn't want any of this. I didn't ask for it. It has been thrust on me against my will.' She breathed as if she couldn't inhale enough air. 'Don't you understand that I don't like you?'

Laurence looked at the proud young beauty who was glaring at him like an enraged angel of retribution and realised that she was on the brink of tears. He felt a twinge of conscience, which he quickly thrust away. 'I know you don't,' he said coldly. 'And you will dislike me a good deal more before I am through.' He turned from her. In the doorway, he stopped and looked back at her, his angry gaze pinning her to the spot. 'I mean it. You are to remain here. If your mother's condition should take a turn for the worse during the night, you'll put me to the trouble of sending for you. And you might be too late. Have you not thought of that?'

On that harsh note he went out, leaving Victoria feeling wretched and thoroughly deflated. Of course he was right. The hard facts were that her mother was too ill to be moved and, if she, Victoria, were to leave the Hall, there was every chance that her mother would take a turn for the worse and she would not be with her at the end.

Sinking down on to the bed, she knew she could not leave and cursed Lord Rockford with all her might for being right. She stared blindly at the closed door for a long time, her heart palpitating with frustration. A whole array of confusing emotions washed over her: anger, humiliation and a piercing, agonising loneliness she had not felt before.

Somehow, all in one day, life had become so much more serious. After just twenty-four hours of not knowing what was happening to her, of what was expected of her, she seemed to have no choice but to live and wait passively in a stranger's house for this time to be over.

Over the following days Victoria didn't come into contact with Lord Rockford. She suspected he was not a man who let down his guard or allowed anyone behind the professionally polite screen he projected to keep everyone at a distance. Everyone around him treated him with cautiousness—like a beautiful, healthy predator, something to be admired and feared, equally.

She realised her presence at Stonegrave Hall was the subject of a good deal of gossip and speculation in the servants' hall—and she seemed to trip over a servant round every corner, there were so many. No one seemed to know how to treat her. She was neither a guest nor family, but the daughter of an old employee. But she had been educated at some posh school in York, so that made her different. However, when they realised she would be taking her meals in the kitchen or her room, and that Mrs Hughs and Jenkins were kindly disposed towards her, they accepted her presence in the house and got on with their work.

Craving some fresh air, Victoria escaped the confines of her mother's sickroom for a little while. The scent of flowers assaulted her and she drew a deep breath. She paused in a secluded area of the garden. Taking an orange out of her pocket, she sat on a stone bench and began to remove the peel, putting it into her pocket to be disposed of later. She began dividing it into segments.

The sight of her stopped Laurence in midstride as he came round a bird topiary and his eyes warmed with fascination as he gazed at her. Seated on the bench, Miss Victoria Lewis presented a very fetching picture. Her head was bent slightly as she concentrated on the task before her, providing him with a delightful view of her patrician profile with its elegant cheekbones and delicate little nose. Sunlight glinted on her rich brown hair, picking out the golden lights, turning it into a shimmering rich waterfall that tumbled over her shoulders. Long curly eyelashes cast shadows on her smooth cheeks as she caught her lower lip between her teeth, dividing her orange.

Victoria was about to bite into one of the juicy segments when she saw Lord Rockford strolling towards her. It was the first time she had seen him since his brother's visit and, recalling the angry words they had exchanged, she wondered how he would treat her. She watched him come closer, suddenly on her guard. Stealing a glance at his chiselled profile, she marvelled at the strength and pride carved into every feature on that starkly handsome face.

Standing before her, he looked down into her upturned face. Her body was tense and the translucent skin beneath her eyes was smudged with dark shadows. 'How is your mother?' he asked quietly.

Victoria was surprised by his unexpected gentleness and relieved to hear civility in his tone. 'Very ill,' she replied, relieved that his anger from their last encounter seemed to have dissipated. 'She doesn't cough as much and she sleeps a great deal. I—I don't think it will be long.'

He nodded, his expression sombre. She was upset, he could see that, and he was determined to treat her with the extra care and gentleness her situation called for. What she needed right now was all the solid strength that he could give her, not the shocking revelation of what would inevitably come later.

'I'm saddened to hear it. I am not completely heartless, Miss Lewis. I am not totally insensitive to your situation.'

'I do know that.'

His gaze swept over the garden. 'I was working in my study when I saw you come out into the garden. It's a shame to think of anything being conducted within doors on such a day as this.'

'So you thought you would come out into the garden.'

'Something like that. I wanted to apologise to you for the other day. You were upset—'

'Upset and angry—and still awaiting answers to my questions,' she interrupted, wanting to appear haughty and coldly remote—anything but miserable, for that was tantamount to weak and helpless.

Laurence glanced away to avoid the puzzlement and scrutiny in those wide eyes, finding it increasingly difficult to maintain the subterfuge and silence Nathan had imposed on him. 'After overhearing my brother's words you had every right to be angry. But I have done nothing to justify your anger. I merely wanted to make sure your mother was cared for.' He looked at her levelly. 'For this, do you honestly think I deserve your bitterness and animosity?'

Victoria's shoulders drooped. She swallowed and looked away. She felt confused and miserable, no longer entirely right, yet not completely wrong, either. 'I—I don't know what to think. I don't know what you deserve.'

To her surprise, the blue eyes watching her showed no sign that he had taken offence. Instead, Lord Rockford's long lips curved. 'Whatever it is, save it for my brother.'

'He was very angry. However, I do apologise for accusing you of interfering when you brought my mother here. I may not show it, but I am indeed grateful—and I assure you, Lord Rockford, that it is not my intention to disrupt your household.'

Those candid eyes lifted to his—searching, delving, expressing her gratitude—only made Laurence feel more than ever like a disgusting fraud. He paused, then, his smile deepening, he said, 'Thank you. I respect your frankness. I hope the servants are looking after you.'

Victoria, her gaze locked in the blue of his, felt a tingling sensation run over her skin. She blinked, then frowned. 'How thoughtful of you to ask. Yes—thank you,' she replied. 'Everyone is being very kind.'

'And you like the house?'

'Very much—but then, who would not?' she said, warm in her admiration. She lowered her eyes. An odd sensation, a ripple of awareness slid over her nerves, leaving them sensitised. It was most peculiar. She would have put it down to the touch of the breeze, but it wasn't that cold.

Beside her, Laurence raised his brows, his predator's smile in evidence. Her dress was hardly fashionable, but it hugged her contours, emphasising their softness, leaving him with an urgent longing to fill his arms with their warmth.

'Are—are you and your brother close?' she dared to ask. Looking up, he trapped her gaze.

'As close as brothers can be. Until he married Diana Ellingham and bought the Grange halfway between here and Cranbeck, he ran the estate in my absence.'

Victoria hesitated, searching his eyes. 'And now you're back you can do that yourself.'

'For now. My business is in London, which is where I'm often to be found. Either there or on board my ship bound for foreign parts.'

'It sounds exciting. What is the name of your ship?'

'I own a fleet, Miss Lewis, but I'm rather fond of *The Saracen*. It was my first vessel, you see. I'm very proud of it.'

'Aren't ships usually named after women?'

'Not in my fleet.'

'Why is that?'

'Because they are more trustworthy.'

She tilted her head to one side. 'And ladies are not.'

His reply was a world-weary crooked smile and a shake of his head.

She smiled. 'I see you're a cynic, Lord Rockford.'

'Absolutely, and I'm not about to change. Have you been to London?'

'No, but I've always wanted to go. My friend, Amelia Fenwick, is to go this summer with her parents. Her grandmother, Lady Elsworthy, lives in the north of the city. I was invited to go with them.'

'And?'

'I declined the invitation. With Mother the way she is, I couldn't possibly.'

'No, of course not. How is your arm, by the way? Better, I hope.'

'Yes, thank you, it's much better.'

'I'm glad to hear it. Come. Walk a little way with me.'

He didn't ask, he stated, Victoria noted. They walked in silence for a moment, then he stopped and looked down at the orange.

'That looks good. You were about to eat it when I interrupted you. Please, go ahead.'

For want of something to do, Victoria popped a segment into her mouth. It was juicy. The tangy sweetness erupted in her mouth and the juice ran down her chin.

Laurence stared at her mouth as she chewed it, tempted to lean closer and claim her mouth in a deep, luscious kiss, to taste the fruit's sweetness on her lips. She fumbled for her handkerchief only to find to her mortification that she didn't have one.

Laurence laughed softly. 'It looks delicious.'

She nodded and offered him a cautious smile, covering her mouth with the back of her hand in embarrassment. 'I appear to have forgotten my handkerchief.'

'Here, allow me.' He produced one of his own and, moving to stand in front of her, he gently gripped her chin with one hand, then proceeded to dab her mouth with the other.

When he was finished he dropped the hand holding the handkerchief, but the other remained. His gaze fastened on her mouth, he brushed her full soft lips with his thumb, which was as gentle as a butterfly's wings.

Victoria felt a shiver of awareness low in her belly and gazed up at him. As though he read her thoughts, he looked deep into her eyes. As their gazes connected, Victoria's voice failed her. She swallowed hard, feeling flushed and feverish all of a sudden. She could not seem to look away. She held her breath, her heart pounding. His deep-blue eyes resembled smouldering sapphires on fire as he slowly bent his head, giving her time, perhaps, to step away from him. Or scream. Or stop him.

She did neither.

They stared at each other uncertainly. Magic quivered like a plucked violin string between them. The garden seemed smaller, the sun more richly golden as it played over Victoria's wary face, caressing her soft cheeks and illuminating her eyes.

Locked in the spell of her amber, sultry eyes, Laurence could not look away. Once again, she defied his expectations. Instead of flying from him in scandalised dread like a genteel miss, she stayed where she was, an innocent temptress, all elegance and demure charm, waiting for him to do what? He found her physically desirable, but he also feared that he might find her irresistible on longer acquaintance. Her chest rose and fell in soft, rapid anticipation, her hands still holding the orange.

They were mere inches apart, their faces close, and still she did not back away. He could feel the warm, beguiling sweetness of her soft breath on his hand lingering beneath her chin—he studied every intricate twist and whorl of her glorious curls.

Laurence could not understand why this girl dazzled him. It was like looking too long into the sun's glare. She drew him to her with a power that enthralled him, overcoming his survivor's sense of caution and his will. Yet the closer he went, the more hopelessly lost he became, his senses climbing to some exalted bliss. She stood before him like some captive goddess. The sunlight played over the gold-silk embroidery of her dress. He stared at her body with a hunger that went beyond the physical. He lusted for her, but as his gaze swept back over every inch of her lovely face, her eyes whispered to him of the elevating companionship he had so long been starved of.

His conscience stirred and the memory of another time, another girl, came back to torment him. His survivor's wariness warned of a thousand dangers, yet hope danced painfully like flickering flames torturing his implacable will.

Maybe—just maybe, whispered his vulnerable heart, there was still something left inside him that was worth saving and this girl could be his salvation, someone to inspire him, someone to hold her ground no matter how loudly he roared. Someone to understand about the deepest problems that troubled his soul.

His smouldering stare took in the sight of her rapt face, so innocent, so ripe for seduction. He gazed at her beautiful, waiting mouth, so pink and soft and simply begging to be kissed. He lowered his lips to hers, but halfway there he paused, checking himself harshly, and quickly berated himself, telling himself that he was running true to form—he never could resist a beautiful woman. But Victoria Lewis in many ways was still a child—and very impressionable.

He could not take advantage of such an innocent. He had come within a whisker of kissing her, but tasting a girl who was vulnerable and soon to be traumatised by her mother's death was simply not good form. He raised his head, unable to believe he was letting the chance to kiss this delectable creature slip through his fingers.

Victoria stared at him, her head tipped back slightly, her rose lips parted. Suddenly wary and on her guard, she drew back, a stirring of anger in her heart. The silence that had fallen between them had thickness and texture. Lord Rockford's behaviour towards her was most improper—indeed, it could be described as flirtatious and not entirely honourable. She was the daughter of his mother's maid who would very soon have to earn her own living, while he was a lord, a powerful man in the world he inhabited. The gulf between them was immense and she could never be to him more than a woman in a hidden house on a back street to be visited in the dark, in secret and in shame.

She stepped back. 'No,' she said. 'Please don't do this. It is not proper and certainly not acceptable to me.'

He smiled at her gently. 'You're right. That was foolish of me. I apologise for having exceeded my place.'

'Yes, you did,' she replied primly, trying to still her quaking heart.

'I don't make a habit of trying to kiss pretty young ladies in gardens—although I have the feeling you wouldn't find it unpleasant.'

'As to that we shall never know,' she told him stiffly. 'I don't know what kind of overtures you think you're making, but I will not accept them. I think you should stop and consider my circumstances and the difference in our stations in life. If you are flirting with me, then you should know that I don't like being kissed because it amuses you. When a man kisses me, I would like for him to mean it.'

Well, damn me for a sinner, Laurence thought, amused by her chastening words. He straightened up and, looking at her hands and the leaking orange, he gave her his handkerchief, hoping to put the incident behind them. 'If you aren't going to eat that, you would be wise to wrap it in this before the juice stains your dress. You can keep it.'

Victoria looked into his eyes, into his face and, despite her harsh words of a moment before, felt a most peculiar shiver slither down her spine. She blushed and blinked, then narrowed her eyes at him, a humorous, playful glint in their depths. 'You're not, by any chance, attempting to make me feel grateful, so that I'll imagine myself in your debt?'

His brow arched, his mesmerising lips quirking at the corners. His eyes, deep blue, intent and oddly challenging held hers. 'It seems the natural place to start to undermine your defences.'

Victoria felt her nerves vibrate to the deep tone of his voice, whilst her heart turned over and her senses sharpened as she registered his words. The most extraordinary things were happening to her. She was buoyed up, excited, filled with energy and confidence and also aware of an entirely new sensation in the depths of her body—a warmth, a quickening, that reached outwards to every corner of herself, and at the same time as she wondered at it she knew precisely what it was. She struggled to regain her wits, to utter some sharp retort, but could think of nothing to say. She lowered her gaze, suddenly shy of him.

'I—I must return to my mother,' she said softly, a little smile parting her lips. 'I've been away too long as it is.'

'Of course.' He looked down at her, giving her a distracted smile, his white teeth flashing from between parted lips. 'You are a strange creature, Victoria Lewis. As pretty as an English rose, with a mind as sharp as the thorns that protect it.' He took the hand not holding the uneaten orange. 'You are,' he murmured, raising her knuckles and brushing them lightly with his lips, 'the most outrageously lovely young woman I have seen in a long time.'

Releasing her, he gently touched her cheek with the tip of his finger. But the reward that outshone any touch was his smile. It was rarely given, much anticipated and treasured. It was a light curve of the lips, an ironic smile, if not lacking in joy. But it was his and, to Victoria's surprise, she loved it.

She left him then and the steps that took her back to the house were lighter than they had been. A little smile curved her lips and her eyes were aglow as she reflected on her strange encounter. To say she wasn't affected by it was a huge understatement. It had left her confused and lightly shaken. In fact, the whole incident had been incredible for her.

Looking ahead, she saw a woman walking towards her. On recognition the smile faded from her lips and she felt a sudden irritation. The woman was Clara Ellingham.

Miss Ellingham was dressed in a coral-silk gown and a matching wide-brimmed hat, which all seemed rather overstated for an informal visit to one's neighbour, but considering her intense greed for Lord Rockford's attention, one could hardly expect a less flamboyant arrival. Possessed of the inbuilt, unshakeable assurance Victoria so admired and envied inherent in the upper class, to her annoyance Victoria knew she was creased and dishevelled, having spent most of the night and morning in her mother's room, and was therefore at a disadvantage.

Clara came to a halt. Her cold appraisal

swept over Victoria. Victoria saw an experienced woman of the world, at ease with men and determined in her goals, while Clara viewed a young, exquisitely beautiful girl barely attaining that full blossom of youth that she herself would soon be yielding.

'So it *is* you,' she remarked when she was close. 'When Nathan told me Laurence had given houseroom to the daughter of a servant who used to work for his family, I might have known it would be you. You are nothing but an ambitious schemer, a trickster who has wheedled her way into this house on some pretext or other.'

Taken wholly by surprise at the intended insult, Victoria's eyes opened wide. 'I beg your pardon?'

'Oh, it's airs and graces now, is it?' she sneered. 'I saw you just now. I saw you making up to him.' Having witnessed Laurence kissing her hand, she seethed to think this nobody shared some secret with Laurence. 'How very touching. You appear to have your feet well and truly under the table, don't you? But don't think it will last, because it won't. Nathan was right to insist that Laurence should make you leave. You have no place here. Do you hear me?'

'It's difficult not to. You have a most unladylike habit of shouting.'

'How dare you accuse *me* of being unlady-like! Don't think for one minute that Laurence is interested in you. He took you in like he would any stray—because your mother left him with little choice.'

Clara Ellingham was taunting her, but Victoria was determined not to let her get under her skin and arouse her to an expression of her personal feelings. Although she felt like she'd been felled and was frozen to a slender sliver of steel, she merely smiled and lifted her eyebrows in pretended surprise. 'Your cutting remarks are wasted. They will make no difference to the situation so you might as well save your breath.'

Clara studied her with unhidden scorn, and when she spoke her voice was low and intense. 'I know Laurence—indeed, we have known each other for many years, Miss Lewis. We are friends—*good friends*,' she informed her, placing strong emphasis on the last two words. 'We have an understanding, so I warn you to have a care. You are an attractive woman, I grant you, and living in such close proximity with each other, I can imagine Laurence might be tempted by you. When he sees something he wants, he takes it with the same dispassionate logic with which he approaches his business transactions. So if he does succumb to temptation, do not imagine for one minute it is you he wants.'

'I think you are running ahead of yourself, Miss Ellingham—and you insult both me and Lord Rockford. I am not practised in the subtle arts of conniving and scheming the way you are.'

'Think what you like, but take care. I won't forget this. You are an outsider, not of Laurence's class. You will never make yourself acceptable no matter how hard you try. I intend to be his wife and I will not let you stand in my way.'

'I am not a threat to you, Miss Ellingham. You are seeing things that do not exist.'

Clara smiled thinly. 'I hope for your sake that is so. Nathan doesn't want you here. He and Laurence have always been close. Your being at Stonegrave Hall is causing a rift between them that may never heal. What kind of game are you playing to set brother against brother in this way? If you have any conscience at all, you will leave.'

Victoria was more disturbed and disconcerted by their conversation than she cared to admit. She had been demoted abruptly from being Laurence's friend to being someone who had no business to be with him, no part of his world. 'Excuse me. You may not be aware of it, but my mother is very ill. I must get back to her.'

'Yes, go, but when she's dead make sure you leave here and don't come back. Be warned. Laurence is mine and I do not take kindly to anyone taking what is mine.'

Victoria merely raised her chin and turned away, refusing to allow this woman to provoke her. 'Goodbye, Miss Ellingham. I can't say that it has been a pleasure meeting you again.'

Despite her hostile encounter with Miss Ellingham, Victoria had left the garden with a warm feeling inside her, strangely affected by what had transpired between her and Lord Rockford and how she was beginning to see him in a different light. But as she sat by her mother's bed, alone with her thoughts, she realised it was not only an awareness of him that Lord Rockford had awakened in her, but of herself.

She burned with the memory of his lips on her fingers and the brush of his thumb on her mouth. When she closed her eyes, she could still see in every vivid detail his darkly handsome face, and mentally traced its outline with her fingertips.

Recollecting her thoughts, she was half-ashamed and vowed she must try harder to ponder the error of her ways, while struggling against her desire for the bold Lord Rockford. The train of her thoughts had begun to unnerve her. His demonstration in the garden proved he did not lack the power to rob her of her wits and better judgement. So whatever thread of connection had existed between them in the garden, she must sever it. It would be for the best.

Clara's visit took Laurence completely by surprise. Living in the same house as his brother and her sister, Clara would know of Nathan's visit and what had transpired, so Laurence was aware of what had prompted her visit. She directed several snide comments about Victoria's presence at the Hall, but she dared not challenge him outright.

'Is it not bad enough to have the mother at the Hall without having to tolerate her daughter as well?' Clara had remarked waspishly.

She eyed him provocatively, but, smiling blandly, he refused to rise to the bait and instead cut her visit short by informing her he had important matters to attend to.

Affronted by his curt dismissal, Clara left.

Laurence had made it a practice to visit Betty's room at least once a day. Victoria was always with her and Betty was nearly always asleep. Although he kept their meetings brief and impersonal, he found himself nevertheless looking forward to them. On one such occasion, he observed Victoria, sensitive to her mother's needs, rise from her chair to comfort her. He looked away—to see such deep connection between a mother and child awoke a particular grief of his own.

Laurence learned the pain of his own mother's indifference was only lying dormant—suddenly, when he was most unaware, the sight of this closeness between Betty and her daughter would open up the old wound again, piercing his fragile soul.

He slipped out of the room. Raising her head, Victoria saw him leave. Sensing his sadness, she went after him, finding him in the hall where he stood staring into the flames with a preoccupied, brooding look on his face, his hands thrust into his trouser pockets.

She hesitated, for at that moment he looked as remote and forbidding as a rock. He looked so hard and so alone. His expression was closed and guarded, his mouth a firm, unsmiling line. Then he turned and saw her standing there. He stared at her as she approached with cautious steps. As she saw the stony look in his eyes, a small corner of her heart despaired. No matter how hard she tried, she would probably never really reach him.

'I'm sorry,' she said quietly. 'I don't wish to intrude—but—when you left the room you looked upset.'

'I'm not upset. Merely beset with memories— being with you and your mother—seeing how close you are.'

'However it looks now, it hasn't always been like that. For the first time in my life, my mother needs me.'

'And your father? Did he need you?'

'Yes, he did. My parents weren't always— close,' she confessed quietly. 'There were times when my mother was so preoccupied with her private thoughts that he often wondered if he existed for her at all. He pretended not to notice, but I know it hurt him dreadfully. His work and I were his purpose in life and both of us were happy.'

'He was lucky.' He turned his head to stare into the flames. 'He had you.'

Victoria watched him, her heart aching, sensing all had not been well between Lord Rockford and his father. She moved to stand beside him. 'Your father had you and your brother,' she said softly. 'Do you resemble either of your parents?'

Whenever anyone else asked about his parents, Laurence changed the subject, but Victoria asked about them in a manner that didn't feel like prying. He believed dwelling on the past and revisiting the pain would make his sorrow worse. Today, with Victoria, he wanted to share it.

'No, I look like my paternal grandfather. Both my parents were fair.'

'Then your brother must take after them.'

He nudged a log further into the fire with the toe of his boot. 'He resembled our father. Nathan was a gentle boy. He looked like an angel. No one could resist him.'

'You said you looked like your grandfather. Are you like him in other ways?'

He shook his head. 'No, thankfully not. He lived a profligate life—reckless, a gambler and a womaniser. He lived each day of his life as if he were indestructible and accountable to no one. He and my father didn't get on. Because I looked like him, my father thought I was in danger of turning out like him.'

'But you haven't,' Victoria said quietly.

He shook his head, his face hardening, and his tone when he spoke was bitter. 'No, and he worked me so damned hard to make sure I didn't.'

Having no wish to pry into his private thoughts, Victoria excused herself and turned away.

'Miss Lewis.' Pausing, she looked back at him. 'Dine with me tonight,' he said suddenly.

His invitation took Victoria completely by surprise. 'Why—I—I don't think that would be appropriate…'

'Please. Some company would be nice.'

'Then—yes, yes, thank you. That is—if I am able to leave my mother.'

Laurence watched her go. He couldn't ignore her, although he was sorely tempted to try, because she was forcing him to recognise and reflect on all the things he had missed in his life and the things that were going to be lacking for all time.

Why couldn't he stop thinking about her? And yet who could blame him? There was something about her, a beauty not just of her face, but in her heart and soul. It shone from her and when he looked at her he recognised it. She was completely unaware of it, of her loveliness, of the glow that shone from her and that was what was so special about her.

For the rest of the day Laurence avoided all thoughts of her as he immersed himself in his work, but as his valet laid out his clothes for the evening, he found himself looking forward to dining with his house guest more than he could remember anticipating a meal in a long time.

Betty's condition took a turn for the worse. After a particular severe bout of coughing that left her struggling for breath, she opened her eyes and stared at Victoria for a long moment, drawing her into focus.

'Victoria—there—is something I must tell you...' She needed to pause frequently for breath. Her speech was halting. Her physical collapse was making everything difficult for her.

'Not now, Mother,' Victoria said gently, taking her hand. 'You are very ill. You must rest.'

'No, there is something you should know...' Her head fell back against the pillows, her eyes closed and her lashes glistening with tears. Victoria held her restless hands and stooped to kiss her hot forehead.

'Does it have something to do with my father?'

She shook her head.

'Then anything else is not important. Now take your laudanum and sleep.' She fed her the medicine from a spoon, gently wiping her blood-spattered lips.

'But I must tell you...' Betty's voice was

very weak—it pulled from her in a raspy whisper. 'I—am afraid of what others might tell you. Don't think bad things of me—I was so in love…'

'Yes, Mother. I know. And my father loved you dearly.'

Betty's eyes met her daughter's. 'No, Victoria—not with your dear, sweet father—always so patient—so understanding. He deserved better than me. All these years—oh, such a terrible secret.' She suddenly opened her eyes wide and clutched Victoria with both hands. 'I have to tell you.'

'Please don't do this now.'

'But—the old master—he—he… He and I…I did the worst thing a woman can do.'

Victoria tilted a brow in confusion. Was her mother yielding to delusions? What had old Lord Rockford to do with her mother? A bad feeling began to stir. 'Not you, Mother. You are not a bad person.'

Betty took in a deep breath. 'I never meant to hurt anyone—I never got to say goodbye… I must explain—tell you about him—your… your… You have to know.' She gasped. Her eyes were wild with fear as she grappled with the reality of leaving this world.

'Goodbye? What must I know? I don't understand,' Victoria said in urgency. Her mother's eyes seemed to look past her, into the distance, as though she were reliving a memory.

'Such love and devotion you cannot imagine,' Betty whispered, desperately trying to get the words out before she ran out of breath. 'What we had was our grand passion, a doomed affair filled with exquisite joy and destined to end in heartbreak. Until I saw him I had always felt nothing. And then I came alive for the first time in my life.'

Victoria stroked her burning cheek in an attempt to calm her. 'Mother, you must not worry. When you wake we will talk, but not now. You are exhausted.'

'But…I must beg your forgiveness.'

'You do not have to ask for my forgiveness—not for anything. You have it always.'

'But there is something you should know—that you have a right to know, I—'

'Later. First you must sleep.' She placed a finger on her mother's lips before she could argue. 'Hush. Later,' Victoria soothed, seeing the laudanum was beginning to take effect. Her mother winced. 'Is the pain very bad?'

'The pain is nothing compared with worrying about you.' She was half-lucid, half-drifting in and out of sleep. 'I am sorry, Victoria—it is almost over.' Her chest rose and fell and, with one last effort, she whispered, 'I didn't want you to wear black before you wore white. Lord Rockford is a good man. Listen to him—do as he says. He has promised to look after you... you will be safe and loved... No money... You are clever... Promise me...' The voice was exhausted, so faint it was scarcely there.

'Go to sleep,' Victoria whispered. 'We will speak of this later.'

Reassured, closing her eyes her mother relaxed and sighed deeply, still holding her daughter's hand, but with a lighter, less agitated grip.

Victoria looked down at her, feeling mortified as she pressed her mother's hand to her lips. Her mother had given her a brief insight into a deeply private corner of her life and Victoria wished she had not. From the stories her mother had told her of her years at Stonegrave Hall, she had always accepted there had been a special bond between her and the Rockfords.

Yet had she realised how special?

As she sifted through her racing emotions, she began to realise she had not. That somewhere, in a deep place she never acknowledged, she had always known her mother was close to the Rockfords in a way that could not be explained. Victoria had no knowledge to support the thought. A memory stirred of her mother telling her in a soft voice of the beautiful Lady Rockford and the handsome lord—like a fairy-tale prince, she had said.

But this was no fairy tale. It was reality.

It was true that her mother had loved Lord Rockford.

This new knowledge, together with memories of the years her mother had spent as the wife of a schoolmaster, revealed a woman who had learned to endure and prevail over the greatest of obstacles. Here at last was the reason for that haunted, almost lost expression so often to be seen in her mother's eyes, for the sad smile and the quiet resignation with which she bore her lot.

It was both strange and hurtful to think that her mother had once loved and hoped and dreamed before she had wed her father. But she didn't wish to think about the wantonness of her mother's actions. All she knew was that she was the one person she had trusted to love her without reserve, and she had not. And yet, despite the love she had withheld as a mother, Victoria could not fault her for anything, nor could she blame her or judge her. She did not have the right to do that.

Her father's face came to mind and she remembered his laugh. It had been a happy, spontaneous laugh that was so contagious it made the most restrained of people smile. He had made her feel comfortable and nurtured and she had loved him dearly.

Chapter Four

Victoria walked into the luxurious dining room, taken aback by the splendour. The chandelier and the candelabra glowed, burnishing the gilding throughout the room and gleaming upon the fine silver and exquisite painted china. Her rich brown hair tumbling over her shoulders and framing her lovely face made her look like an exotic *ingénue*. She wore a soft, deep-rose-coloured dress with a square neckline that just managed to call attention to the tops of her firm breasts and accent her narrow waist.

Laurence would have been surprised to know how Victoria had agonised over joining him for dinner—and even more about what to wear, for this was the first time she had been invited to dine with a gentleman alone and she could visualise Miss Carver's frown of disapproval that she had decided to do so. But with circumstances as they were, propriety seemed like a petty irrelevance.

Shyly avoiding his frankly admiring gaze, Victoria nodded graciously at the two aloof-looking footmen standing to attention near the mahogany sideboard containing platters of food, complimented the silver bowls of delicate spring flowers on the table, then slid into the chair that Lord Rockford held for her before he walked round the table to his own.

'You look extremely lovely,' he said, his eyes warm and appraising.

Victoria blushed. Never had she felt so self-conscious in her life. She felt a sudden quickening within, as if something came to life. Something was happening, something rather golden, and when she spoke, she could only stammer, 'Th-thank you. The dress isn't new, but it is the best I have.'

'The gown becomes you, but it is not nearly as lovely as the woman wearing it,' Laurence replied, and when she looked down as if she were truly embarrassed by his remark, he reminded himself very firmly that he had not invited her to dine with him to seduce her, and that considering the circumstances, it was an inappropriate time to evoke thoughts of a soft bed and swelling breasts to fill his hands.

In view of that he turned his thoughts to safer issues and enquired after her mother.

'She is sleeping—very deeply. The nurse is with her, but I must not leave her for too long.'

'No, of course not, but I am sure the nurse will send for you if you are needed.' A flick of his eyes told the footmen to serve the wine and the meal.

Victoria declined the wine the footman would have poured her in order to keep a clear head for the night to come. Throughout the delicious courses they spoke of inconsequential matters. Afterwards, when the footmen retired, they sat across from one another by the fireside, Laurence drinking an after-dinner brandy and Victoria her coffee.

They fell silent, each preoccupied with their own thoughts and content to listen to the wind that had risen and was buffeting the great house on the high moor. Seated thus, Victoria felt a strange sense of security she had not felt in a long time.

'Thank you for inviting me to dine with you,' she said softly. 'The food was delicious.'

'I'm glad you enjoyed it. You seem more relaxed.'

'That is how I feel—just now.'

He watched the youthful, graceful line of her neck at the back of which her hair fell, soft and shining. He saw the sensitiveness of her small hands folded in her lap and the dark sweep of her long, curling eyelashes against her flushed cheeks. 'You have spirit and courage, Miss Lewis. I commend that. In fact, you are a complete contradiction in terms and appearance.'

'A contradiction?' she queried, looking slightly bewildered.

'I already know that you are direct and intelligent—and quite lovely. I saw that when I first met you on the moor. You give me the impression of being rather delicate and extremely vulnerable, yet I believe you are both strong and determined—and more than a little obstinate. I suspect you are not always the easiest person to get along with.'

Encouraged and warmed by his words, she tilted her head to one side, a slow smile tempting her lips. 'I have my moments,' she told him. 'I should hate to be predictable. And speaking of someone who is difficult, I encountered Miss Ellingham when I left you in the garden the other day.'

'I take it your opinion of Miss Ellingham remains unchanged.'

'I have the same opinion of her as she has for me. She—doesn't like me.'

He grinned. 'Miss Ellingham doesn't like anyone she might consider a threat.'

Victoria cast him a sharp look. 'I cannot see that I pose any threat to her.'

He lifted a dark brow and a smile quirked his lips. 'Believe me, Miss Lewis, from where I'm sitting, I can.'

There was a soft, caressing note in his voice that had the power to make a feral cat lie down and purr. Victoria looked at him and smiled, enjoying the warmth and the intimacy of their conversation though she knew she shouldn't.

With a mixture of languor and self-assurance, Laurence shifted to a more comfortable position, propping one well-shod foot casually atop the opposite knee and absently fingering the stem of his brandy glass as his gaze swept over her in an appraising, contemplative way. She looked relaxed and her eyes were soft, her cheeks flushed with the heat from the fire. He was touched despite himself by her youth and perhaps also by some private scruples. She had an innocence and warm femininity that touched a deep chord inside him.

His instinct detected untapped depths of passion in the alluring young woman that sent silent signals instantly recognisable to a lusty, hot-blooded male like himself. The impact of these signals brought a smouldering glow to his eyes. So much innocence excited him, made him imagine being the one to arouse the pleasures and sensations in Victoria Lewis that she could not yet have experienced.

The ugliness of what he was actually thinking hit him and it sickened him. Every time he saw her, a part of him yearned for her. What was happening to him? Was his absence from society making his mind vulnerable to his basest impulses? Why could he not see her and feel only simple friendship? After all, he had only taken her in out of duty to her mother.

Besides, she was a naïve virgin and much too young for him. Fortunately he was not so utterly lacking in morality to actually offer her an arrangement that would have robbed her of all chances of respectability. Henceforth, he would see that she was made to feel secure. He also resolved to fulfill his role as her protector from that moment forwards and to think of her only in the most impersonal terms. Besides, just two days ago her mother had made it impossible for him to consider her in any other light.

Victoria was reluctant to raise the issue that was prominent on her mind lest it spoiled the atmosphere between them, but because he seemed to be genuinely concerned and approachable, her mother's confession could not be shelved any longer and it was important to her that it was brought out into the open.

'I—I have something I would like to speak to you about,' she began hesitantly. 'Indeed I find the matter highly embarrassing and I hope you will understand it is not something I say lightly. There is no need for you to protect me from the truth any longer. I know everything.'

'Oh?' Laurence eyed her sharply, his look suddenly uneasy. Victoria Lewis might not be of his society, but she was sharp—clever enough to work things out for herself. He tilted his head slightly, a speculative gleam in his eyes as he waited for her to continue.

'I know your father was a handsome man with a certain charm. I also know my mother was an attractive woman before she met my father. They—I mean your father and my mother—had an affair, didn't they?'

The defiance in her eyes as she held his gaze warned Laurence his reaction to her question would determine everything between them. Lifting his glass, he took a long drink, as if the brandy could somehow wash away the bitterness and regret he felt on having to withhold the whole truth from her.

He nodded. 'My dear Miss Lewis, you have

divined the truth exactly.' It was no use denying it. It would also go some way to explaining
to her the reason he had brought her mother to
the Hall. 'How did you find out?'

'My mother told me herself. I'm usually very
good at figuring things out for myself, but I
never imagined anything like this.' She stared
at him for a moment, then lowered her lashes.
'It did happen, didn't it?' she said, raising her
eyes again.

'Yes. Accept it, Victoria,' he said, making
use of her given name for the first time.

'I shall have to. That is why your brother
is against her being brought back here. I can
understand that. It—it must be awkward—for
both of you.'

'Something like that. You are right. Nathan
is finding it difficult to deal with. I will let him
stew awhile. Perhaps it might ease his dispo-
sition. He was offhand to you when he came
here. I'm sorry about that because it's not in
his nature to be rude to anyone. Quite the opposite, in fact. Nathan is the kind of man who
can charm his way out of anything, especially
when it comes to the fair sex. Women adore
him. They can't seem to help themselves. I have
seen small girls ask him to marry them when
they grow up and titled dowagers of advanced
age have been seen to give him the eye. In the

end he fell for and married Diana Ellingham, a girl he has known almost all his life.'

'Why didn't you tell me about my mother and your father?'

'It was not my place. Besides, it is in the past. No point in dragging it up again.'

'And your mother?' she asked, searching his face in confusion. 'Did—did she know?'

'Yes.'

His expression was so perfectly open and earnest that it threw her. 'I'm sorry. Forgive me if I appear confused, but why was my mother not dismissed? How Lady Rockford must have suffered.'

'On the contrary. Your mother proved a trustworthy and steadfast companion to my mother in a confusing and often difficult arrangement. She had a difficult time when I was born. When the doctor told my father that another pregnancy would probably put her life in danger, that part of their marriage was over. Although she craved another child, which she achieved when Nathan was born, she accepted his liaison with your mother with good grace— in fact, it may surprise you to learn that she sanctioned it. My father was a virile man. His affair with your mother kept him from looking elsewhere.' He smiled wryly. 'He was not cut out to be a monk.'

'Mrs Knowles always says restraint is good for the soul.'

'I doubt Mrs Knowles was referring to making love, Victoria.'

'No,' she replied, pink-cheeked. 'I don't suppose she was.' Victoria was shocked at his irreverent reply about his father. 'But—you cannot be serious. No woman would endure such humiliation in her own home, surely.'

'Your mother took nothing away from her. My parents loved each other in all the ways that were still possible. My mother was everything to my father and he loved her to the very depths of his soul—despite his affair. The three of them were discreet about it. Love is a strange thing, Victoria. My mother never thought my father had betrayed her. She was very fond of your mother, which was why she requested that she be taken care of should anything happen to her.'

'Do you mind telling me your feelings on the matter? It cannot have been easy for you growing up with this knowledge.'

'Naturally I would prefer it not to have happened, but it did and there is nothing to be done about it.' Careful to keep his expression nonchalant, he lifted his eyebrows wryly before saying, 'But how do you feel now you know, Victoria? Are you shocked?'

'Yes. It is very painful for me knowing this—and sad, too—for my mother—and my father. I'm not even sure how I feel—confused, yes, shocked, yes, but beyond that I don't know. How much do I mind? That my mother had been in love with another man—not her own kind, a gentle schoolteacher? How did it happen, how could she have done such a thing? All these things I have probed, cautiously, carefully, as if exploring the extent of a wound—and I cannot begin to find any answers. I—I think she loved your father deeply. But I will not judge her or blame her. I don't have that right.'

Relief skimmed Laurence's features at her smooth acceptance of her mother's secret, even though she could not understand it.

'Your brother is not as understanding about the affair as you are,' she went on, 'and I cannot say that I blame him. Little wonder he cannot bear to think of us being here. If you were so determined to abide by your mother's wishes, perhaps you should have thought of some other way of taking care of her maid.'

'Bringing her here is what she would have wanted.'

'Not if it meant causing a rift between her sons.'

'Nathan will get over it.'

'I have to ask you who else knows about this. It cannot have gone unnoticed—not in a house with so many servants.'

'Mrs Hughs knew what was going on—as did Jenkins. They are old retainers and both are discreet. Others who might have known have either passed on to their maker or moved on to find employment elsewhere.'

'I see. I am glad of that—fewer people to gossip. Where are the things that were taken from the cottage?'

'They are quite safe here at the Hall. You can see them whenever you wish. What will you do with them?'

'There are some things I would like to keep—personal things. I suppose I must sell the rest.' Her face dropped in sadness. 'It will be difficult, though. Apart from the time I spent at the Academy, I have lived all my life in Ashcomb. I had a happy childhood and good memories are there. All the things I associate with my parents.' She bent her head and her hair fell across it in a cascade of darkness. 'What am I to do with them? Where are they to go?'

'They can stay here until you decide.'

'They cannot remain here for ever. Eventually there will be decisions to make. When all this is over and my mother is…' She bit her lip, swallowing down the tears that threatened. 'I will leave here and we need never think of each other again.'

'I am not sure that is possible,' he said, with the candlelight shimmering on her hair and glowing in her warm amber eyes, eyes that did not know how to deceive, eyes that could not know of cruelty. Deep inside he felt a stirring of tenderness, a protectiveness towards her that surprised and disturbed him, and he lifted his glass, drinking the liquor to cover his own bewildering emotions.

The silence was punctuated by the crackling of the logs burning on the grate. Laurence continued to watch her covertly from beneath his lashes as she stared moodily into the flames of the fire. She looked unhappy, which was not unusual in the circumstances, he supposed, but there was a droop to the corners of her mouth, like that of a despondent child, which he found heart-rending. The firelight had turned her dark-brown hair to coppery black, glossy and tumbled, and touched her lips to a full poppy red.

Roiling with bewilderment, suddenly Victoria got to her feet and, putting his glass down, Laurence did the same.

'Surely I cannot have rendered you speechless,' he murmured teasingly.

'It's dreadfully late,' she said. 'I really should be getting back.'

At that moment the door opened and Jenkins entered. Laurence glanced towards him.

'What is it?'

'The nurse is asking for Miss Lewis, sir.' His gaze shifted to Victoria. 'Please come quickly. Mrs Lewis has taken a turn for the worse.'

Victoria and Laurence exchanged worried glances.

'I'll come at once.'

Victoria hurried to her mother's room and her heart wrenched. Her head had sunk into the pillow, her face had gone a deeper pallor.

After an hour the doctor arrived, and he was silent as he stood by the bed and looked at the unconscious woman.

After a slight examination he took Victoria's arm and led her from the room, and when they were in the corridor, he said, 'She will not regain consciousness. You should be thankful of that. She is in no pain. I doubt she will last the night.'

Betty died just before dawn. Having kept vigil since the doctor had left, Victoria closed her eyes, her chest seized with the pain of her loss. Whatever it was her mother had wanted to tell her had died with her.

With the feeling of death and the oppressive weight of the house pressing in on her, draping a woollen shawl about her shoulders, Victoria walked outside for some fresh air. The filmy grey half-light before dawn rang with birdsong. The air was moist and cool. She could smell the moor and taste the salt of the sea on the languid breeze.

She began walking with no particular destination in mind, but it was not long before she stood before the wrought-iron gates looking out over the moor. Behind her in the east, the sun was edging up over the horizon. Its pink light turned the moorland turf a soft gold and green. The loveliness of it went unobserved for she was encased in grief and shock. A cluster of wild hyacinths on the edge of the drive seemed to mock her with their promise of life and hope to come.

She closed her eyes, drawing a deep breath of the salty air. Perhaps it was the discovery that her life was about to change for ever, or the close look she had just had at death—or perhaps it was merely the lack of sleep—but she had never felt so alone or so wretched. She didn't know if the pain would ever go away.

Drawing the shawl about her, she turned to retrace her steps when she saw Lord Rockford walking towards her. She waited for him, her gaze softening as she took in his dark and brooding expression. His strides were long and purposeful. His hair was tousled. When he stopped in front of her she looked at him standing there. His expression was serious, anxious even. She was oddly moved.

'I'm sorry about your mother,' he said, his voice low with compassion. He scrutinised her face. He felt her despair. She looked up at him with her great amber eyes smudged with weariness and grief, and just for a moment, before the defences went up, he saw in those eyes, not just grief, but desperation and fear—and relief that he was actually there. 'How are you?'

Her face contracted in pain and her eyes were lost and lonely, those of a child which finds itself amongst strangers. It seemed she was asking something of him, something to do with the problems that beset her and which she begged of him to help. 'I—I don't know what to do.'

She stepped a little closer to him, her gaze held by his and there was something in them, some intuition in his compelling blue eyes which drew her to him. It was as though he had put out a hand and taken hers, held it close and was telling her to relax and confide in him.

Laurence saw the great wash of tears spring from her eyes and flow down her face. His heart jolted for her pain and he strained to give her something, anything which might ease her hurt. Holding his arms out to her, he said gently, 'Come here.' She walked into them and placed her face against his chest. His arms closed round her and he held her like a father, like a brother. He was surprised to realise the urge to comfort her came from a place of authentic compassion, not simply desire.

'Cry, Victoria. Let it go. Betty was a good woman, a dear friend and her death will be felt and grieved over by those who knew her. She is worthy of your tears—and mine.'

Victoria wept, her face pressed into his chest. He felt her body shudder with the force of her anguish and her voice was muffled as she cried out the words of love and loss for her mother. He had to fight the urge to place his lips on her bent head. His heart contracted with pain and pity, for never had he seen or heard so much desolation in anyone before.

When the weeping was done she stood back. He saw her eyes soften gratefully as her mind dwelled wonderingly on the compassion she had seen in his eyes and the consolation she had found in his arms. He had been so tender, so infinitely soothing, comforting her in her grief at a time when she was at her most vulnerable and emotionally insecure.

He had just returned from his ride, which he took every morning, and Victoria could smell him—horsey, faintly sweaty. She smiled wanly, wiping her face with the back of her hand.

'Here, have my handkerchief.'

'Thank you. I never seem to have one when you're around.' She blew her nose hard. 'I didn't mean to cry on your shoulder again. I didn't mean to cry at all. It's just that—well, I can't seem to help it.'

'It's natural that you should cry. Feel free to cry whenever I'm around. I have a strong shoulder.'

'And an incredibly comforting one,' she added, her lips trembling in a wobbly smile. 'I know I should be thinking about what I'm going to do now, but somehow I can't. I'm floundering, I'm afraid.'

It was not surprising that she was unable to think properly, and who could blame her, Laurence thought, and not for the first time he was filled with a sudden urge to protect her. An urge he had never felt for anyone before. Something strange was working in him, something new. It was an uncomfortable, unsettling feeling and he was not sure he liked it.

'You don't have to think of anything for the time being.' He took her small hand in his. As he did so his heart seemed to flip, for it was so delicate, so fine, the nails oval and polished and perfect. 'I shall personally make all the necessary arrangements for the funeral so you don't have to worry about that.'

'Thank you.' She gently withdrew her hand. 'That's very kind of you.'

Laurence watched her walk back to the house before he turned and headed back to the stables to instruct the groom to have his horse saddled for mid-morning. He would ride over to the Grange to call on his brother. It was not a visit he relished, but it had to be done.

Ever since Victoria Lewis had taken up residence in his home he had gone about his work in a calm, fluid state of suspense, his senses charged by an inexplicable sexual tension. No one had ever drawn such a response from him—perhaps Melissa had at one time, but he quashed all thoughts of her immediately.

It was wrong to think of Melissa at the same time as Victoria. It was as if, in Victoria, fragments of his life and self that had been blown apart suddenly came together, finding their place in spaces inside himself that he'd thought empty and cold. Victoria brought warmth and made things whole. Her presence occupied and healed his mind, his body and his heart.

As he strode along and saw the gardeners beginning their work for the day, the smooth running of his estate—and his worldwide company, for that matter—inspired him with a most gratifying sense of solid order, security, and accomplishment. And yet...

He was plagued by a deepening awareness of a large gaping hole in his life. An emptiness. He had sensed it vaguely and ignored it for a long time, but it had sharpened of late into a kind of hunger, a gnawing urgency.

Over the years he had built up an empire and possessed a fortune, but he had no one to share it with. He had Nathan to leave it to, but Nathan was proud and had made it plain that if Laurence did die unexpectedly, he had neither the desire nor the right to any part of his fortune. So if anything should happen to him, the company that he had created would die with him.

The solution was obvious. He needed offspring, sons, but to have sons he needed a wife, a prospect he little relished after his ill-fated betrothal to Melissa, and, with a reluctance to repeat the process—unless he could find a wife who would bear his children and make no demands on him—he had shelved the idea.

Until Victoria Lewis had taken up residence at the Hall.

She really was very lovely. When he had taken her in his arms and held her, caressed the soft cloud of hair that tumbled loose and fell in wanton disarray about her face, he had cursed softly, aware of his own inadequacy to ease her grief and knowing that Victoria had made a deep impression on him, penetrating his tough exterior and finding a way into his heart as no other woman had done since Melissa. When he thought how spirited she was, how young and vulnerable, despite her quality of mind to show self-possession, how ripe she was for being initiated along the secret, mysterious paths of womanhood, he smiled.

Recollecting himself, he pulled himself up short, disgusted with his unfulfilled yearnings and dreams. He had almost married Melissa, believing she could make those dreams come true. How stupid he had been, how incredibly gullible to let himself believe a woman cared for him enough to light up his life with love and laughter and to give him children, when all she cared about was wealth and rank. His smile vanished as he realised Victoria Lewis was suddenly bringing all those old foolish yearnings back to torment him.

* * *

It was mid-morning when Victoria went searching for Lord Rockford to discuss the finer points of her mother's burial that he might not know, only to be told that he had left for the Grange. This came as no surprise. No doubt he had gone to inform his brother of her mother's demise and to assure him that she would soon be gone.

Victoria's mouth had set in a grim line against her grief, grief she could feel just below the surface—so much grief confined in so small a place. Her face tight and closed, she felt herself sway slightly as they lowered the coffin that contained her mother's body into the ground on top of her husband, but the touch of Mrs Knowles's hand on her arm steadied her.

'Bear up, lass,' she whispered, the words heard by no one but Victoria and Ned on the other side of her. 'It'll soon be over.'

The day was cold in the Ashcomb church yard. Though not exactly raining, the damp clung to the handful of mourners. They stood with their heads bowed, hands clasped respectfully, their faces bearing every expression from sadness and sympathy to curiosity, for Betty's removal from her cottage to the Hall had given rise to much speculation in the village. There were subdued greetings for Victoria and the usual funereal platitudes.

'I am the Resurrection and the Life, saith the Lord...' the parson intoned.

Raising her head, her face wrought with sadness, Victoria looked about her. She was in the deepest black. She could feel the sympathy of those gathered, all those who had known her mother when she had lived in Ashcomb. A handful of servants from the Hall had come to pay their respects.

'It's over, lass. Let's get you back to the carriage.' Victoria came back from her detachment to feel Mrs Knowles's hand drawing her away from the grave, guiding her round the freshly dug soil and on to the path.

Lord Rockford was there to assist her into the carriage, his face stern on this sad occasion but his deep-blue eyes were soft with sympathy. He had stood on the other side of the gaping hole, ready to leap across it if necessary to give her his arm to cling to, wondering why he should think like this. He supposed it was because she had no one but Mrs Knowles to cling to, the woman who had been such a good friend to Betty.

After embracing Mrs Knowles, Victoria took Lord Rockford's hand and climbed inside, unconscious of the fascinated stares of the mourners. Lowering her head, she sat across from him as the carriage headed back to the Hall. Victoria was her mother's only family. Because of this she had decided there would be no formalities following the interment.

The funeral over, Victoria realised that her entire future was hanging by a thread. What was she to do? A section of her mind was already planning ahead. She would write to Miss Carver and explain her situation. Perhaps, depending on how much money she had, she would be able to afford to return to the Academy. If not, then she was young and healthy and there was nothing to stop her from doing something to earn a living. Perhaps she could find work outside the village—at Cranbeck, maybe, or Malton. She had hoped to go and stay with Amelia and her family in York until something came up, but she had received a letter from her friend that very day informing her that in two weeks she was to accompany her parents to London where they would be staying with her paternal grandmother for several weeks.

Before she could put pen to paper to write to Miss Carver, Jenkins came to inform her that the master was asking to see her. She hastened downstairs, knocked on the study door and, in response to Lord Rockford's call to enter, she

went in, closing the door behind her. She stole
a glance at him, at the chiselled profile, marvelling at the strength and pride carved into
every feature on that starkly handsome face.
With that lazy, intimate smile of his and those
deep-blue, penetrating eyes, he must have been
making female hearts flutter for years. She was
saddened that they would soon part, but now
her mother was gone there was nothing to keep
her here.

Besides, she couldn't stop thinking of what
her mother had lived through in this house. As
she walked the corridors and rooms in which
her mother had once lived and worked, her
imaginings crowded in on her so that she could
hardly bear it—the hopelessness of a young
woman in love with the master of the house,
her mistress's husband—a lady who sanctioned
her husband's affair with her maid. Victoria had
said she would not judge her mother's actions,
but there was something most unsavoury and
sordid about the whole situation.

But how her mother must have despaired,
for she would have known that their affair was
doomed from the start. They were all of a pattern underneath, these men born into the gentry, who were bred to think of themselves as
above ordinary mortals. Their opinions on most
things might be diverse, but when it came to

class and the division between the servant and the master, there they stood firmly together and her mother could never have risen above what she was—the mistress of the master of Stonegrave Hall.

Laurence looked up and, seeing Victoria, gentled his voice, for this young woman was grieving badly and he was afraid that what he had to disclose might just send her over the edge. 'Victoria, come and sit down.'

Laurence got up from his massive, intricately carved desk and, walking round it, pulled out a chair. Instead of returning to his seat, he perched a hip on the edge of the desk, crossed his arms over his chest and studied her seriously. She smiled up at him, then the smile slipped away. When he spoke his voice was calm and authoritative.

'Now the funeral is over there are matters to be discussed. Naturally you will want to know the contents of your mother's will.'

Bewildered, Victoria sat on the edge of the chair and stared up at him. 'Yes—but I thought Mr Collinson, my mother's solicitor, would be handling this.'

'That's usually the case, but she made some changes when her illness worsened—making me her executor. I know Mr Collinson would like to speak to you regarding your mother's affairs and he will call tomorrow. In the meantime I thought I would put you in the picture.'

She clasped her hands in her lap, suddenly wary of what he was about to tell her—and more than a little hurt that her mother had taken Lord Rockford into her confidence without consulting her. Her ire at his condescending superiority was almost more than she could contain just then.

'Forgive me if I seem a little surprised,' she said tersely, 'but I really had no idea she had made you her executor and I cannot for the life of me understand why she did.'

'You will, in a moment.'

'Before you say anything else, I must tell you that I have given some thought to my future. I am grateful for everything you did for my mother, but now she is gone I have no intention of staying here a moment longer than I have to. I shall write to Miss Carver to ask her if I can return to the Academy. After all, my father left us well provided for, so I would like to gain the qualifications that are necessary for me to seek a teaching post or that of a governess.'

Laurence's heart flinched and he turned away from her so that she would not see the expression on his face. Why should he feel the gnawing in his gut which her words had caused him, for this girl, whom he had never seen until he had met her on the moor? And why had he let her mother talk him into becoming her executor? He must have lost his mind. But something about this girl, this young woman, drew him to her, to her sadness, which he wanted to alleviate.

He looked at her once more. 'There is no money, Victoria,' he told her flatly. 'Your mother was penniless when she died.'

When he fell silent she waited in expectant anticipation, expecting him to continue, to tell her there was more, until she realised there was nothing more. Her heart rose up to choke her and she stared at him in absolute confusion and astonishment and more than a little desperation.

'But—but that's not possible. There must be some mistake. There has to be. My father's assets! When he died he—he left my mother a substantial amount of money. There has to be something.'

'There is no mistake,' he said quietly, his voice penetrating the mist of Victoria's bemused senses. He was aware of the pain she was suffering. She was young and unable to deal with the dilemma in which she found herself. As he looked at her his gaze was secretive and seemed to probe beneath the surface, but he could see by the terror in her eyes, how her face had become drained of blood and the way her fingers clutched her throat, that this unexpected blow had hit her hard.

'I know the Academy was expensive—but I had no idea…' In helpless confusion she looked up at him. 'Why didn't she tell me? Why, she—she must have spent a fortune on my education—and the fine clothes so I would not feel different from the other girls. If only I'd known, everything would have been so different.'

'How could you know? Your education was important to your mother. She was very proud of you.'

Unable to sit still, Victoria got to her feet and walked restlessly across the room. Her thoughts were beginning to take on some semblance of order. 'This has come as a terrible blow. In fact, I am quite devastated. I had no idea things were so bad. But I have already given some thought as to what I would do if such a situation should arise.'

'Have you now,' he said. She was not in a position to make decisions, but he saw no reason to point that out to her just now.

She stopped and faced him. 'I thought I might go and stay with Mr and Mrs Fenwick in York until I find some kind of employment so that I can be self-supporting and continue with my education at the same time.' She smiled thinly. 'I'm sure you will be relieved not to have me rattling about your house any longer and I know your brother will be thankful to have me gone.'

'Forget about Nathan. This is about you. I am here to help you.'

'Thank you, but I will not take advantage of your kindness any longer. The only thing I can make of all this is that my mother has spent every penny my father left us on my education. Now there is nothing left I will not throw myself on your mercy. My financial situation is not your problem or your concern. I will make my own way. Indeed, I am looking forward to beginning my teaching career.'

Laurence's jaw hardened. 'Not without my consent, you won't. So you can forget the idea of finding work. Damn it, Victoria, you are eighteen years old and alone in the world. You need looking after.'

With superhuman effort, she took control of her rampaging ire. Lifting her chin, she looked straight into his enigmatic eyes and said, 'I am not a child. I am more than capable of looking after myself.'

'I won't allow it!' he barked, relinquishing his perch on the desk to confront her.

She drew herself up before him and her eyes

blazed with golden copper. 'How dare you raise your voice to me, ordering me about as though I am yours to direct, just as though you have a perfect right to do so?'

She did her best to hold in the resentment she felt, to be as dignified as a lady of his class would be, but it was difficult and her expression was icy. He had been very kind, but, if he had not brought her mother to the Hall, she could have managed perfectly well without him. And now she must extricate herself from the Rockford snare. She had set herself a demanding task, and in the midst of loss she knew she must find the strength to put aside her grief and fix her sights firmly on the future.

Something swelled up in her, a powerful surge of emotions to which she had no alternative but to give full rein. It was as if she had suddenly become someone else, someone bigger and much stronger than her own small self.

'So,' he said coldly, moving closer, his face working with the strength of his emotions which were in danger of getting the better of him. 'Are you going to abandon this nonsense and settle down to—'

'Nonsense!' she flared. 'What are you talking about?'

'This notion you have of being a teacher,' he said. With the patience of a teacher discussing an absurd rhetorical issue with an inferior student, he said mildly, 'If not, would you care to tell me how you intend to accomplish that?'

His infuriating calm made Victoria long to kick him on the shin. 'I have already told you. I will not repeat myself. And who do you think you are, laying down the law and telling me what I can and cannot do? I am a grown woman and I am quite capable of running my own life without you interfering.'

His face whitened, the rush of furious blood under his skin ebbing away at the implication of her statement. He seemed to tower over her. 'Interfering? Is that how you interpret what I have done?'

'No, of course not,' she replied, instantly regretting her choice of word. 'But whatever commitment you felt you had to my mother, it ended when she died.'

'Not quite. I promised her that you would be provided for. I think your mother would be best pleased if you were to set your sights on being a lady instead of a teacher.'

'That is where you are wrong. She always encouraged me in my ambition. I am not a lady and never will be. My father was a schoolteacher and I suppose he managed to gather a sheen of gentility about him, and at least I am perfectly able to hold my own in what is called polite society. But I would like to realise my dream to become a teacher. I, not you, will be the one to determine my future. You have no power over me.'

'I think you will find that I have,' he said on a softer note. 'You see, Victoria, just two days before she died, your mother made me your legal guardian until you reach the age of twenty-one.'

Victoria became still. The atmosphere was charged with something she did not like. It was a tension that had a sharp needle piercing it. One that she feared could hurt her, though she was not sure why.

Chapter Five

'So that's what all this is about. From the very beginning I knew there was something amiss in all of this—something didn't make sense. Now I know why. But eighteen is rather old to be someone's ward, don't you think?'

'Not at all. In most families young ladies are either under the control of parents or guardians until they reach an age or until they marry.'

'Which, if I understand correctly, is to be my lot.'

'It was your mother's wish that I should see you betrothed to a man of means and consequence, and I promise you that, with my connections, we won't have a problem finding one of those.'

Victoria's expression was one of disdain.

'The whole scheme sounds mercenary and cold to me.'

Laurence shook his head, his next words practical. 'You're a female and you have to wed some time, you know that—all women must wed. You're not going to meet anyone eligible cooped up here, so at the appropriate time I shall take you to London. And I'm not suggesting we accept an offer from just anyone. I'll choose someone you can develop a lasting affection for, and then,' he promised, 'if you wish, I'll bargain for a long engagement on the basis of your youth. No respectable man would want to rush a girl who has just turned eighteen into matrimony before she was ready for it. That is what your mother wanted,' he warned her when she looked as if she was going to argue.

Sheltered though she'd been, Victoria knew he was not being unreasonable about expecting her to wed. He was only pointing out to her that it was her duty to marry in accordance with her mother's wishes. In this case, as her guardian he was in charge of making the selection and she resented it bitterly.

'I shall provide a respectable dowry,' he went on. 'Without that you will be at a disadvantage no matter how desirable you may be.'

The absurdity of that scenario was not lost

on Victoria. 'But why should you provide a dowry for me? That is something only a father can do. You're not my father. Why did my mother do this? For what reason?'

'Because she knew she wouldn't be here to take care of you. It worried her a great deal that you would be alone in the world. She wanted the best for you.'

Tears of outrage stung her eyes. 'And she considered making *you* my guardian the best?'

'No matter how distasteful you find it, that is the way things are.'

Her face became one of furious indignation. 'You can go to the devil, Laurence Rockford, and take your idea of protecting me with you. I can look after myself. I don't need anyone and I certainly don't need you. Just because you took care of my mother, don't think you own me.'

'I don't, but since she made you my ward, I have a right to say what you will and will not do.' His voice was mocking and his eyes gleamed sardonically though he was still white-lipped with anger. He gazed at the tempestuous beauty standing before him, her eyes flashing like angry jewels, her breasts rising and falling with suppressed fury, and his anger gave way to a reluctant admiration for her courage in standing her ground.

'You will make Stonegrave Hall your home.'

His voice was very serious. 'You know that now, don't you, Victoria?' It was not a question but an order.

'I do?' Slowly she raised her eyes to look into his face, a face that was at last ready to smile with satisfaction, for it seemed to him she was willing to allow him to do this for her. Laurence Rockford was a wealthy man. She would live in luxury in this house—but at what cost to herself?

All her future plans were to disappear. The tragedy of the loss, the pain of it, went deep into her soul and was almost too much to be borne. The hopes and dreams that had driven her on since childhood were to dissolve like the morning mist.

'I am to give up my ambitions, then? You are taking it for granted that I must give up what I have always wanted and come and live with you in this fine house, is that it?' Her voice was expressionless, flat and empty.

'And what is wrong with that?'

'Have you any idea what that will do to me?'

'You will find it difficult, I know, but here you will have everything you need.'

Victoria glowered at him with stubborn, unyielding pride, her chin pert, her hands balled into tight fists by her sides as she tried to conceal the hurt she felt. 'Am I to have no say in the matter?'

'What is there to say?'

'Plenty. Is your lofty rank supposed to intimidate me?' she asked, her voice shaking with the force of her anger. 'Is it your high-handed belief that I will give up my dream? That I will sit at home, *your* home, and do nothing.'

With his hands fixed firmly on his hips, Laurence thrust his face close to hers, his eyes glittering with a fire that burned her raw and his eyebrows drawn close, giving him an air of fiendish intensity. 'There will be many things you can do to occupy your time. While you live in this house—*my* house—you are under my care. You will do well to remember that and the sooner you accept it the better it will be for us all. You will be accountable to *me* for your actions. Is that understood?'

Victoria didn't even recoil from the fury in his eyes. 'You can go to blazes, Laurence Rockford, and the sooner the better. Ever since my father died I call no man my superior—and least of all you. I have been accountable to no one for my actions but my parents. Now they are gone I do not intend replacing them with you.'

'Yes, you will. Someone should have taught you some sense and drummed that wilful pride out of you some time ago,' he said, anger pouring through his veins like acid, his fury making him carelessly cruel. 'I am not daunted by your defiance.'

'You wouldn't be daunted by a stampeding herd of elephants,' she retaliated. 'I will not sit at home twiddling my thumbs when I could be better employed.'

'You told me you have not been to London. I am to go there shortly. You can accompany me.'

'Suddenly it has lost its appeal.'

She started to turn away, but his voice stopped her. 'Where are you going?'

'To my room. To pack.'

'I can appreciate your desire to take charge of your own future, Victoria, but you will not carry out any plans involving your departure from here without my consent. I refuse to give it.'

Like a cat, Victoria turned and slowly walked back towards him, a feral gleam lighting up her eyes as she faced him, so close that she could feel his hot breath on her face. 'Tell me, Lord Rockford, does everyone march to your orders?'

'Always.'

'Not me,' she flung back. 'I shall match you stride for stride; I won't answer to you.'

His eyes turned glacial. 'Do not address me

in that tone. If you flout my authority and do anything else to inconvenience me while you live in my house, I will personally make your life a misery. Is that understood?'

'My life is miserable already. It cannot get any worse. What can you do?' she scoffed.

'Out of respect for your mother and your sex, I will curb my temper. But if you brazenly defy me, do not depend on my ability to exercise similar restraint. If you want to win my approval, you are going to have to change your attitude and make yourself more agreeable to me. *That* should be your first concern.'

Victoria's ire at his condescending superiority was almost more than she could contain. 'Why on earth should I want your approval? And as for my attitude, no one else finds it a problem. Perhaps it is your own attitude that is at fault.'

Laurence glared at her. 'You are the most outrageous, outspoken and obstinate young woman I have ever met and your behaviour is deplorable. You certainly don't act like a female who has spent the last five years at a respectable Academy for young ladies. I will not have it, Victoria.'

Rigid with accumulated pride and rebelliousness, Victoria dominated the situation as much as he. Her eyes were shining assertively, alive with the hidden mysteries of a rare jewel, her breasts rising and falling with suppressed fury as she struggled with the sensation burning in her veins.

'*You!* This is not about *you!* You may be the master of Stonegrave Hall, but you are not the sun around which the world revolves. In fact, you are quite the opposite, for you are the most inconsiderate, overbearing, selfish man I have ever known.'

'You needn't go on. I get the picture,' he drawled.

'You have no regard for the feelings of others and you are arrogant enough to believe that your rank entitles you to behave that way—' She broke off and looked away as if attempting to contain her emotions. As well she should, for this torrent of inexplicable criticism was both unjustified and unpardonable, and he was right. Her behaviour was deplorable.

Laurence opened his mouth to continue giving her a dressing down for her impudence, as he would any other person who spoke to him in the way she had just done, but she spoke before he had the chance to do so.

'I apologise. I should not have said those things.'

'No, you shouldn't.'

'I spoke in the heat of the moment...' How she wished she could retract the words.

Laurence had no intention of letting her off the hook lightly. He moved to take a dominant, indolent stance by the fireplace, one arm braced on the mantelpiece. His jaw was set hard, his eyes intense as he slanted her a look. 'I don't know who taught you at that school, but they should have told you that to speak to people like you have just spoken to me is an extremely unpleasant and alienating thing to do. Not to mention the height of rudeness.'

'I have said I am sorry,' she retorted tightly.

'I heard you. I am a reasonable man, Victoria, and I am perfectly willing to allow you as much freedom as you wish, but that does not mean for you to act brazenly and irresponsibly—and running off to York or anywhere else for that matter would be an exceedingly irresponsible act on your part.'

Neither of them had seen the door open and Diana, Laurence's sister-in-law, come striding in. She was taken aback by the quite unexpected heated altercation between these two. She found it hard to believe that Laurence, a man so self-assured and masterful when in the presence of some of the most powerful men in England, had been stripped of his composure and was being baited with such boldness by an eighteen-year-old girl. They were such a combustible combination and it was quite evident that Miss Lewis, who looked magnificent, glorious and indestructible as she faced the master of Stonegrave Hall, had a will every bit as strong and stubborn as Laurence's own.

'Pay no attention to my ill-tempered brother-in-law,' she said, casting Laurence a slightly imperious though smiling look in an attempt to ward off further argument, for the air fairly vibrated with tension. She went to him and proffered her cheek for a duty kiss and turned to Victoria, whose face was beetroot red with embarrassment at being caught behaving so very badly. 'I must express my admiration for your courage. You have my profound sympathy for what you must have endured—having to put up with my dear brother-in-law at Stonegrave Hall alone whilst your mother has been so ill. It cannot have been easy for you.'

'No—but then I've found myself in far worse situations than trying to keep on the right side of an irate lord,' Victoria replied, meeting the eyes of the slender young woman dressed in a fashionable gown of emerald green and matching hat atop her auburn curls.

Diana laughed, a pleasant, warm sound, which went a long way to relieving the tension in the quiet room.

'Diana! This is an unexpected pleasure,' Laurence said, relinquishing his stance by the hearth. 'I take it you have come alone?'

'Yes. Clara was otherwise engaged.'

'And Nathan?'

'He—he's meeting with an acquaintance in Cranbeck.'

Knowing perfectly well that his brother was adhering to his promise not to come to the Hall until Victoria had left, Laurence didn't pursue the subject. 'Diana, may I present Miss Victoria Lewis—although I believe the two of you have already met.'

'Yes, we have—in Malton. I truly thought my husband had done you a mischief that day. I was so sorry to hear of your loss, Miss Lewis,' she said, her voice warm with obvious sincerity. 'I would have been over sooner, but I've been visiting friends down the coast and I've only just heard.'

Victoria gave her a hesitant smile. It was hard to believe that this polite young woman was married to the man who had been so rude to her—although it did cross her mind that maybe she had come on behalf of her husband to enquire when she was leaving. 'Thank you.'

'Why don't we sit down?' Diana suggested. 'Some tea would be nice, Laurence.'

Laurence rang the bell and in no time at all

a maid came in bearing a tray of tea and fancy cakes.

'I do hope your stay at the Hall has been comfortable, Miss Lewis,' Diana said, leaning forwards and beginning to pour the tea. 'It must have been a worrying time for you, your mother being so ill. I am sure that now the funeral is over you will be looking to the future.'

'Victoria is to remain here, Diana,' Laurence informed her quietly. He sat across from them, crossing his long legs in front of him and leaning back in the chair. 'Mrs Lewis made her my ward. She is to make the Hall her home— although I must tell you that she has her heart set on leaving.'

Silence exploded in the room. Diana had gone perfectly still, the cup lifted halfway to her mouth. Instead of drinking the tea she put it back on the saucer and placed it on the tray. 'I see. Does Nathan know about this?'

'No, but he will.'

'Well, if I seem surprised, that's because I am surprised. I don't seem to get past the staggering discovery that you are not only a sentimental at heart, Laurence, but also terribly protective as well.' She looked at Victoria, who was holding her head at a determined angle. 'You don't wish to live here, Miss Lewis?'

'My father was a schoolteacher, Mrs Rockford,' she answered as her dire predicament reclaimed her thoughts. 'It is my ambition to follow in his footsteps and become a teacher myself.'

'Teaching is an admirable profession. I can see you are an independent young woman and if that is what you want to do then I see nothing wrong with that. However,' she said, her eyes settling on her brother-in-law, 'might I suggest that in persuading Miss Lewis to stay, you make use of the charming aspects of your character, Laurence? You might have better success in changing her mind if you remember that she is a woman with needs and feelings and dreams of her own.'

She turned to Victoria. 'I think,' she said, looking as if she were trying to smile when she felt concerned about this latest turn of events, 'you are very brave, Miss Lewis, to take up residence with my formidable brother-in-law.' And then, as if she'd belatedly thought of it, she held out her hands and exclaimed with a bright smile, 'Oh—and, welcome to the family. I shall make a point of visiting you often. We are going to be great friends. I know we are.'

Something about this forced, desperate cheer in her voice set off alarm bells in Victoria's brain and she felt her hands tremble as she held them out to Lord Rockford's sister-in-law. 'Thank you.' That sounded so inadequate that an awkward pause followed. 'Lord Rockford only informed me of my changed circumstances a few minutes before you arrived, so you will have to forgive me if I seem a little shocked. I would like it very much if we could be friends—and please call me Victoria.'

'I would like that and you must call me Diana.'

'I am sure Diana will be a great help in introducing you into society, Victoria.'

'I will gladly help her in that task.'

'I have not had much of that,' Victoria remarked. 'Oh, an occasional party when I was at the Academy in York, but that is all.'

'But you do know how to dance?'

Victoria laughed. 'Yes, of course I can dance. That was one thing our teachers made sure of.'

'Then that is all right then. You should come with us to London. You have been to London?'

'No, I'm afraid not.'

'I would love to show it to you! It is the most exciting city. We can go shopping and I will be happy to assist you to make appropriate acquaintances and introduce you to eligible young gentlemen.'

The moment she had said those words, Diana wished she had remained silent. Laurence had never been one to refuse a challenge. As she expected, her brother-in-law met her gaze and replied, 'There will be ample time for that', observing the scene with mingled irritation and interest. 'Do not forget that Victoria is in mourning for the next twelve months.'

'I am perfectly aware of that, but in the meantime there is no harm in looking to see what is on offer,' Diana said with a tranquil smile while a teasing light danced in her eyes. 'I'm sure you wish to marry, Victoria,' Diana said, breaking into her thoughts.

'I…' She took a deep breath and bent her head, feeling her new friend's eyes on her. 'Truly, I have not thought about it. It is unlikely to happen.'

'But it will.' Diana laughed not unkindly at Victoria's naïveté and glanced at Laurence, who was listening to the conversation with quiet interest. 'Victoria is charming and, as pretty as she is, you will soon have a stream of suitors knocking on the door.' She was also unique, Diana suspected. Based on what she had witnessed, she could not believe Laurence was immune to this young woman's attractions. But her immediate concern was for Nathan and how this would affect him—and Clara. She must not forget Clara.

'But there is one important factor you have

not considered, Laurence. Victoria cannot possibly stay here alone and unchaperoned. If we were to do that, nothing we could say or do would salvage her reputation or enable her to make a suitable match. By the time the *on dit* have circulated through the city, she'll have become your paramour, and you cannot risk that sort of gossip.'

'Fine,' Laurence agreed. 'What do you suggest?'

'You need a chaperon of unimpeachable character and reputation who can stay with her at all times. The obvious choice is Aunt Libby. She would make a perfect duenna. Aunt Libby is Laurence and Nathan's unmarried paternal aunt who lives with us at the Grange,' Diana explained to Victoria. 'This was her home before she moved to the Grange. No one would dare question her acceptability.'

'Will she come?' Laurence asked.

'I'm sure she will be happy to help out. Besides, you know how she loves being at the Hall. Aunt Libby has a wide circle of friends, Victoria—' Diana smiled '—so be prepared to be invaded. I'll speak to her when I get home.'

Laurence nodded with approval. 'Do that. I'll bring the carriage over in the morning. I also have to speak to Nathan. He will be at home, I trust?'

'I'll tell him to expect you.'

When Diana had left, promising to call again very soon, Victoria escaped to her room, still feeling raw after her bitter altercation with Lord Rockford and the terrible pain she felt on having to abandon her dream of being a teacher.

What was she to do? Tears of self-pity and outrage stung her eyes. What did Lord Rockford know, sitting in his fine house, what did he know about being lonely and scared and needing money and no way, it seemed, of getting any, and how dared he talk to her as if he had some claim over her? She didn't need him or his help. She didn't need anyone. She would manage perfectly well on her own...

'No, you won't,' she said aloud. 'You won't manage at all.'

She went on to reflect just how badly she was managing, how much she did need help and that it had been kind of Lord Rockford to take her on at her mother's request. She certainly needed it. Earlier she had furiously rebuked him and now she had an insane urge to beg him to forgive her and to ask him to put his arms round her.

Knowing she was risking a cutting rejection, she went in search of him.

He was seated at his desk engrossed in his ledgers. She looked at his handsome, ruggedly lean face with its stern, sensual mouth and hard jaw, and her stomach flipped over. She felt as she always felt when confronted by him— slightly weakened as if the huge force of his energy somehow attracted some of hers and drew it off.

He appeared to be the image of relaxed elegance, looking not only casual but supremely self-satisfied, his expression so bland and complacent, that once again she felt there was more behind her being at Stonegrave Hall. She asked herself the question—how did she feel about this man who she seemed unable to banish from her life? She searched her mind carefully, frowning as she looked away from him, trying to be completely honest with herself. He was capable of plucking at the strings of her heart and turning her bones to water with a single glance.

Glancing up, he quickly looked down again. 'What is it? I'm very busy.'

Feeling rather like a bothersome child who had just been firmly, but politely, put in her place, Victoria said hesitantly, 'I—I'm sorry for interrupting you.'

Throwing down his quill, he sat back in his chair and looked at her. 'It's late. I thought you'd be in bed.'

'I couldn't go to bed until I'd—I'd…'

Shoving back his chair and getting up, he walked round the desk and held out his hand to her. 'Come and sit down.'

She did as he bade and he seated himself opposite.

'I—I will leave in a moment, but what I want to say cannot wait.'

Steepling his fingers together and balancing one ankle atop the other knee, he looked at her perched on the edge of her seat, her hands clasped in her lap. It was obvious that she was nervous and uneasy about something.

'Well—let's hear it,' he said.

'I—I want to apologise to you for my behaviour today. I was rude and insulting towards you and now I heartily beg your pardon. I was awful, wasn't I?'

'Pretty much.' His face relaxed and a ghost of a smile twitched his lips. 'But since you apologise most charmingly, you are forgiven.'

Victoria glanced at his paper-strewn desk. 'You're always working. Do you have to work so hard?'

'I have a lot to do.'

'Don't you have people to do it for you?'

'I do—and they do, but I like working.'

Gazing across at him, she plucked up her courage and said, 'Considering my disgraceful behaviour earlier, I can understand if you think I'm the most tiresome and unpredictable female alive.'

'You are quite unlike any female I have met before, but you had just buried your mother. You were upset and grieving—and disappointed and deeply hurt at having to set aside your ambition of becoming a teacher. Victoria, I do understand and commiserate. That said, I would like to enjoy your company better. I would like you to be more amiable towards me. I find you quite challenging.'

She had difficulty suppressing a smile. 'You make me sound like a mountain you would like to climb. Why do you find me challenging? Is it because you want to bring me to heel and, when you have done so, trample me under your foot?'

He arched a brow, amused. 'No, but I would like you to be less hostile towards me, less stubborn, and accept your situation. It is new to us both. We both have to adjust.'

'I know and I will try to make the best of what I find to be an extremely difficult situation. I would like to tell you that I don't belong here. I never will. I want to go home, back to Ashcomb—but I can't go home. My mother saw to that when she made you my guardian and I had to abandon my dream of becoming a teacher.'

'You are right. Accept it. Your former life is over—permanently.'

'I know, but that doesn't lessen the pain of what I have lost.'

His gaze swept over her face. He had to admit he found her oddly disturbing. It wasn't just her beauty, the fair skin, the fine features—not even her sensuality or the undoubted presence of strong hungers in her—it was the odd blend of vulnerability and intense courage, of toughness and tenderness and her insistence she needed no one. He thought of her more than he cared to admit even to himself.

His expression softened. 'Did anyone ever tell you that you have lovely eyes, Victoria? You have a lovely mouth as well.'

She looked away, staring out of the window. 'Please don't say those things.'

'You're right. But you really are a beautiful young woman. I can see I'm going to have my time cut out fending off your many suitors.' Standing up and leaning over her, reaching out, he placed his forefinger gently on her cheek and turned her face back to his. He arched a questioning brow.

Victoria lifted her small chin and met his gaze unflinchingly, feeling his finger scorch her flesh. Firmly she removed it with her own. 'If it is your intention to gentle me, my lord, you will have to use brute force to subdue my rebellion rather than seducing me. Those are the only tactics I know.'

In spite of himself Laurence threw back his head and exploded with laughter.

Wounded by his reaction, Victoria scowled at him. 'You're enjoying this, aren't you?'

'Every minute of it,' he confessed, still laughing, his eyes dancing with merriment. 'It appears to have slipped your mind that seduction is a time-honoured tradition in my family—one that we're good at.'

'As my mother found out to her cost when she encountered your father.' She gave him a prim look. 'You're supposed to be taking care of me and setting a good example—not seducing me. Do guardians take such advantage as this?' she asked him, her words more effective at stopping him than a slap across the face.

'Not if they can help it and you are quite right—and I am rightly chastened.' His wickedly smiling eyes captured hers and held them prisoner until she felt a warmth suffuse her cheeks.

'You do like the Hall, don't you?'

'It's a beautiful house. I always thought so. As a child I would often see it from a distance when we played on the moors and wondered what it must be like to live in such a splendid house.'

'Did your mother not tell you of the time she worked here?'

'Yes, and the balls and everything, but the telling is never the same as experiencing it for oneself.'

'Then you shall. When your period of mourning is over, we shall have a ball—or a party at the very least.'

'I would like that. Tell me, Lord Rockford—'

'Won't you call me Laurence?'

After thinking it over for a moment, she smiled. 'Yes, all right,' she conceded to his immense surprise and satisfaction. 'Laurence it is then. Tell me when you first knew my mother. She often told me of her time here, but she never talked about you or your brother.'

She looked at him. His blue eyes were very tender, very thoughtful, and there was a long silence before he spoke. Then he said, 'She left the Hall when Nathan was born. This may seem strange to you, but I knew your mother for a very long time—since I was born, in fact. She was a person of extraordinary strength of character, loyalty and kindliness—characteristics not usually found in one so young and placed as she was. Because she was in attendance on my mother, we became as close as two people could be, coming from different classes and different backgrounds. There were times when, as a boy, I needed a friend. She tried to be that friend. I was very fond of her and I think she was fond of me.'

Victoria sat speechless, staring at him.

'When she left and married your father, there wasn't much that happened to her over the years that I didn't know about.' He shot her a look. 'You, too, for that matter. So now you are here, I would like you to know that you don't have to worry about anything.'

'And your brother? Will he accept me—living here? As I recall, he was not in the least happy to see me.'

Laurence's expression hardened. 'Nathan does not feel as I do. He came along later and did not understand the way things were. But I don't want you to worry about that. You have met Diana, seen how charming she is and how eager she is to befriend you. She'll talk to him, make him see how things are—and I intend to ride over to the Grange in the morning and explain everything. He'll come round.'

Victoria's heart was thumping painfully. She didn't believe him—at least, she did believe him, but she felt there was quite a lot he wasn't telling her—and she needed to know—and he wasn't going to tell her. He was clearly trying to shield her from something out of kindness, however misplaced. He had certainly done more than anyone to try to help her. She smiled at him and said, and meant it, 'Thank you. Thank you for telling me about your relationship with my mother. It does help—but— I'm sorry if my being here has upset things between you and your brother. He must love you. You must try to make things right.'

'Make things right?' he echoed. 'My dear Victoria, you are unbelievable. For your information I am not the one who made things wrong.'

'I never assumed that you were,' she assured him. 'I'm only trying to help. Whatever unpleasantness lies between the two of you, I don't want to think I am the cause.'

'You're not,' Laurence said tightly. 'Now please leave it. The conversation is tedious.' His tone was irked, but inside he was trembling.

'I'm concerned, that's all. You and your brother have a problem and I want to help.'

'We don't have a problem and I don't need anybody's help. I never have.' He pinned her with his gaze. 'I never will.'

She looked at him impatiently. 'Please hear what I have to say. Nathan is your family. If I had one more day with my dear father—and my mother—I would pay a king's ransom for that, but I can't. They are gone. And some day you are going to know how that feels.'

His response to her words was quick and fierce. 'I was never adored by my parents, Victoria—particularly not by my father as you were, and you're never going to know how that feels.'

She stared at him, deeply moved by his revelation. If, as he said, he was not close to his parents, after what he had told her about his relationship with her mother, she hoped she had brought some warmth and happiness into his life during the time she had worked at the Hall. She smiled softly. 'So what happens now?'

'That's up to you.'

'You mean I have a choice?'

'Within reason.' And then he smiled and Victoria was dazzled.

Dear Lord, he made her heart beat faster, but she struggled to maintain at least an outward show of calm. The human heart was such a strange thing, she thought. There was no control over this chaotic beating thing that lusts and yearns. It was its own master and went where it would, the paths it travelled traverse and secret—even to the mind that claimed to be superior.

The following morning, after visiting the Grange, Laurence returned to Stonegrave Hall with Aunt Libby, having spoken at length to his brother. As the younger son of the deceased Lord Rockford, Nathan had inherited neither title nor substantial fortune, yet he had managed through dint of will, unstinting work and a prestigious marriage to Diana Ellingham—whose father had grown rich from shipping and property, his wealth split evenly between his two daughters on his death—to amass a considerable fortune.

To his relief, Nathan's anger had abated somewhat since Laurence had last seen him at Stonegrave Hall, but he would not accept the situation. It had come as no surprise to him that Mrs Lewis had made her daughter Laurence's ward. Nathan knew Diana had been to see her and tried to talk him into accepting her—indeed, she had tried to tell him that he would like her, but he had very firmly shut her up on that subject.

He had looked at Laurence when he strode into the room. 'You cannot seriously mean to go through with this.'

'I intend to do exactly that.'

Nathan's face whitened at his words. 'Why?' he demanded. 'You can't expect me to believe that you feel responsible for her.'

'Yes, I do.'

'But why, for heaven's sake?'

'Because her mother asked me,' Laurence said with brutal frankness.

In this instance, he was correct and he was feeling nothing stronger than a certain grim, angry resignation towards what Betty had asked of him when she had been close to death. In his hands he hoped Victoria would not lose her wide-eyed innocence and naïveté and not acquire the veneer of bored sophistication and droll wit that was as much a requirement for admission into society as were the right family connections. He owed it to her mother to do his utmost to see she made a suitable marriage.

'Like it or not,' he said to his brother, 'I do feel responsible for what happens to her. Based on what little I know of her, I like her well enough. I cannot shrug her off as easily as you would like me to. You are not the one her mother made her guardian. You would not find it so easy to fulfil that role without finding her so damned attractive.'

'I wouldn't—at least not in that way.'

A look of contrition clouded Laurence's eyes. 'No, of course not. That was thoughtless of me. I'm sorry, Nathan.'

Nathan had been waiting for Laurence to explain his willingness to make Miss Lewis his ward, but his last revealing sentence banished everything else from his mind. 'So she appeals to you in *that* way, does she?' he pressed.

'In exactly *that* way,' Laurence bit out. He stared at his brother. He longed to explain away the extraordinary circumstances that drew him to Victoria Lewis, to make excuses, but the look on Nathan's face stopped him.

'I see, then I can only hope you come to your senses and don't do anything that you will come to regret.'

Laurence shook his head and his strong face lost its penitent cast and became soft. The shamefaced play of his features died away. His eyes were steady and honest and he did not avoid Nathan's gaze as he spoke. 'Nathan, I will not lie to you and deny that I am attracted to her. There is something special, something fine about her, an indescribable magnetism which draws me to her.'

Nathan gave him a wry smile and when he spoke his voice was dark with disapproval. 'It's little wonder you find her attractive. Diana herself finds the girl utterly delightful.'

'That may be so, but I am adamantly opposed to doing anything that will jeopardise my position as her guardian—and the welter of events that took place so long ago renders me helpless to even consider her.'

'I do know that. Based on your previous attitude toward the female sex—which, by the way, has me in complete despair of ever seeing you married—you have rejected Clara at every turn. She has taken it hard. Miss Lewis may not be as easy for you to dismiss as the others have been. You find her physically desirable and my fear is that on longer acquaintance you might find her irresistible.'

'You have nothing to fear.'

'And for the second time in your life you have no reason to fear the loss of your cherished bachelorhood?'

'Are you quite finished?' Laurence enquired blandly.

'Quite,' Nathan quipped.

'Victoria is very vulnerable just now and will be easily hurt, so I must tread with care. I am thinking of her best interests. I promised her mother that I would see to it that she makes a suitable marriage.'

'It can't be a moment too soon as far as I'm concerned,' Nathan retorted.

'Actually, there are several problems associated with this plan. There is one difficulty.'

'And that is?'

'I need some female input.'

'I understand Aunt Libby is to provide that.'

'Come on, Nathan, Aunt Libby is seventy-five-years old and spends a great deal of her time dozing in a chair or in bed.'

'You want my wife to call on her?' said Nathan, reading his mind.

'Precisely.'

'I am against it, but if it will get Miss Lewis off our backs I will agree to it. I am sure Diana will be happy to lend her enthusiasm and assistance.'

'You really should meet her, Nathan. You will have to at some time. She is completely innocent in all of this, innocent of any blame. She is struggling to come to terms with her mother's death and the change it has brought to her life. She has had to abandon her ambition of becoming a teacher and she is feeling it very badly.'

'I don't want to hear anything about her,' Nathan had told Laurence, 'good or bad. If you want to play nursemaid, then go ahead, but I'd rather just think she wasn't there at all.'

'I'm sure you do and I would like to reinforce what I have said before, that she deserves to hear the whole truth and will be able to handle it better than she could handle confusion and deception. I carry a great burden of guilt and remorse over depriving her of the truth.'

'What can I say except that I am sorry you are finding this whole thing difficult.'

'It's quite horrendous, Nathan. Victoria is as much a victim of the events as you are. Try to remember that.'

'I'd rather not, if you don't mind.'

They regarded each other across the room, two fiercely indomitable wills clashing in silence. Then Laurence had shrugged and said he didn't mind at all, but he hoped Nathan would change his mind. Nathan told him he wouldn't. He simply closed his mind, in a way that was half-fierce, half-frightened.

Just the thought that Victoria Lewis was at Stonegrave Hall, just over the moor from him, was a permanent reminder of his father's infidelity that was almost like a physical pain in his life. It was something he had to endure and try to cope with.

And yet it was with sombre concern that he watched Laurence mount his horse and ride away. Despite his brother's words to the contrary, Nathan had an uneasy feeling that he was not as immune to Miss Lewis's charms as he would have him believe. He had not heard him speak with the same degree of gentleness and warmth, had not seen that gleam in his eyes for a long time—not since Melissa.

Chapter Six

The neighbouring gentry responded to the news of Lord Rockford's new ward in various ways, but all showed astonishment by the unconventionality of it all. Generally, the reactions came from those neighbours near at hand who could not believe that the illustrious master of Stonegrave Hall had taken Betty Lewis's daughter under his wing, and her just a slip of a girl. It was indecent, some said, a young girl alone in the house with a relative stranger—and she only a schoolmaster's daughter. True, Mr Lewis had been a well-respected man, but that didn't elevate him any higher than that in their eyes.

Particularly was it being asked how a chit like that was going to make anything of herself,

not being of the master's class. And that same
question was quietly asked in the house itself as
soon as she moved out of her room in the servants' quarters to a more desirable one in the
main part of the house. In keeping with her ele-
vated position, she was appointed a young maid
called Sally. Since they all held Lord Rockford
in high esteem and valued their jobs—and because neither Jenkins nor Mrs Hughs would
speak against her—as long as she remembered
her place and didn't start giving orders, then
they would keep their opinions among themselves below stairs.

When Victoria first met Aunt Libby, her new
duenna, she'd taken one look at her and been
pleasantly surprised. Instead of the stern-faced
old Amazon she'd imagined, she was a small
elderly lady who, with rosy cheeks and silver
hair tucked beneath a lacy cap, looked more
like a china doll. As Victoria had looked into
her sharp grey eyes and listened to her happy,
friendly chatter, she decided that she was an
excellent choice and would suit her very well.
If anything, she amused Victoria, rather than
intimidated her.

'It's very good of you to come here to look
after me,' Victoria said, ringing for tea.

'Not at all, dear,' she replied, making herself comfortable on the sofa and plumping the

cushions around her. 'I was thrilled to be asked and so very pleased to be of assistance. Stonegrave Hall was my home before I went to live at the Grange with Nathan and Diana. I always like to come back.' She smiled. 'You're such a pretty girl, Victoria. I'm sure Laurence will have no trouble making you a good match, and in the meantime we are going to have a lovely time. Yes,' she said, chuckling happily, 'a lovely time.'

Later, when she was ready to go down to dinner, Victoria caught sight of the dreary figure in black in the gilt framed mirror and wondered for a moment who she was. Was it really her? Pale, listless, dull and graceless. She was eighteen years old and though she would love her mother to the end of her days, was she to drift about looking as dead as she was? Despair was doing its best to enslave her. Then, determined not to be sad tonight, she lifted her head high and, turning on her heel, went to join her guardian in the candlelit dining room, hoping he wouldn't find her appearance too dour.

How she would have liked to wear one of the gowns she wore for special occasions at the Academy—her favourite lime-green silk, which complemented her figure and her hair. But she reminded herself that her mother had wanted her to be a lady and ladies did not discard their mourning and change into lime-green gowns so soon following a bereavement.

Laurence was standing by the sideboard, pouring red wine into two glasses. Victoria was struck by his stern profile outlined against the golden glow of the candles. She saw a kind of beauty in it, but quickly dismissed the thought. He turned when she entered and moved towards her, his narrow gaze sweeping over her with approval.

'I hope I'm not late,' she said. 'I've been settling into my room.'

'Is it to your liking?' he asked, pulling out a chair at the damask-covered table decorated with orchids.

'Yes, thank you. It's a lovely room,' she said, slipping into it and taking a sip of wine.

'I hoped you would like it. Facing south, it gets most of the sun.'

'It also faces Ashcomb. The rooftops are just visible.'

'I'm glad you decided to join me for dinner,' he said, seating himself across from her. 'I hoped you would.'

'I could hardly ignore a royal command, could I?' she replied, unable to resist taking a gentle stab at him, an impish curve to her lips softening the tartness of her reply.

His glance darted across the table. 'It was not a royal command—but this is how things are going to be from now on. This is your home, Victoria. You must treat it as such.'

'Yes—thank you, I will try to.'

'Good. Now that is settled, perhaps we can enjoy our dinner.'

'I shall endeavour to do so.'

'As long as you don't upset the cook by not eating. As you will know by now she is very efficient—and being a woman, she is extremely temperamental and takes it as a personal criticism if anyone refuses to eat.'

'What! Even you?' Her eyes sparked with laughter.

'Even me.' He smiled in response, spreading a napkin over his knees.

'Is your aunt not joining us?'

'Aunt Libby is not as young as she was and gets very tired. She prefers to dine in her room.'

'But is not the whole point of her being here to chaperon me at all times?'

'I think she can be excused now and then,' he replied with a wicked gleam in his eyes.

It was a delicious meal, excellently cooked and served by the aloof footmen who came and went. Laurence talked of the Hall, giving Victoria a brief insight into what her life was going to be like from now on.

'You have quite a problem. Moving in society will be difficult enough when you have not been raised to it—which I shall do my best to help you overcome.'

'And how will you do that? I have no doubt whatsoever that I shall be ostracised when word gets out that you have become my guardian.'

'You needn't concern yourself over the attitude of others while I'm about. My shoulders are broad enough to deflect any slings and arrows aimed in your direction.'

'And when you're not here?'

'We'll face that when the time comes. For now I will start by teaching you how to ride. You are the only female I know who doesn't. Riding, I'm afraid, is *de rigueur* for all young ladies.'

Victoria groaned. 'Not all, surely.'

'Most of them, and I am certain you will benefit from it.'

'Don't be too sure about that. I am not ashamed to admit that I have a strong aversion to horses—especially when they come too close. I have never been on one in my life and I have no intention of doing so.'

'Come, Victoria,' he said teasingly. 'Where is your spirit of adventure?' His laughing eyes communicated with hers in silent challenge. 'Afraid?'

'Yes, if you must know, I am rather terrified.'

'Then I shall help you to master your aversion. You will have them eating out of your hand in no time at all and wonder what all the fuss was about.'

'You sound rather confident about that.'

'I am. You may be a little sore from the experience at first, but I can assure you you will soon get the hang of it and enjoy yourself.'

Victoria looked at him in alarm. The man was insufferable. He was positively revelling in her discomfort. 'Of course that is what you would say. You are quite pleased about my distress.'

'It will be short lived, I assure you. I intend to embark on a course of action that will make you overcome your fear of the beast.'

'I'm surprised you would agree to teach me anything. If I have to do this, then couldn't one of the grooms teach me? Your time is valuable.'

'I will make time. I shall enjoy teaching you.' He began to smile.

She pounced on his pleased expression at once. 'You see?' she said, pointing at him in an accusing fashion. 'My ignorance of horses and the possible consequences of my being a social failure no doubt fills you with amusement. I am sure you are looking forward to watching me make the most complete fool of myself when I am tossed over a horse's head.'

He laughed. 'Do not think so ill of me as that. I have many faults, Victoria, but taking pleasure in someone's social embarrassments is not among them. And don't come all missish on me. It will give me pleasure to do this for you, so indulge me.'

She looked away, then back again. 'I did not mean to insult you. However, I cannot help but question your motives.'

'In general or the matter of teaching you to ride?'

'Both, I suppose.'

No one had questioned Laurence's motives since he had become master of Stonegrave Hall and he seldom felt the need to explain them. In this case, however, he knew it was important that he do so.

'I mean what I say. I am a man of honour. If I cannot succeed in my objective by fair and honest means, I would rather fail. I intend to do all I can to make your life comfortable here at the Hall. In the light of your distrust, I should like to prove it to you.'

'How?'

'I have no desire to see you disgraced, which is why we will begin your riding lessons first thing in the morning. Nine o'clock on the dot.'

'Will anyone else be there?'

He looked at her in puzzlement. 'Why should there not be? Does it bother you?'

'Only in the most general sense.' She glanced away and then back again. 'I—I would rather not have an audience.'

Laurence was becoming curious. 'You will have an audience. The grooms will be around.'

Her cheeks turned pink. 'I understand that. It cannot be helped, I suppose. They have their work to do. But any of your friends and neighbours are a different matter.'

Laurence could not make this out at all. In the face of his obvious bewilderment, she went on, 'It's just that whatever I undertake, I seek to do it as well as possible.'

Laurence suddenly understood completely. He could expect no less of her. 'What you are saying is that you do not wish to do anything in front of people unless you can do it faultlessly?'

'Well—yes.'

'Victoria, you are far too severe upon yourself. No one can do every single thing without flaw.'

'Yes, I know, but…' She paused, bit her lip and looked away. After a moment, she drew a deep breath and let it out on a sigh. 'The truth is, whenever I did anything wrong at the Academy, the other girls would laugh at me—and

now I have a horrible fear of being laughed at,'
she confessed in a small voice, returning her
gaze to his. 'I couldn't bear it if Miss Ellingham should come to call and see me tumbling
out of the saddle. Until I become proficient on a
horse, I should prefer not to have an audience.'

Laurence looked at her—the smoothness of
her countenance that never gave anything away,
the discretion in her that never revealed a secret, this need to do things perfectly. He felt an
unexplainable surge of anger at the other girls
at the Academy.

'*I* will see you make mistakes,' he pointed
out, his voice gentle.

'That's different. You don't count. I don't
care what you think,' she lied, hoping she
sounded convincing.

He laughed at her. 'Now *that* I can well believe. Very well, Victoria, we shall keep your
riding lessons to ourselves. There are plenty
of places where a lord, his pupil and a horse
can hide.'

'Thank you. I would appreciate that.'

By the time Victoria reached the stable yard,
she had the bit firmly between her teeth. She
was determined to take Laurence's advice and
learn to ride. It was all very clear in her mind.
If she was to mix with society, then she would

have to learn how to, and if learning to sit atop a horse was to be part of that initiation, then so be it.

Wearing a black woollen dress and bonnet and sturdy boots, she strode into the yard on the dot of nine o'clock. Grooms and stable boys were going about their daily tasks. Having just returned from riding out, Laurence sat upon a massive chestnut hunter with elegant ease, effortlessly controlling the restive beast. In his dark-green jacket and white-silk neckcloth, buckskin riding breeches and gleaming black-leather boots, his dark hair ruffled by the slight breeze, he looked happy and relaxed as he blithely chatted to a groom, Victoria noted. She halted in the shadows of the stable arch, her attention riveted on him.

Amelia, who was an experienced horsewoman, had often remarked that true gentlemen looked uncommonly dashing on horseback and, looking at Laurence Rockford, Victoria conceded that her friend had a point. With that lazy, intimate smile of his and those deep-blue penetrating eyes, he must have been making female hearts flutter for years.

Dismounting, he handed the reins to the groom, taking a moment to fondly rub the mount's nose. Victoria couldn't tear her eyes from him. She was struck by his stern profile and was able to see a kind of beauty in it, but quickly dismissed the thought. All thoughts of her reason for being there fled as her breath was suddenly caught in her throat and her heart beat painfully fast. Not wishing to intrude on the moment, she took a step back, but she realised she must have made a sound or he sensed her presence, because without warning he turned his gaze directly at her. She felt heat in her face—felt it spread at that naked, desirous look. It was a look that spoke of invitation and need.

Laurence saw her hesitate and had no mind to let her escape. 'Here you are.' He strode towards her. 'Nervous?'

Victoria felt her legs begin to shake and cold fear race down her spine—her pulse accelerated wildly. 'All my life I've been nervous around horses—I feel it is not about to change.'

'We shall see.'

'Then since all civilised young ladies know how to ride, I have decided to let you civilise me.'

A dashing smile spread slowly over his handsome face. 'An intriguing proposition.'

'I believe it should prove an amusing project, yes.'

'It is the least I can do. I consider it my duty to help those less fortunate than myself,' he joked, a teasing light dancing in his eyes, 'and, forgive me, but it is very clear that without my guidance, you will never know the joys of sitting on a horse.'

'Well, I am your most eager pupil—clay in your hands. Mould me as you will,' she said, eyeing the horses nervously.

Noting her apprehension and the way her eyes darted to his horse as it was being led into the stalls, Laurence was determined that by the time he had finished she would have conquered her fear of horses. A slow, lazy smile swept across his face and Victoria braced her trembling body for him to say something mocking, but his deep voice was filled with admiration. 'You look lovely—although we shall have to see about getting you a riding habit. Are you ready for your first lesson?'

'I think I'd prefer pistols at twenty paces,' she remarked, eyeing the grey mare a groom was leading towards them.

'Whoa—easy now,' the groom murmured soothingly to the horse when it shook its head and snorted loudly.

Laurence took the reins from the groom and nodded for him to disappear. 'Try not to be nervous. Don't let the horse see your fear. Horses need to be taught obedience by their rider. Once that has been established, a good horse will always recognise its master—or, in your case, mistress.'

Victoria tried to swallow her fear. 'I will try.'

'Good girl. Come and make friends with her—her name is Misty. She's as docile as a lamb.' Taking something out of his pocket he offered his hand to the horse. Misty snorted. Taking the piece of sugar, she crunched appreciatively. Laurence placed another piece of sugar in Victoria's gloved hand. 'Now you try.'

Gingerly she approached the horse and held out her hand. She was tempted to withdraw it at the last minute, but she didn't, and her lips broke into a wonderful smile when Misty nuzzled her hand and took the sugar.

'There, see how easy that was? Time, patience and a lot of friendship can make anything happen.' Laurence casually caressed Misty's nose, urging Victoria to rub her neck. After several minutes more, in which Victoria tried to familiarise herself with the mare, Laurence said, 'Are you ready to mount her?'

Taking a deep, fortifying breath, Victoria said, 'I suppose it's now or never.'

He took her hand as she ascended the mounting block, then climbed into the side saddle, holding the horse steady while she arranged her skirts and picked up the reins. She felt so high up her head spun but, taking a deep breath, the feeling passed after a moment. Laurence let her sit there and get the feel for the horse before leading it out of the yard and on to a bridleway that was concealed on both sides by foliage. It was frightening at first and Victoria was terrified she would fall off. Walking along beside her at a slow, measured pace and holding the side of the bridle, Laurence was wonderfully patient, giving her instructions and correcting errors. Gaining confidence all the time, she began to relax and enjoy herself.

Laurence looked up at her, tracing with his gaze the soft lines of her face, the brush of lustrous dark lashes, the strands of hair that rested against her cheek, her features rosy with the exhilaration of the ride. 'Still nervous?'

She shook her head. 'No. I'm feeling much better—better than I imagined.'

'You're doing well.'

'I think Misty has something to do with that. She knows how to be gentle with me and has helped me to build up my confidence.'

'She does have a natural gift for patience, I grant you, which is why I chose her.'

Glancing down into his eyes, Victoria saw the soft, smiling warmth there and the last of her fear evaporated. 'It's clear you have a way with horses.'

'I like them and enjoy being around them.'

The bridle path opened up on to moorland, the ground littered with giant boulders. The air was crisp and clear. Pale-grey clouds dotted the sky—the smell of damp heather and earth was all-pervasive. They paused by a knoll and Laurence lifted her from the saddle. Sitting on a boulder, one knee drawn up, he gazed at her, a half-smile curving his lips.

'Why have we stopped?' Victoria asked.

'To rest the horse. No good tiring it.'

'But we've only been riding for half an hour—at a sedate pace, I might add.'

'True, but I'm trying to be a responsible and considerate riding instructor,' he joked, his eyes twinkling with humour. Her face was rosy, her eyes bright from the ride. 'You're doing so well, I see no reason why tomorrow we don't progress to a trot.'

'Is that not a little ambitious?'

'You can do it. I have every faith in you.'

She laughed happily, pleased that she was progressing better than she had imagined. 'You have more confidence in my ability than I have.'

They were content to look about and let the cool air refresh them. Victoria's gaze took in the panoramic view. 'This is such a beautiful place,' she said, her gaze caressing the gentle rise and fall of the moors.

'Did you miss it when you were away?'

She glanced at him, his arm resting on his knee, deceptively at ease. 'Oh, yes, but in York everything is so different. We were always busy—and York is so large I was able to disappear if I felt like it and to be anonymous. Here you're awfully visible.'

Laurence smiled lazily. 'Careful, Victoria. You're beginning to reveal your insecurities. Do you feel you have the need to disappear?'

'Sometimes.'

He patted the boulder beside him. 'Come and sit down. We'll resume the ride in a moment.'

She did as he bade, perching her hips on the edge close to him. Removing her bonnet, she shook out her hair. She liked to feel the sun's warmth on the top of her head.

Laurence was completely transfixed by the heavy mass tumbling about her shoulders. It was thick and silken, shot through with tones of russet and chestnut, dark with the gloss of good health. His expression said he liked what he saw. It was in his eyes and the curling expression on his well-cut lips, which were ready to smile with pleasure.

'You have lovely hair, Victoria,' he murmured softly. 'It is almost a sin to cover it with a bonnet.'

She turned her head and met his gaze, her heart slamming into her ribs when she saw the inexplicable hunger flare in the depths of his eyes. 'I cannot imagine why you are concerning yourself with something as trivial as my hair. I've always considered the colour to be quite ordinary and the texture to be of a wilful nature, which makes it awfully difficult to arrange.'

'To a man, a woman's hair is never trivial. Imagining a woman with her hair down, imagining how it will feel in his hands and how it will look spread out across his pillows, can become a man's obsession.' Reaching out, he caught one of her long curls and wrapped it around his finger before pulling it gently, unfurling it to its full length, his knuckles brushing her cheek. 'I confess it has been mine on occasion.'

Waves of heat flooded through Victoria's body at his words and his touch as the image of her hair spread across his pillows flashed across her mind, followed immediately by horror at the very thought of such a thing. She forced herself to look away. 'A woman's hair is your first priority, then,' she said as if they were discussing the weather. 'Are all men concerned with women's hair rather than what is inside their heads?'

He continued to twine the lock of hair around his finger. 'Where women are concerned, Victoria, men are not very deep.'

'That is not very complimentary about the character of your own sex.'

'Men have no character when it comes to women. Love turns us into complete idiots or dishonourable rogues—or both.'

'Even you?'

He dropped his gaze to the lock of hair, his brows drawing together in a fierce scowl. 'Even me,' he answered quietly.

'I'm sorry,' Victoria murmured. 'I should not have mentioned it—only, when two people marry, there must be love,' She gazed at him. 'Have you ever been in love, Laurence?' she enquired quietly.

Inwardly, Laurence recoiled from the mere mention of the word. 'As I've discovered, with age and experience, very few of your sex are actually capable of feelings or behaviour that even approximates that tender emotion— though women talk as if it were as natural to their sex as breathing.'

'Dear me, you are a cynic.'

'I am. I instinctively mistrust the word and any woman who mentions it. I will not utter false protestations of undying affection that I don't feel.'

'I do not share your feelings in that regard.'

Something in the soft romanticism of her words irritated him, for they brought memories to the surface, memories he thought he had buried for good. He ruthlessly shoved those memories back down deep and concealed his irritation with an air of indifference. 'That is your prerogative.'

'When two people marry there must be love. How else is it to succeed?'

When he spoke again his voice had a hard edge to it that evidenced his irritation on the subject. 'Love, Victoria, has no place in marriage. On the whole, in my world, marriages are arranged for profit and gain. Those who believe they are in love find their pleasures elsewhere. They throw caution to the wind. Have you ever been in love, Victoria? But, no, I doubt it,' he said shortly. 'You are young and still innocent of love's joys.'

She met his gaze. 'You are right. I know nothing of what you speak of. You are talking in riddles.' It began to register with Victoria that, as he continued to twirl her hair around his finger, he looked almost—admiring. 'You really do like it—my hair?'

Laurence liked it. In fact, he liked every single thing about her. 'I do like it,' he said casually, releasing the curl and watching it bounce back. 'Does my opinion count?'

'Well, since you ask…' Victoria said, feeling shy and warm beneath the heat of his smile. He was so handsome—in a dark, manly way—that it was difficult not to stare at him. 'I can't help feeling—flattered. But why do you speak of love in such a derogatory manner?'

'Do I?'

'Actually, yes, you do.' She tilted her head to one side. 'Why aren't you married?' she asked pointedly. 'Most men who reach your age are.'

'And how old do you think I am.'

She thought for a moment. 'About thirty—give or take a year. But you didn't answer my question,' she said quietly, thinking what an attractive man he was. He infected her with his own enthusiasm and made everything seem oddly pleasurable. But most of all, and this was where the real miracle of resistance came in, he was inordinately desirable.

The more they were together the more she became aware of him. She felt as if a huge spring coiled somewhere in the depths of her body. She could feel it physically, its stirring, its pressure, trying to unwind and prevented from doing so only by the casing of her body. One day that spring would become unleashed and when she allowed herself to dwell on it, it was almost beyond her wildest imaginings.

'Why have you never married?' she persisted.

He shrugged nonchalantly. 'What does it matter?'

She dropped her gaze. 'I just don't want to see you end up alone.'

Laurence let out a bitter laugh and turned away from her. 'Why not? I'm used to it. It gets a little dull at times, but at least this way no one can stab me in the back.'

'Is that what happened?' she asked softly. 'Did someone betray you?'

'Stay out of it, Victoria,' he told her curtly. 'It's none of your affair.'

'Maybe you're afraid that I'll betray you, too. But I won't, Laurence. I promise.'

No, he realised, he did not feel that Victoria would stab him in the back. But he still didn't want to open his heart to her. He never explained himself to anyone.

'I remember when I began at the Academy, everyone in Ashcomb knew you were to marry—a woman from London, I believe. What happened to her?'

At the mention of that traitor, the one person he had believed for a while had really cared about him back in those days, the past engulfed him like a swarm of locusts, swirling around him with mocking, ghoulish laughter. Rather than tell Victoria the whole humiliating truth, he said, 'We decided we didn't suit. Since then I've never found a woman I wanted to be my wife.'

'Not even Miss Ellingham?'

He smiled thinly. Since he had arrived home, Clara had embarked on a campaign with amusing—and increasing—perseverance to draw a proposal of marriage from him—to no avail. 'Clara is not my type.'

'And what is your type?' she asked, pushing back her hair. 'You must be very hard to please.'

'I am.' He smiled at her, and then suddenly he stopped smiling and all around them, and indeed time itself, seemed to freeze. Victoria stared at him, feeling she had never seen him before, or rather as if he had always been out of focus before and now he had come clear and sharp. She felt she was not just discovering him with her eyes, but with all her senses—she was drawn, pulled towards him. She could hear no sound but his breathing, was aware of no movement except his own eyes, exploring hers.

And then, very slowly, very carefully, as if afraid of breaking the spell, he reached out and cupped her cheek in his hand, his thumb feathering over the fullness of her lower lip. It was the most extraordinarily and powerfully sexual thing Victoria had ever known. She put out her hand and touched his face, very gently, and all the emotion of the past few days, the pain, the remorse, all centred somewhere deep within her, became less emotional, more physical, a huge shifting, violent force. Without taking her eyes from his, she moved nearer.

He stared at her, studied her face. For the first time since he was a boy, he felt the agony of uncertainty. Guilt abruptly doused his pleasurable contemplation of her appealing assets. Her mother had made him her guardian, for goodness' sake! He had no right to be mentally undressing her and thinking what it would be like to take her to bed—lusting after her. His attraction to her was insane! If he wanted diversion of any kind, he could choose from among the most beautiful, sophisticated women in the country. There was no reason on earth to feel a wild attraction to Victoria Lewis, no reason to react to her like some randy adolescent or ageing lecher.

But he couldn't help himself. She stood so close and smelled so sweet—and with her face upturned to his…

The next moment she was in his arms and his mouth descended on her soft lips. She kissed him with the whole of her being. Her artless passion took his breath away. It was a kiss unlike any other. He could not remember being kissed like this before. All the women before her faded into obscurity.

Gathering her close, it would have been absurd to deny that Victoria was already connected to him more deeply than any previous involvement, even Melissa—in the furthest reaches of his past—his first real love, who had rejected him. No, this was nothing like that. And Victoria was nothing like her. But he could not allow this to happen.

Suddenly his conscience tore at him and he set her back, looking shocked. 'Dear God,' he said, mentally flaying his thoughts into obedience. 'This is insane.' His hoarse whisper was dredged from his throat. 'Devil take it! I can't keep my hands off you.'

With an abruptness that left her swaying, Laurence stood and tore himself away. He stood there at arm's length, staring at Victoria in the gasping silence as if seeing her for the first time, as if she were an apparition, his expression one of dismay, a look halfway between pain and pleasure. His mouth tightened as he stared at her softly heaving bosom and the tantalising mouth that was still full and hot from his kiss.

'I think we'd better stop this.'

Unsteadily, Victoria fixed her gaze on his mouth, not comprehending why he had broken off their embrace. She was as shocked as he by her desire for him, by what had happened.

Laurence hardly understood it himself as he looked at her sitting there, wide-eyed and vulnerable and trembling. And lovely. Dear Lord, she was lovely. He wanted her with a fierceness that took his breath away.

'I'm sorry, Victoria. I should not have done that. By making me your guardian, your mother placed me in a position of trust. I will not—cannot—contravene that trust. I promise you that my barbaric display of passion will not be repeated. When the time is right I want you to have an opportunity to enjoy the acquaintance of other men, to look over eligible suitors. I will not allow myself to get in the way of that.'

Victoria stared at him. How could he kiss her with such passion, raising her hopes that he wanted her, when all the time he was trying to rid himself of her? She could see it in his eyes. She could feel it, and why not? She meant nothing to him. She was merely someone who had been thrust on him by her mother whose wishes he felt obliged to carry out—and the sooner the better.

But she didn't want anyone else. She wanted Laurence—but she wasn't suitable.

She felt as if something were breaking up inside. Tears of humiliation burned the backs of her eyes, which she struggled to control, fighting desperately to recover her shattered pride and not to weep for her stupidity, for her gullibility—and for falling for a man who felt nothing for her but a responsibility. Some protective feminine instinct warned her that she must never again let herself trust him, never again let him touch her or kiss her, for if she did she would be well and truly lost.

'I'm not ready for any of that,' she said quietly. 'But I suppose…given time…I will have to put my mind to it.'

'It will be for the best,' he said, trying to ignore the wounded look in her eyes which tore at his heart, fighting the desire to wrap her in his arms and beg her forgiveness. From now on, he would stay well away from her. He wouldn't lose control of himself again.

Victoria looked away, swallowing hard. 'Yes, I am sure you're right. I—I thought I might visit Mrs Knowles tomorrow—if that is all right,' she said awkwardly, considering it best to draw a line under the kiss—which had been a dreadful mistake—and change the subject.

Laurence looked at her, trying to pull himself together. 'You are not a prisoner, Victoria. Of course you may visit Mrs Knowles. Now I think we should resume your lesson. Matters of this sort bring out the worst in me.'

Since Aunt Libby had taken up residence at Stonegrave Hall, being a popular and well-loved figure of the community, not a day passed when carriages didn't arrive to deposit friends and neighbours at the door. Some came out of curiosity to see Lord Rockford's ward, and, not surprisingly, when word of Victoria's beauty got out, some of the district's eligible young gentlemen found their way to the Hall on some pretext or other to see for themselves.

Victoria was flattered by all the attention, and since Laurence seemed to be avoiding her, she welcomed the distraction.

Laurence watched it all from a distance. On one particular day when a hopeful young male came calling with his mother, while she was taking tea with Aunt Libby on the terrace, the youth was promenading Victoria round the garden paths. From the window of his study, Laurence observed the happy pair, his eyes colder than an icy winter sky. The sight of Victoria with another man, and laughing as though she had not a care in the world, was crucifying him. The desire she had ignited in him with that one kiss was still eating at him. He wanted her so badly that he ached with it.

Dear Lord, what was wrong with him? How could he let a woman affect him as this one did? He had told himself that the kiss they had shared had meant nothing to him—and yet he had felt the glory in her. She was an obligation he could not escape, not until she was wed to another—which was a situation he could not bring himself to contemplate. As he continued to watch her, he wanted to go out and shake off her companion's hand, to fling him away from the lovely girl whose rosy face was smiling up at him. How dare he put his hand on what was his... And yet who could blame him?

There was something about Victoria Lewis, a beauty not just of her face but in her heart and soul. It shone from her like the sun, and when men looked at her they were drawn in by that glow.

Turning from the window, he shook his head to clear his reeling senses. His strategy to avoid her had backfired with a vengeance. Perhaps, he thought disparagingly as his inner turmoil turned to self-scorn, he should never have allowed himself to get so close to her in the first place. Had his past encounters with women taught him nothing?

Disgusted with his body's relentless craving

for her, he knew something had to be done. Because he lived in the same house as Victoria there was no escape.

It was when she was going to her room after dinner that he told her he had decided to leave Yorkshire for London.

'But—why?' Victoria asked, pausing at the bottom of the stairs, so disappointed she could hardly think. Ever since he'd kissed her he'd been avoiding her, passing the duty of teaching her to ride to one of the grooms and only speaking to her when Aunt Libby was present.

'It's a matter of business,' he told her. 'I have clerks and managers who do an excellent job, but I like to keep my finger on the pulse so to speak.'

Victoria was unprepared for the wave of distress that swept over her—and she certainly didn't relish being all alone at the Hall. 'Oh—I see. So the minute I become your ward, you abandon me,' she remarked in a prickly tone.

He raised his eyebrow. 'I have no intention of abandoning you. I would never do that.'

'Do you expect to be away long?'

'Six weeks at the most.'

'Then might I suggest that I travel to York to stay with Amelia. I know Mrs Fenwick won't mind.'

'I would prefer you to remain here for the present. Aunt Libby will be here and Diana will call on you so you won't exactly be devoid of company.'

'But she won't be here all the time. Can't you understand? And I would so like to visit Amelia. Besides, there are times in this house, where my mother—and your father... Oh,' she cried, thrusting her hair back from her brow in frustration, 'there's no point expecting you to understand.'

Laurence looked at her, and then he looked away. For the briefest instant she saw a flash of—what? Remorse in his dark-blue eyes? Then he looked at her again and said, 'I'm sorry, Victoria. I do understand how difficult this must be for you and you are quite right. I think you should go and stay with your friend for the time being. Write to Mrs Fenwick. If she is in agreement, then I shall take you there myself.'

The quietness, the gentleness, startled her. She stared at him, frightened, and at the same time oddly moved. Then he suddenly reached out and took her hand, looking at her, studying her. A lick of desire, entirely unexpected, shot through Victoria. She was startled by it, by its intensity, contrasting with her other emotions—her anger, her fear, her sense of loneliness—it seemed absurdly, ridiculously sweet. When he had kissed her she had felt things, things that were completely alien to her, and she was still unsure how to deal with them. She stood quite still, staring at him, wanting him to kiss her again more than anything in the world.

And as Laurence looked at her, still quiet, still gentle, he recognised that, saw it—and said, 'I'm not completely heartless, Victoria. While you are in York you might like to do some shopping and see the sights, even though you are familiar with them. You have to begin building up your wardrobe some time— although it's a wonder you learned anything of fashion at that Academy of yours. I imagine you mostly wore uniforms.'

'Only in the latest styles,' she replied with a puckish smile.

'Then I can only hope that time spent in York and Mrs Fenwick will be your salvation.'

'You are very generous, Laurence.'

'Nonsense. The clothes you have are adequate, but as my ward it is imperative that you have a fashionable wardrobe. Does that appeal to you?'

'Oh, yes, but I cannot discard my mourning for frivolous gowns and such for some time.'

Having no desire to look at her dressed in funereal black for the next twelve months, Laurence felt a stab of disappointment. 'No?'

'A definite no. If I am to acquire a position in society, I must not deviate an inch from the path that society demands.'

'That's true. But there's nothing wrong with preparing for the time when you are no longer in mourning. However, for the present, since you are so recently bereaved we won't get mired down with that just now. Plenty of time later.'

Laurence didn't pursue the subject, but he had every intention of raising the matter again very soon. She was young, eighteen years old, and could not be expected to suffer the living death of mourning for twelve long months, living in partial seclusion. That was the last thing Betty would have wanted for the daughter she had so passionately dreamed of being a lady.

Chapter Seven

Mrs Fenwick had replied to Victoria's letter, expressing her condolences for her recent loss and saying how pleased they would be to have her stay with them. Two weeks more of being alone in the house with Laurence, night after night dining together. He was always so proper and distant, never hinting by word or deed that he even remembered what they had both felt on that first riding lesson—how they had become physically aware of each other, that they had kissed and touched each other's faces, the gesture both intimate and ridiculously sweet.

The Fenwick residence was a large, imposing house along The Mount just outside York. Mr Fenwick was a respected lawyer in the city, his wife wrapped up in all manner of charity work. With three sons, Amelia was their only daughter and the youngest.

Arranging to collect her on his return in about six weeks' time, telling her he would write and let her know the exact date, Laurence carried on to London. As much as Victoria was sad to see him go, her sadness was set aside when she became caught up in the household she had come to know so well from the times she had spent there whilst attending the Academy.

She was happy to be with Amelia again, a vivacious brunette. So much had happened to Victoria since she had left the Academy that they had plenty to talk about. On a day of pale-yellow sunshine, when white clouds drifted gently across the River Ouse like cotton wool, they entered York to do some shopping, returning three hours later after visiting shops popular with those who could afford the exorbitant price of garments made specially. All were to be delivered to the Fenwick residence, most of them for Victoria. She sighed, but there was no sadness in that sigh—only the sheer pleasure of satisfaction.

Victoria enjoyed herself in York as much as her mourning allowed. After six weeks she received a letter from Laurence, informing her that business commitments meant he had to remain in London longer than he'd expected and that she should make her own arrangements for returning to Stonegrave Hall. She stared at the letter, thinking of Laurence, and she lifted her hand to touch her cheek with the tips of her fingers, just as she had done countless times during the past few weeks. She closed her eyes and imagined far more—a kiss, a touch, his hand on her breast. With these thoughts uppermost in her mind, she decided to return to Stonegrave Hall.

Laurence stretched out his long legs and lifted his head, encouraging the light breeze which had just sprung up outside the open upper window to lay its coolness upon his face. Shadows lengthened as the sun sank rapidly in the sky over London's docklands, where he sat in his office at Rockford Enterprises. Then the night, deep and swift, was upon him.

Brandon, his secretary, appeared from nowhere, shaking the floorboards with his heavy tread.

'Your brandy, sir, and shall I be lighting the lamp?'

Laurence sighed, reaching for the drink and sipping it absently. He would stop off at his club in St James's before going home. He glanced at Brandon.

'You were saying, Brandon?'

'Shall I light the lamp, sir?'

'Oh, yes, and bring me another brandy.'

The lamp was lit and, in the glow, shared suddenly by a horde of tiny moths, Laurence put down his pen, and his thoughts, as they did so often of late, darting like swifts about his head, quick and hard to grasp, turned to Victoria. He stared blindly across the black sheet of water littered with mighty sea-going vessels of all kinds—a great many of them his own, the breeze plucking at the rigging with a tuneful hum—thinking of the time he had spent in the company of the young woman, which would be the beginning of a relationship that would be important to them both.

Whenever she was in a room with him he had difficulty keeping his eyes off her, and when they were alone, it took all his control to keep his hands off her. When they were apart he couldn't seem to keep his mind off her. She had intrigued his male sensibilities from the start, stirred his senses, her sharp mind stimulating his own, and had captured his imagination with her bright, spirited opinions on everything from literature to sailing ships.

She was possessed of strong determination, waywardly confident, and she showed a capacity to think for herself and to assess what went on around her. He admired her spirit and her sweetness—especially her honesty. And she made him laugh. He could see her now, laughing and shaking her head when her horse had almost thrown her, and he remembered how her brow clouded as she argued some point with him.

He stared into the deep-purple blackness of the night sky. His hand reached out again for the tumbler of brandy before him and, as he sipped it, he began to marshal his thoughts with the precision taught him by years of doing business with pirates and gentlemen alike. His head cleared and in the gloom a strange elated gleam, a pinpoint of clarity, shone in his deep-blue eyes and a smile, lurking at the edges of his mouth, quivered as though longing to burst into laughter.

He had a choice to make. Either he could go on fighting this—denying it—the ever-strengthening bond between him and Victoria. Or he could believe that someone could actually love him—not his money, not his power, not his flesh—but him. Victoria Lewis was the only woman he knew for whom he could ever imagine risking his heart again—baring his soul.

Suddenly, with enormous vitality he sprang up and the blood raced through his veins. He'd had enough of London. He was going home to sort out this muddle Victoria's mother had left him—and to hell with finding her a suitor. His mood veered from grim to thoughtful to philosophical, and finally relief and gladness when he decided he would act out his desire without surrendering all claim to honour and decency, for he knew, deep down, he could not consider handing her over to another and he had no idea to what irrational lengths he might have gone when other suitors started appearing at his door.

She had already turned nineteen years old and was ripe for marriage. He'd known he wanted her from the moment he'd looked into those mesmerising amber eyes of hers. It had started then and strengthened the more time they spent together. Victoria wanted him, too. He'd known that from the beginning, and she hadn't changed, no matter how much she tried to behave otherwise.

A long time ago Melissa Piggott had dealt him a blow that had wounded him deeply. He'd had many affairs since, but not one woman he'd considered proposing marriage to. He'd been reluctant to repeat the process. As a consequence, he had not come near to forming an association with another woman that was anything approaching permanent—until Victoria. At the risk of upsetting his brother, which would be complicated, he contemplated for the last time his decision and the desirability of acting on it at once.

Since he was now determined, he considered only the advantages of haste and ignored any disadvantages. After one past mistake, of almost marrying a woman who hid avarice behind inviting smiles and ambition behind lingering glances, who pretended passion when all she was capable of feeling was for what he could give her, Laurence had finally found a woman who wanted only him. Now, ready for domesticity, he was grasping it with both hands. Should he find it was a handful of broken glass he held, so be it, he would bleed, but at least he would know he was alive.

Shrugging into his coat and telling Brandon to lock up, his spirits flew like the moths still circling the lamp in demented circles, as excitement gripped him.

As he drank with some of his most intimate friends in St James's, he could see only two clear and candid eyes shining in the sunlight and in his anticipation, uncharacteristically, he let down the barrier of reserve which had always stood between himself and those with whom he socialised. They were amazed to discover that not only did he have an intended, but he would be married as soon as he arrived back at Stonegrave Hall.

'By god, you devil, you!' one of his companions shouted, raising a glass, the champagne in it sparkling in the light from the lamps, its pale amber lucidity shot through with a thousand tiny bubbles. 'Are you not the dark horse? Here we all were thinking you married to those ships of yours when all the time you have a delectable young beauty hidden away in the darkest reaches of Yorkshire.'

'And why did you not tell us this before, you sly dog?' shrieked another.

Swept away upon a wave of hopeful exultation, by the time Laurence sought his bed some time during the early hours, he was, in his own mind, firmly and irrevocably engaged to Victoria Lewis.

'Where is Miss Lewis, Jenkins?' Laurence enquired on arriving home four months after he had left.

'Out riding, sir. I believe she was to ride into Ashcomb and return by the river.'

Laurence was pleased to hear her riding had progressed to such an extent that she was both competent and confident enough to go off on her own. The day was pleasantly warm, but with a summer storm threatening to break at any minute, concern for her safety was paramount. Thinking he would surprise her, he set off over the moor.

The horse's hooves thundered over the turf and down the hill to the river. The rain began to fall steadily at first, but it was soon sweeping across the landscape in sheets, parting and lifting now and then to reveal the boulders and sheep that littered the ground. He could hear the thunderous sound of water in full flow and exploding against the rocks as he neared the river. Sparks flew from the rocks over which he galloped. Hoping to meet Victoria at any moment, he pulled on the reins and slowed his horse to a walk, his shoulders hunched and his head bent to avoid the sheeting rain.

Following the course of the river he looked about him. He came to a place where the water cascaded over rocks and into a pool below. The noise was overwhelming, but Laurence was deaf and blind to all, his whole sum and substance concentrated upon the young woman standing knee deep in the swirling, frothy flow, icy yet fresh against her tender flesh. At that moment the rain stopped and the sun slid out from behind a cloud.

Holding the hem of her dress and dark-red cloak high, she gingerly stepped from the water and sat on a low rock, staring down at the river. He was disconcerted by the expression he saw in her face, and bewildered by it. He could not name it, though he felt he should, for it was one that was familiar to him. She had a look of absorbed concentration as she gazed into some other world which she would enter if only she could—a look of yearning for a prize just beyond her reach. Her clear amber eyes had warmed to a soft, subdued shade, and her lips were parted as though she were about to speak.

From beneath the hood Victoria looked up. She detected a strange surge of electricity fairly crackling in the air, like the change in atmosphere that came before a storm. It made the hairs on her nape rise, but the pounding of her heart was entirely due to the man's presence. He sat atop his horse in the shade of the trees, his wide shoulders visible beneath his drenched cape. He nudged the horse out of the shadow and came towards her, into the sunlight. He was smiling, with white teeth and an incredibly handsome face—it was the old irresistible smile. They faced each other across the short distance, each held by the same uncanny fascination.

'Laurence,' she whispered.

From the day he had left her in York she had tossed and turned in her bed until the early hours because of this man, and then her dreams had been filled with such longings and yearnings as she had never thought possible. These past months she had missed him more than she would have believed—his lazy smile, the laughter they shared, the arguing and his quiet strength.

She appeared to be as little surprised as he. The rain had soaked through, the moisture dripping about her face. Her boots and stockings were beside her.

The horse stopped and Laurence slid down from its back.

'Stand,' he said quietly, and though his voice could not be heard above the roar of the water, the animal heard and obeyed. Laurence walked towards her. They looked at one another steadily for a long moment and a spark flared, then Victoria glanced away and got to her feet, retrieving her shoes and stockings.

Taking her arm, Laurence led her to where she had left her horse, where they could speak and be heard above the noise of the river. She spoke first.

'I did not expect to see you.'

'Obviously,' he said, glancing at her boots and stockings dangling from her hands.

His voice surprised her, as always, by its depth and resonant strength, the richness of its quality reminiscent of sultry nights under open skies. 'I thought you were still in London,' she said, liking the feel of his hand gripping her arm.

'I concluded my business and thought it was time I came home.'

Victoria was silent. She was fascinated. Standing there in the rain next to a man she had known for such a short time and whom, she knew with absolute certainty, she would follow anywhere he asked her to go, everything else—the Academy, her friends, her career, those aspects of herself that she had not even been aware of—suddenly fell into place.

'What made you come this way?' he asked. 'Had you not come by the river you would have been home before the rain and safely ensconced at the fireside. You are absolutely soaked, Victoria.'

'The rain doesn't bother me and I'm not one for sitting by the fireside. My friends and I used to come here a lot. Children are always drawn to water.'

She fell silent, feeling awkward suddenly. Her eyes, which had been avoiding his, began to cling now. They never left his face. She was enchanted, it seemed, by the line of his strong jaw and the curve of his throat.

It was as though the day and this place

had cast a spell on them and they had not the strength, nor perhaps the desire, to escape it. He smiled, and then the smile slipped away and his eyes darkened to the deepest blue. They narrowed and became hazed, and his face softened. His lips parted and he wet them with the tip of his tongue. They were each aware that they were completely alone. Signals passed from one to the other and the invisible cord, denied by Laurence himself, stretched between them, as it had done from the moment he had first laid eyes on her. The closer they drew to one another, the tighter the tension became. They were conscious of it, but it did not matter. Like a jewel which glows on the edge of one's vision, Laurence had been aware of Victoria.

It began to rain once more and Laurence watched as it fell on to her face. He looked down at her, smiling slightly as he stared into her eyes before allowing his gaze to travel, slowly, over every inch of her face. He was fascinated by the wisps of hair that clung to her flesh. Droplets hung from her eyelashes and slipped down her cheeks, and her pink tongue licked the moisture from her lips in an innocently sensual gesture. He felt heat pulsate through his veins and he could not look away.

'I've missed you,' he murmured.

The husky whisper was as potent as a caress. 'I've missed you, too.' For weeks she had been telling herself that she was drawn to this man because of his compelling good looks and his powerful animal magnetism. She had almost convinced herself that it was so, that this strange hold he had over her was merely his ability to awaken an intense sexual hunger within her. But that was just the tip of the iceberg, for what she felt for Laurence Rockford went way beyond anything physical. It was something deeper, something dangerously enduring, which had been weaving its spell to bind them inexorably together.

He removed his riding gloves and, without being aware of what he did, he gently touched her face, trailing his finger down the curve of her cheek and brushing raindrops from her nose.

Once again she felt that melting sensation between her legs as his finger made sensuous movements on her flesh. She did not speak or move, but her eyes darkened as her pupils dilated.

More than anything in the world Laurence wanted at that moment to take Victoria Lewis to bed. Had she then made the smallest seductive gesture—had she indicated that she was willing—he might have taken her quickly on the slick, wet grass there in the rain. But Victoria was inexperienced. She was not merely a body, a thing of the flesh. He lusted for her—oh, yes—but as his gaze caressed every inch of her lovely face, her eyes whispered to him of the gentling influence—the elevating companionship—he had so long been starved for.

They were standing close, she with her head tilted back to meet his gaze. At that moment, all that existed in Victoria's world was this man's eyes upon her, and his low voice. His eyes were so tender and she could not bear it if he did not kiss her.

Laurence could feel the warm, beguiling sweetness of her soft breath on his skin. His heart slammed. Moving with care so as not to alarm her, he lifted his hands and slowly ran his palms down her arms beneath her cloak. He felt her quiver under his light touch, heard her breath catch in her throat. He caressed her again, gliding his hands up her arms, past her low neckline, until he came to the creamy expanse of her neck. He could feel the hectic beating of her pulse as he touched her, gently stroking her neck with his fingertips. Her long lashes drifted closed and her rosy lips parted with desire.

His smouldering stare took in the sight of her rapt face, so innocent, so ripe for seduction—her mouth beautiful and waiting. And yet, though she was innocent, he knew an invitation in a woman's eyes when he saw it. Slowly he lowered his lips towards hers, then he claimed her mouth in a kiss.

Nothing in all her nineteen years could have prepared Victoria for what she was experiencing beneath Laurence Rockford's touch, the heat of his mouth on hers. Pleasure unfolded inside her like a butterfly opening its wings to fly. Never in her imagination had she experienced anything so piercing and sweet as this. The movement of his mouth on hers, the warm taste of it, the strong touch of his fingers at the nape of her neck and along her spine—all these things were strangely confusing. She responded slowly at first, then faster with bewildered movements of her own body and little graspings at his arms and shoulders. She did not understand and she did not care. The confusion spread through her whole body and she could not stop it, she did not want to. Her heart raced with guilty pleasure. Her body came keenly alive, all her senses heightened and focused on him and herself and the touch of his mouth until nothing else mattered. His kiss was deep, his lips teasing hers apart. In his arms, with his hand gently cupping her breast, she felt wanton and joyously alive. Caught up in sensation, she was floating on a cloud of euphoria.

This, heaven help her, was exactly what she had wanted, needed him to do. She slipped her hands inside his cloak and slid them over his chest, marvelling over the breadth of his shoulders. Then they were about his neck like tendrils of ivy, clinging to him as an ache spread through every part of her, a sensation never felt before, yet oddly familiar. She slid her hands up into his hair and pressed against him, wanting to bring him even closer. It was as if her entire body knew what to do, even if her mind did not.

With an abruptness that startled her, he tore his lips from hers and turned his face away, breaking the kiss, his breathing uneven. His arm around her relaxed and fell away. Taking her cue from him, she relaxed against him. Still touching her face, he bent his head to rest his forehead close to hers. 'You see,' he said, his breathing ragged as he looked into her eyes, 'how much power you have when you choose to wield it.'

She did see that she, who had convinced herself she had no influence over anything in her life, felt as captivating and alluring as the most beautiful woman on earth, and a joy she had never felt before blossomed inside her. 'Thank you,' she whispered, 'for making the kiss one of the most enjoyable moments of my life.'

He gazed down at her seriously. 'High praise indeed, but I think I should let you go while I still can.'

Weak from the turbulence of her emotions, Victoria rested her head on his chest and felt his heart beating as fast as her own, which meant that he, too, must have been affected by their kiss. There was something different about him, something indefinably more tender, and more authoritative. With confusion making her feel dizzy, she said, 'What we just did—what does it mean?'

She sounded so defeated by the amazing passion they shared that Laurence smiled against her hair. 'It means we're here because we're attracted to each other.'

'But—I hardly know who you are. I know you are a businessman...'

'I also gamble great sums of money on ships and cargo. Does that improve my character in your eyes?'

'Of course it does—but...'

'And as to needing to know who I am, that's very simple to answer.' His hand lifted, grazing her flushed cheek, then smoothing backward, cupping her head. Gently he explained, 'I am the man you're going to marry.'

She stared at him, completely bewildered. 'But—we can't—it's impossible. What I mean is, you may be my guardian, but we are worlds apart.'

'Not for much longer, Victoria. I want you to be my wife.'

'Oh, dear Lord,' she whispered, fear and a sense of euphoria gripping her heart.

'I think it's too late to start praying,' he teased huskily.

'But—but it's madness,' she said, her voice quavering.

'My thoughts exactly,' he whispered. 'You were not in my plans.'

'Please don't do this to me,' Victoria implored helplessly. 'I don't understand any of this. I don't know what you want.'

'I want you,' he said in a tone of tender finality. He took her chin between his thumb and forefinger and lifted it, forcing her to meet his steady gaze as he quietly added, 'And you want me. Ever since that day on the moor when I kissed you I have been in purgatory. You have no idea how much I wanted you. And then I thought it was not all that impossible. You're going to marry me. I'm determined.' He stepped back. His serious expression remained as he studied her upturned face. Her eyes were still languorous, her lips soft from his kiss. 'You must know it cannot end here.'

'But I am not of your world. We aren't at all suited.'

'Aren't we?' he whispered, curving his hand around her narrow waist and moving her closer against him, his tender gesture demonstrating quite clearly that he disagreed with her. 'Marry me, Victoria. Do me the honour of becoming my wife.'

Victoria looked at him. She saw the purposeful gleam in those heavy-lidded eyes and drew a swift breath. This had come unexpectedly— before she was ready—taking her by surprise. Surely there should be more to a courtship, a period of mutual discovery and delicious anticipation. If she said yes, would she be giving in too quickly? And yet, that kiss had been too urgent to be contained for long. She wanted to move on to the next stage as much as she regretted the lost dance of courtship. And by marrying Laurence, she would at once dispatch her mother's concerns for her future.

Her mind shied away from delving too deeply into the exact nature of her feelings for Laurence. She had little faith in trying to judge her own emotions. But she did care for him, there was no use denying it. She had always responded warmly to his nearness and she certainly wasn't indifferent to him. He desired her, this she knew, but he didn't love her. He cared enough about her to want to marry her and it seemed silly to pretend she hated the idea of marrying him, considering how she felt about him.

She looked at his lips and then into his eyes and her panic smoothed away. They were smiling. With those eyes watching over her she would never feel afraid and insecure again, not until the very end and that was a long time away. Marrying Laurence would be like going into a castle, a thick walled place, a safe place where no one else could enter. The feeling was so strong that she could only stand quietly and let the warmth envelop her. Not that her thoughts were quite so cogent in the minute that she made Laurence wait—but those were the strands that swirled around in her head before resolving into the force that made her slowly but definitely reach out her hand and take his.

'Yes,' she whispered. There were tears in her eyes. Tears for the speed of her surrender, tears for all the other futures there might have been. But then he drew her into his arms and kissed her again, touching her mouth with an exquisite gentleness that stunned her into stillness. His mouth brushed back and forth over her lips, lazily coaxing, shaping and fitting them to his own while his hand curved around her nape, stroking it sensually. He kissed her endlessly, as if he had all the time in the world to explore and savour every contour of her mouth. The man who was kissing her had suddenly become the concerned man who had taken her mother in, who'd extended his hospitality to her daughter, the man who'd teased her to laughter and taught her to ride—only now there was a subtle difference in him that made him even more lethally effective—his seeking mouth was possessive as he held and kissed her. Whatever the difference was, she found him utterly irresistible.

When he relinquished her lips her face was flushed and she pushed the wet hair from her forehead with both hands. It was still raining. For the first time Laurence noticed her discomfort and, reaching out, he covered her head with the hood of her cloak.

'So it is settled then,' she said quietly.

'It looks like it. The two of us are headed for the altar.'

'When? I am still in mourning.'

Laurence frowned. 'For another six months. Do you really want to wait another six months? I doubt your mother would have wanted that.'

'No, I don't think she would. But it would have to be a quiet affair.'

'Well then, we won't wait any longer. Now we should be getting back before you catch your death.'

'How do you think your brother will react to this? He will not approve.'

Laurence's expression became grim. He was prepared to be open and honest with every aspect of his life, but Nathan's insistence that the issues that concerned both Nathan and Victoria be kept from her continued to trouble him. 'As to that, we are going to find out.'

Nathan must be told, and soon. Laurence knew he appeared to Victoria as though he wasn't concerned what Nathan thought, but of course he was. He would never say it to her, but he was more than a little apprehensive of his reaction.

Victoria knelt beside the shallow river and, cupping her hands, scooped up some water and drank. The water tasted sweet for she was thirsty. Looking into the water she saw a reflection of her face, noting that her eyes on the rippling surface were dark with unease, for she could not believe she was to be Laurence's wife. She reminded herself that had he not wanted to marry her, he would not have asked her and that she trusted him. But a wrenching pain twisted in her gut, perhaps a premonition of some kind which she had not experienced before now. She closed her eyes, telling herself that the excitement of his return had gone to her head.

Suddenly she was afraid and she shuddered at the thought that the decision she had made was the wrong one. She was in a place she did not choose, with people who were not her own kind, and all she knew was that the nagging feeling of doubt within her had replaced reason in her mind. She took a deep breath to calm herself. She told herself that she was just surprised by Laurence's proposal and not thinking straight, but these uncertainties created chasms she could not fill.

When she stood again there were damp patches on her skirt and water dripping from her chin. Laurence smiled and wiped the droplets away with his fingers. Shelving her unease, Victoria laughed at him, the memory of the kiss still warm and happy inside her.

They swung up on to their horses, gathered their reins and splashed through the water, the horses bounding up the far bank. They moved across the moorland, sitting loose and relaxed in their saddles.

Laurence was well satisfied with the way things had turned out. He could only marvel at how much Victoria had lowered her defences toward him, like a wild horse gentled to his touch only. It was no small honour, for he knew how reticent she had been towards him, yet she had opened herself to him. Even now, he could feel her vulnerability and it made him tremble inside to see how much she trusted him when he wasn't even sure if he could trust himself.

Victoria was a new world—a place of endless mysteries and unexpected delights, an enchanting mixture of woman and child. She could discuss most things with a clinical objectivity and a minute later blush all over when he looked at her in a certain way. She was as stubborn as a mule, haughty when it suited her, serene and inscrutable at times and at others a young girl. On their rides she would test his patience by riding off at a gallop and provoking him into chasing her. She would giggle for minutes at a secret thought. Sometimes she was so naïve that Laurence thought she was joking until he remembered how young she was. She could drive him from happiness to spitting anger and back again within the space of minutes.

But once he had won her confidence she responded to his kisses with a violence that startled them both. Laurence was completely absorbed in her. He told himself she was the best thing he had ever found.

* * *

During those halcyon days, as Victoria planned for her wedding, she was as happy as a bird at daybreak. And yet, although her feelings for Laurence were changing, her fear and uncertainties remained. She told herself that she would strive to overcome them, and when she looked at him they did ease, and all she felt was a deep and abiding tenderness and love.

'I feel like a guest in my own house,' Laurence laughingly remarked to Diana as they waited for Victoria and Aunt Libby to join them in the hall two days before the wedding.

At Aunt Libby's suggestion, he'd moved into the Grange, where he planned to remain for the three days before the wedding. He'd graciously agreed to her suggestion because Aunt Libby was an adequate chaperon and Victoria's reputation might suffer now that local society knew she was to marry him. In an isolated community, every scrap of gossip was pounced on and painted in dramatic overtones. And so it was with Lord Rockford and Victoria Lewis's wedding. Victoria prepared herself for the coming event by ignoring the inevitable clouds of gossip and speculation collecting about her.

Impatient to see her betrothed, Victoria ran down the stairs to meet him in the hall. For a few seconds, Laurence and Diana remained stock still and looked at her in silence. She was so vividly alive, so radiantly beautiful in a dark-grey silk gown. A pair of the daintiest slippers peeped from the whirl of soft skirts and petticoats as she ran towards them.

'I thought you were never coming,' she announced. 'You're so late.' She stopped, her face wreathed in smiles, and gazed at her future husband. Never had she seen him look so striking and handsome as he did now. His dark-claret jacket and trousers set off his broad shoulders and emphasised his long legs with a perfection that bespoke the finest London tailoring—his snowy-white neckcloth was tied to perfection and his hair was perfectly groomed. Even in his relaxed pose his tall body gave off the muscular power of an athlete, while his handsome features were stamped with the cool arrogance of his title.

'Did you think I wouldn't come?' he asked, taking her hand and raising it to his lips. There was an intensity in his voice. It was apparent in his gaze that seemed to scorch the very air between them.

'If it hadn't been for me, Victoria,' Diana said apologetically, 'we should have arrived long ago. I was having a glass of wine with

Nathan and spilt it down my skirts and had to change. I'm so sorry it made us late.'

'Think nothing of it. It really doesn't matter. I'm so sorry about your husband, Diana—that he isn't here.' Victoria would have had to possess the hide of an elephant not to know how deeply both Laurence and Diana felt Nathan's absence from the wedding celebrations, but there was nothing she could do about it. At least he had received the news that Laurence was to marry her better than Laurence had hoped, but he'd refused to accompany him tonight.

'You don't have to worry, Victoria,' Diana said with a smile. 'He has agreed to stand with Laurence in the church. We will have to be content with that for the present.'

'I'm so glad.' Victoria would like to think that Nathan was beginning to soften towards her, but deep inside her she didn't hold out much hope.

In an effort to put her anxieties concerning the wedding out of her mind, Victoria was determined to enjoy herself. Unfortunately the evening passed as if it were minutes, not hours, and all too soon it was time for Laurence and Diana to return to the Grange. Victoria went with them out to the carriage and when Laurence had assisted Diana inside, he turned to Victoria and took her in his arms.

'I'll see you in the church the day after to-morrow. And don't worry. Everything will be fine.'

'I know it will,' she answered with a confidence she did not feel, for as the wedding came closer, her anxiety about what she was about to do increased. She had the insecure sense that she did not know the rules of the game Laurence was playing. They lived on separate islands in a society divided by an ocean of money and privilege. The thought troubled her.

Laurence kissed her for the last time. She returned his kiss, but her anxiety remained.

The day had come at last. The sun shone bright, shrouding the moors with golden promise.

Victoria was in a different world, peopled by beings quite different from those she had known. The wedding was to be a quiet affair, the ceremony at Ashcomb Church. She would have no relatives of her own at the wedding— not a single male relative to give her away. None of her friends would be there to give her encouragement, no kind, supportive Amelia. Not wanting to appear too frivolous, the only thing that had given Victoria pause for thought was the question of a wedding gown. Diana, sensitive to her mood and saying that she was sure her mother would have wanted her to look like any other bride on her wedding day, suggested an ivory-silk gown.

Victoria could not believe what was happening, for not only did her mind and her whole body churn with a mixture of feelings—she was sad because her mother was not here to see her married—but she was full of wonderment that she was to be the wife of a successful businessman and a rich landowner and would be mistress of his estate, but above all these feelings she was fearful of what lay ahead.

She was pale with nervousness. Diana came to help her prepare and Aunt Libby was fussing about like a mother hen. When she was ready they departed for the church, and it was left to Ned to take her in the carriage.

Alone in the drawing room, waiting for him to arrive, she restlessly walked up and down, wishing he would come so she didn't have time to think. She told herself that she wanted to marry Laurence more than anything else. She loved everything about him—his smile, his looks, the brisk authority in his deep voice and the confidence in his athletic movements. She loved the way his eyes gleamed when he laughed and the way they smouldered when he kissed her.

Tearing her thoughts from Laurence, she

stared bleakly out of the window. Yes, she loved many things about him but she was not a good judge of men. She had no experience of them. Laurence was attracted to her, this she did know. She had tried to convince herself that what she felt for him was gratitude and friendship, but she knew it had gone much deeper than that and she was more than a little in love with him. But did he want her love?

Fear raced through her and panic began to set in. In less than an hour she was going to commit her entire life to a man who had once told her in the plainest terms that love had no place in marriage. Every instinct for self-preservation that she possessed warned her not to marry him. For the thousandth time she reminded herself that she was not of his world and never would be, and that instead of making him happy and making him love her she would make him miserable and herself, too—but her heart begged her to gamble everything on him and not to be a coward. Her mind, however, told her to turn and run.

Suddenly she was overcome by a heavy feeling of foreboding. The day had darkened—great clouds were rolling from the west over the moors and the sky was streaked orange and red behind them, dramatic, threatening. She felt chilled, anxious about the day. A sense of great

unease stirred inside her along with a premonition of approaching danger. Giving herself
a mental shake, she told herself she was being
absurd, that it was the sudden change in the
weather that had provoked this, but when Clara
Ellingham stepped into the room from the terrace, she knew it wasn't the weather.

Clara smoothed down the lustrous velvet of
her riding habit, savouring the feel of the rich
and expensive material beneath her hands. Her
smile of self-satisfaction was evident, the diamonds in her ears as she threw back her head
sparkled even in the dim interior of the room.

Looking into her eyes Victoria saw something swimming in their depths. A *frisson* of
alarm slithered down her spine. Whatever it
was she saw reminded her of a shark circling
in deep water. She saw the malevolence, saw
the paleness of Clara's face and the high red
colour on her cheek-bones.

'Good morning,' Victoria said tightly. 'Visi-
tors usually come in by the front door.'

Clara looked her up and down as if she were
some beggar who had the temerity to accost her
in the street. She smiled, showing her perfect
teeth. 'I'm not averse to using the back door—
the servants' entrance, which you will know all
about.' Her smile deepened. She would never
forgive this upstart who had stolen the man she

had earmarked for herself. But all was not lost. She still had hopes of getting him back, for she meant to destroy Victoria Lewis.

'Look at you,' she purred, 'you scheming upstart.' Clara looked down her long nose at Victoria. 'You thoroughly believe yourself the equal of him, don't you? You are of a different class and ill equipped to deal with the society he inhabits. Ever since you came here you have started to behave like the entitled rich, giving yourself airs of privilege without the pedigree that define them. You think that because Laurence is marrying you you can keep him, don't you?' She moved closer, her hostile eyes never leaving Victoria's. 'Well, when I've told you a few facts about your precious Laurence Rockford, he will be the last man in the world you will want to marry.'

'Will you please leave? I have nothing I wish to say to you.'

'I have plenty I want to say to you.'

'Haven't you said enough in the past?'

'I think you need to hear what I have to tell you,' Clara smoothly declared.

Her entire body vibrating with panic, Victoria faced Clara Ellingham. 'And I have told you I don't want to listen. Ever since I left the Academy and came to live here you have hounded me with your obsession for Laurence.'

'And who do you think paid for that fancy education you received at the Academy in York? Who do you think bought you your fancy clothes?'

'My mother.'

Clara thrust her face close to Victoria's and laughed vindictively. 'That's what she told you, was it—what you assumed?'

Victoria stared at her. 'What are you saying?'

'That every penny of your education was paid for by Laurence. He knew how difficult it was for someone in your mother's position to find the necessary funds to pay for your education. How lucky she was to have a *male friend* to pay for it all. I suppose he felt somehow beholden—which was why he sent you to that fancy Academy in York. Now how do you feel knowing that?'

Paralysed by her revelation, Victoria felt the blood drain from her face and her eyes had a haunted, almost desperate expression. 'You're lying.'

'And you're sure of that, are you?'

'And for what reason would he feel beholden to my mother?'

'Well, there is the matter of your mother and her morals.'

'Her *morals*—good or bad—are nothing to do with you. She's dead and cannot speak for herself.'

'No, she can't, can she—but the truth will out.'

'Truth? The truth about what?'

'Her sordid affair with Laurence's father—and how she shamelessly flaunted it underneath his wife's nose—but then I suppose gentlemen of the old Lord Rockford's ilk are allowed their little indiscretions, are they not?'

Victoria looked at her and a searing white light seemed to dance in front of her eyes. She felt hot, blazingly, ragingly hot, and physically sick as she faced Clara Ellingham, and felt each of her enraged words as if it was a blow to her head, her voice speeding up faster and faster, spinning so quickly the next one appeared before the other had spun away. Clara held nothing back: *Laurence financing her education—her mother's scandalous affair with his father—something about a child, a son—Victoria's half-brother—her mother had given him up to Lady Rockford and agreed with Lord Rockford that she would never see him.*

Standing in the wreckage of her dream of marrying Laurence, the one just blasted by Clara Ellingham who had once threatened to bring her down, Victoria looked at her and started to speak, and all the hurt, all the betrayal she had ever felt were in her words.

'Please leave. I think you have said everything you came to say.'

For the rest of her life Victoria, remembering that moment when the bottom had dropped out of her world, had thought of all the things she might have said and done, what appropriate, clever, sophisticated remark or gesture she might have made. What she actually did was to ask Clara to leave and then, with no emotion in her voice, she asked Jenkins to instruct Ned to bring the carriage, before going to her room, taking off her wedding gown and dressing in something more appropriate for travel.

She realised that beneath everything she had just learned just how much she actually loved Laurence, but now the security that she had found with him was gone. A lump rose in the back of her throat at the realisation that he was going to walk into Ashcomb Church thinking he was about to be wed, only his bride would have deserted him. On top of her earlier doubts about the marriage, the unease and insecurities, Clara Ellingham's revelations had come as the final straw.

Deep down Victoria was furious, furious at

the injustice done her. The walls of her castle had proved to be made of paper. She had felt the first cold draughts blowing through them as Clara Ellingham had walked into the room, and she had felt the walls tremble and the wind howl stronger outside when Clara had spoken her first condemning words—then they had collapsed into ruin around her feet.

The bloom on her face had withered until her expression was dead—blank and as dead as a statue—and she wondered if the strange pain in her heart would ever go away. Standing in the half-darkened room with her wedding dress and the frothy pile of her petticoats on the bed, she looked down the long, lonely corridor of the future. It was worse than tears would have been, that silent acceptance, thinking of the man she had trusted so completely and who just as completely had deceived her, had betrayed her. She felt more lonely than she could ever remember being in her life. She knew she could not stay. There was only one alternative.

'What shall I tell his lordship?' Sally asked as she was leaving.

Carrying her valise, Victoria turned in the doorway. 'Tell him—tell him it was a mistake. Tell him I couldn't go through with it.'

By the time she left the house the rain had

begun, light and powdery, more mist than anything. After half an hour it was raining harder,
grey sheets of water, and a driving wind had
set in.

Chapter Eight

His expression unreadable, Laurence waited for his bride in Ashcomb Church. Nathan was at his side, the vicar in front of him, the marriage book open in his hands. As the minutes passed and Victoria failed to arrive, Nathan turned to look at his brother.

'What do you intend to do?' he asked.

'We'll wait.'

Laurence waited another thirty minutes in the asinine belief that Victoria would come. Refusing to believe that history was about to repeat itself, he waited. His eyes were colder than an icy winter sky and there was a thin white line about his mouth. Still they stood there, the two of them, facing the altar.

When the vicar came to have a word with

Laurence, excusing himself, Nathan went to find Diana who was in the vestibule, looking worriedly along the road for any sign of the bride's carriage.

'I've heard of brides being late for their wedding, but this is taking it too far,' Nathan complained crossly.

'Something must have happened,' his wife said. 'You may be certain Victoria will have an excellent explanation for being late.'

'Let us hope so—for her sake. To be jilted once at the altar is bad enough, but twice is not to be borne. Laurence will tear her to shreds if she doesn't go through with it. I knew it was madness for him to propose marriage, but he wouldn't listen.'

After a further half an hour and Victoria hadn't arrived, Laurence sent the driver of his carriage to the Hall to see where she was. Eventually he was apprised of the fact that she had vanished from the Hall with Ned. Sally, her maid, was unable to throw any light on why she had suddenly discarded her wedding dress and gone, taking very little with her.

'But she must have said something,' Laurence demanded.

'She did, my lord,' Sally uttered nervously. 'She—she said it was a mistake and she couldn't go through with it.'

Laurence turned his back on her. The plain and simple fact was that Victoria had run away.

'She must have good reason,' Diana said to her husband.

'It won't matter,' Nathan said in a harsh voice. 'Unless she can convince Laurence she was forcibly abducted, she's as good as dead to him.'

'Please don't say that. He loves her. Anyone can see that.'

'I know my brother better than you, Diana,' Nathan replied, remembering Laurence's actions on the day Melissa Piggott left him standing at the altar. 'He'll never give her another chance to hurt him. If she's left him voluntarily, she's as dead to him. Look at his face. He's already killing any feelings he had for her.'

'It isn't so easy to put someone you love from your heart.'

'Laurence can,' Nathan argued. 'He'll do it so she can never get close to him again.'

When Ned returned to the Hall, he affirmed that he had taken Victoria to Malton where she had boarded the coach for York.

There was no way to avoid the truth and not enough liquor in the world to douse the rage that was beginning to consume Laurence. Unable to bear being married to him, Victoria had run off. After all his experience with women, he thought bitterly, as his wrath continued to build, he'd fallen prey to a damsel in distress.

Twice!

'What shall I do with her wedding dress, my lord?' Sally asked when Lord Rockford came to her mistress's room.

'Burn it,' Laurence bit out, 'and get rid of everything else she left behind.'

Nathan was right. Victoria Lewis was already dead to Laurence. Beyond that monumentally handsome skull of his was a brain as quick and unforgiving as a guillotine.

On reaching York, Victoria's bitter tears of hurt and disappointment had been burning at the back of her throat for almost the entire journey. She wanted nothing more than to be in the quiet of her room in the Fenwick household, where she could give vent to them and, please God, emerge on the other side of this crushing experience.

Thinking of her mother was agony, but she was able to think more clearly now she was away from Stonegrave Hall. If what Clara Ellingham had told her was true—and deep down she believed it was, for it explained so much that had remained unsaid—her mother had been delivered of Lord Rockford's child.

She wasn't sure what she felt as she wondered if the strange pain in her heart would ever go away again—confused, yes, shocked, yes, but beyond that—what?

How much did she mind that she had a brother, that her mother had been in love with and borne a child to another man, not Victoria's own kind, gentle father—a child she had never mentioned. How had it happened, how could her mother have given it away? How could she have done that? What kind of a mother could form such an agreement? How could anyone just hand over her child with so cool a detachment? Or be able to hold herself to it? How could she, all these years, have remained silent?

Finding all this out explained why her mother had kept herself withdrawn from her and her father. It broke Victoria's heart to think that she might have loved her son more than she loved her daughter, but being unable to acknowledge him, to talk about him, must have tortured her every waking moment of her life.

All these things Victoria probed, cautiously, carefully, as if exploring the extent of a wound, and she could not begin to find any answers. She felt terrible. Part of her was in shock, another part acknowledged that she had known, or instinctively suspected, that there was more than Laurence had wanted her to know about the affair between her mother and his father. The state of rage she had been in since Clara Ellingham had spilt her vitriol into her ears had cooled. It was an awful, sad, sordid story, but at least it was no longer a total mystery. She could begin to face it head-on and meet it in the eye, and get to know it.

A terrible thought clutched at her. Had Laurence asked her to marry him to stop the scandal getting out? Where she was concerned, how could she have agreed to marry him? It had been a mistake, she could see that now. Her whole life had been one big mistake. The biggest mistake, of course, was allowing herself to fall in love with Laurence. And, the strangest thing of all was that she loved him still—after all this upheaval, she thought angrily. That was the shameful bit. She still loved Laurence. She always would.

What did become clear to her was that Nathan was her half-brother and that he knew, and had suffered his own kind of torment because of it. Clara Ellingham's malevolence had reached out and suffocated her. She wanted Laurence, and she would move heaven and earth to get him. She, Victoria, stood in her way and must be removed, and with a few acid words she'd succeeded.

On Victoria's arrival at Fenwick House, in the space of seconds, Amelia considered Victoria's dejection and knew something had gone dreadfully wrong. She noted the total absence of her normal, unaffected warmth and correctly assumed her current attitude of proud indifference was a façade to conceal some sort of deep hurt. Since Laurence was the only one who had the power to truly hurt her, that meant he was the likely cause of the problem.

'What has happened to make you say you no longer wish to be married to Lord Rockford?'

When she looked into Amelia's sympathetic eyes, Victoria promptly succumbed to a fresh wave of grief-stricken tears. 'It didn't work out as we expected,' she cried, unable to tell her the truth, that there was something inside her that cried out against Laurence's deceit and pretence.

'But what has happened? I thought you would be married by now. Has something happened to Lord Rockford?'

Victoria shook her head. 'There was no wedding, Amelia. We—we decided we didn't suit after all.'

With her mother looking on sympathetically,

with the ties of childhood friendship and long-standing affection tightening around them, Amelia sat down next to Victoria on the sofa. It was more serious than she'd thought. 'Whatever the argument was about, I am sure it can be sorted out.'

'No, Amelia, it can't. How I wish I'd never seen him. He is too high born for me—a lord—an important man,' she said through her tears, 'and I am only a school master's daughter. I am nothing to him. I never was. I should never have reached above my station.'

'Oh, Victoria, come now,' Amelia scolded tenderly, patting her shoulder. 'Lord Rockford wouldn't have asked you to marry him if he hadn't wanted to.'

'Where is he now?' Mrs Fenwick asked.

'At the Hall,' Victoria whispered through her tears.

'Then I will write to him.'

'There is nothing more to say. I can't go back. Can—can I stay?' she asked tentatively. 'Until I find employment of some kind—which is what I intend to do. I will not impose on you longer than necessary—but I really have nowhere else to go.'

'You can stay as long as you like,' Mrs Fenwick said, getting up and ringing for tea, convinced there was more to this than Victoria was letting on. 'You are Amelia's closest friend and you are very dear to us, Victoria. You are most welcome.'

What had happened had hit Victoria hard. She longed to talk about it, to tell Amelia and Mrs Fenwick, to receive comfort, support and understanding, but she couldn't. This was too private, too painful, something she was locked into alone, quite alone now. She felt shocked, almost bereaved—she ached, physically— bruised, dragged through an assault course. She had trouble sleeping—her appetite, usually so healthy, so hearty, failed her. Tears overcame her—suddenly, shockingly. Amelia and her mother noticed, asked her if she was all right.

'Victoria, I know there is something you haven't told us. Would you like to talk about it?' Mrs Fenwick asked, her gentle face soft with concern.

She shook her head, and forced a smile. 'I don't think so. No. But thank you. You're being very kind.'

Mrs Fenwick smiled back and said she understood and hugged her very close.

Realising she owed Laurence an explanation for her actions on their wedding day, Victoria wrote him a long and extremely painful letter, telling him of Miss Ellingham's visit and that she hoped he would understand why she had acted as she had when he learned what was behind it. She stressed that he should have told her that her mother had given birth to his father's child and that Nathan was that child—her half-brother. She told him he'd had no right to keep the truth from her, that she had a right to know. She went on to say that she was deeply sorry for any hurt he might have suffered because of her actions, but his deception over this matter had distressed and angered her almost beyond bearing, and the crushing humiliation she had felt when she had learned she owed her education to him and not her father, as she had believed, was unforgivable.

The letter was duly sent. Victoria would have been furious and hurt had she seen Laurence take the letter and crumple it in his hand before consigning it to the fire without bothering to read it.

He did, however, write to Mrs Fenwick—he was, after all, still Victoria's guardian. The letter was brief and to the point. As far as he was concerned he had been inconvenienced enough of late and if it was agreeable to Mr and Mrs Fenwick, Victoria had his permission to stay with them until she was twenty-one. If she should wish to marry in the meantime he would raise no objections to that. There was only one thing he insisted upon and that was that Victoria should never contact him again for any reason.

'Inconvenienced!' Victoria railed on reading this. Her colour mounted high in her cheeks and warmed her ears. She was incensed. Mrs Fenwick was taken aback by her outburst and went on to explain that Lord Rockford was prepared to meet his obligations and was to provide a generous allowance for her keep and clothing.

On hearing this, Victoria's humiliation was complete. She accepted that she could not expect to live with the Fenwicks indefinitely without contributing something towards her keep and, since she had no income of her own, she had no choice but to accept what she considered to be Laurence's charity. But where her clothes were concerned, she had acquired an adequate wardrobe—albeit paid for by Laurence, which galled her to think about—and she did not intend to accept more of his charity than she could afford.

The fact that he made no mention of her letter or its contents and made no further effort to contact her in any way sent anger ripping through her—hot, violent rage. And then her brain turned full circle and she told herself instead that if he had any feelings for her at all, he would want to know at the very least how she was.

In the weeks that followed she coped in the only way she knew how. Trying not to think about Laurence, she immersed herself in helping Mrs Fenwick with a dozen civic and church activities, and she kept herself going until she dropped into bed at night, exhausted.

Christmas came and went and the days merged into weeks that passed in a blur of activity, but slowly she began to find her balance again. But Laurence was never far from her thoughts. Despite the bitterness still eating away inside her, she found it extraordinarily difficult, even after this considerable time, to think about much else. He obsessed her— she saw his face, heard his voice, remembered him—oh, dear Lord, she remembered him, everywhere, all the time. Time, if anything, increased her desire for him, but she could not forgive his deception.

There was great excitement when the family prepared to journey to London to partake of the Coronation celebrations for King George IV. He had become king following the death of his father, George III, in January of the previous year. Wishing it to outshine Napoleon Bonaparte's Coronation, the king declared it would be the grandest ever.

The Fenwicks were to reside with Mrs Fenwick's mother, the dowager Lady Elsworthy, who lived in a fine mansion in the north of London. Unlike Amelia, who was tremendously excited about visiting the metropolis and the social gatherings she would attend, Victoria viewed London as a wider scope to seek employment.

'What you need,' Amelia said as she surveyed her extensive wardrobe, 'is some fun. You've never been to London and I just know you are going to love it. Perhaps you'll meet someone who will make you forget that you ever knew Laurence Rockford—when he no longer matters.'

Victoria looked at her friend with quiet dignity. 'When he stops mattering to me, then I'll be ready for someone else. Not before.'

Amelia knew better than to pursue the subject, but on reaching London she had every intention of drawing her dear friend out of the doldrums and into society at every opportunity.

Amelia was right. Victoria found London a delight, but she would have preferred to spend her time quietly seeing the sights and visiting the galleries than attending the many social events Amelia insisted upon.

It was at one such gathering that she overheard it mentioned that Nathan Rockford and his wife were in town for the celebrations and that his sister-in-law Clara Ellingham had accompanied them. They had taken a suite at the grand Pulteney Hotel, which, like every other hotel, was full to bursting with people converging on London to celebrate the Coronation. She also heard some gossip concerning Laurence, of how he had been left waiting at the altar while his bride—one Victoria Lewis with no connections and of no possible consequence—absconded.

Clara Ellingham was right. Victoria was ill equipped to deal with society. The noble tribe was arguably the hardest of all in which to gain acceptance. Its language, its customs, its initiation ceremonies were all absolutely exclusive, no experience of any other people could prepare for it. While Victoria was only trying to gain acceptance as a member, when it became known that she was the same Victoria Lewis who had jilted Lord Rockford, she was seen, by the women within the circle, as an interloper of the highest order, a thief stealing a glittering and unearned prize. Most people in Lady Elsworthy's circle treated her with an initially overt and gushing politeness and then proceeded to ignore her, occasionally tossing her a courtesy smile.

She tried to cope with it all, to learn to act quite skilfully at the life there, the self-indulgent, egocentric gatherings, to sit and smile at least at the homes and the parties, but she didn't like it. She felt lonely, small, of no importance.

She was there on sufferance because she had nowhere else to go.

She had made the Fenwicks aware of the full extent of the events leading up to her cancelled wedding to Laurence, and although they were understanding of her situation and tried so hard to protect her from the humiliation of the gossip—which made her feel guilty in itself—it was a situation she could not accept for much longer.

The answer to her dilemma came from Lady Elsworthy. Aware that Victoria was seeking employment as a governess, she had heard from a reliable source that a Mr and Mrs Levinson, a wealthy American couple, were looking for an English governess for their seven- and five-year-old daughters. They were staying at the Pulteney Hotel and were to return to America shortly.

Victoria lost no time in writing to apply for

the position. An appointment for an interview came almost immediately. Knowing Nathan was resident in the same hotel, she wrote asking if he would meet her. It was something she had been thinking about for some time. Giving the day and the time, she told him that if he didn't wish to meet her, she would understand. Whether it was a reckless gesture or not, she felt it only right that she approach him. He would still probably not want to have anything to do with her, but she had to try.

Her interview went well and she liked Mr and Mrs Levinson immediately. They were warm and friendly and their children polite, well behaved and absolutely adorable. They had two more ladies to interview and would contact her when they had made their decision. Victoria was hopeful.

The interview had finished with time to spare before her meeting with Nathan—if he deemed to show up. It was early afternoon and the hotel was quiet. Glancing through the open doors into the luxuriously appointed dining room, the candelabras glowed, burnishing the gilding throughout the room and gleaming upon the fine silver and exquisite painted china.

She sat waiting in the vestibule among an arrangement of palm fronds and huge white lilies

and neatly arranged chairs, her heart thunder-
ing with dread and hope and uncertainty. She
saw him before he saw her. Rising, she looked
at him with new eyes as he strode in her direction. His hair was fair like her own, but that
was where the similarity ended. He had their
mother's eyes and he had a way of holding his
head that reminded her of their mother. An inexplicable pain penetrated her heart.

Then he saw her and stopped, taking her in.
She could feel his eyes examining her, exploring her. There was a barrier of aloofness about
his manner and lines of strain about his mouth
that moved her. The fact that he had agreed to
stand beside Laurence at their wedding told
her he might have been softening towards her.
But that was then. As Laurence's brother and
knowing how close they were, Nathan would
despise her for leaving Laurence, for hurting
him, and the scandal that ensued.

He approached her slowly. His eyes holding hers seemed to be trying to say something
to her. She was disconcerted by what she saw
on his face. He seemed oppressed and weary.
Instantly the look was gone, replaced by cool
formality, but thankfully the hostility that had
governed their last meeting at Stonegrave Hall
was absent. But what took its place bewildered
her even more. Looking into his eyes she saw

compassion, a certain wariness and regret, and despite herself, Victoria felt her heart go out to him. Despite her misgivings, he was her brother.

'*So here you are!*' he said, staring woodenly at the young woman who'd deserted his brother at the altar, which had caused a furore of pain and scandal. He had watched Laurence closely in the weeks following that day. He brooded and worked and the only activity he enjoyed was riding—except that now he ruthlessly forced his mount over impossible obstacles and rode with a reckless, bruising violence that struck genuine alarm in Nathan. When he could stand it no longer, Laurence had headed for London to immerse himself in his business. 'How very *good* of you to find the time to pay me a social call. Would it be too pushing of me to enquire where you are staying?'

'I have come to town with the Fenwicks. We are staying with Mrs Fenwick's mother, Lady Elsworthy. I—can imagine what you must be thinking,' she began in a conciliatory manner.

Nathan interrupted sharply, 'Oh, I don't think you can. If you could, you'd be quite horrified at this moment. You'd be surprised at what a man can imagine,' he said, the words punishing but without malice.

'I fear I would not,' she answered calmly, her reticule clutched in her fingers at her waist.

'You have much to explain, Miss Lewis.'

'I have already done so—to Laurence. I will not repeat myself.'

Nathan frowned and glanced at her curiously, but did not pursue the nature of her reply. 'I fail to understand why you wish to see me. Have you any idea of the scandal your desertion caused—in Yorkshire and here in London? I dare say all of London will be eager to hear what you have to say for yourself.'

'I am not going to say anything. I have not come here to pacify the gossips. I have no reason to.'

'Then I must ask you to stay away from Laurence. Don't shame him more than you already have! I congratulate you, Miss Lewis. You have managed to reduce a great man to a laughing-stock in the eyes of the world.'

Victoria's chin came up in defiance. His judgemental attitude struck sparks of rebellion in her. 'I suppose I could make amends if it would make you feel better. I could put an announcement in the papers telling the world that *he* jilted me,' she said with quiet sarcasm.

'That is encouraging at least,' he uttered, equally sarcastic, 'but I know that Laurence would not want to buy back his pride at the cost of your own. You might offer to do it, however. That would help convince him you are truly repentant.'

Victoria's eyes darkened. 'Repentant? Oh, no, I don't think so. I, too, was wronged that day.'

'What are you talking about?'

'About you, Mr Rockford—or perhaps I may call you Nathan since I believe you are my brother—my half-brother, that is.'

Nathan stared at her, momentarily stunned. Ever since he had found out he had a sister some years ago, the very sound of her name had been anathema to him. But now he had met her, he didn't know what to think any more, how to react to her. He usually concealed the pain and the hurt done to him by all those who had colluded in the shameful events of his birth in anger. 'You know?'

'Yes. I know we share the same mother. I didn't have to come here, but I wanted to see you.'

Nathan's face was rigid, as though he had determined upon a path of self-control that threatened to break at any moment. 'I have nothing to say to you,' he said, his voice hoarse as his emotions threatened to get the better of him. 'I don't want to get into this—not now. I think you should leave.'

His back was straight and Victoria recognised the stance, for it was one her mother had taken when something or someone disagreed with her. Stubborn, her father had always said she was, stubborn. 'Don't you want to know about our mother?'

Swallowing his hurt, he averted his eyes. 'Why should I? She cut me out of her life when she gave me away. What kind of person could do that but a heartless, unfeeling woman.'

Victoria refused to be drawn into an argument with him, but despite the hurt she herself had suffered all her life, she felt she had to defend her mother. 'She didn't give you away. And she wasn't heartless. She was good and kind, loyal and loving.'

Nathan's lips twisted bitterly, and when he looked at her again Victoria saw all the pain and hurt that was in her own heart mirrored in his eyes. 'Was she? Well, I'll never know, will I?'

For a brief moment Victoria thought she heard a note of regret in his voice and saw it in his eyes, but it was quickly gone. 'No,' she said quietly, with empathy and compassion. 'You won't. She left you with your father. I don't know the facts myself, but I imagine she didn't have a choice.'

'Forgive me if I find that a little hard to believe,' he said, his voice hardening.

'What kind of life do you think she could give you—an unmarried mother! How did you find out?'

'What? That I am a bastard? My father thought I should be told before someone else did it for him. And you? How did you find out about me?'

'Your sister-in-law took great delight in informing me about that moments before I was due to leave for the church—and several other matters she couldn't wait to divulge. She certainly has a penchant for twisting the knife. From the very beginning she made it plain my presence at the Hall was unwelcome.'

'Clara has never been one to mince her words. She was right. The manner in which you ingratiated yourself into our lives was bad enough, but to agree to marry my brother was beyond speaking about.'

'Why? Because the home from which I come cannot be described as one of genteel domesticity?'

'I imagine it was far from it. You have much to learn.'

'And you would know that, would you? You don't know anything about me.'

'And you know even less about me.'

Victoria put up her chin and managed to say with great dignity, 'No, I don't. I don't know who taught you your manners, but they should have told you that it's an unpleasant and alienating thing to do to speak like that. It doesn't matter how you choose to look at it, I am your sister—you are my brother. I had hoped we could at least acknowledge each other. Perhaps this isn't the right moment to tell you about our mother—I imagine it's still very painful for you—but if you feel like speaking to me you can find me at Lady Elsworthy's house. Otherwise,' she said, shoving her hands into her gloves and turning away, indicating that the meeting was over, 'you can climb back into your self-pitying little shell and stay there.'

Nathan was looking at her in outrage. 'How dare you?'

'Oh, I do dare,' she replied calmly. 'I dare do a lot of things I wouldn't have dreamed of doing before Miss Ellingham's visit. How is Laurence?' she asked, pausing and looking back at him.

'Why this sudden interest in my brother's well-being? Do you honestly care?'

'If you must know, I do care. Very much.'

'Then try telling him that—in fact, you can do it now—if you can get him to listen to what you have to say.'

Victoria swung her head to the door and saw a tall man just coming in. An uncontrollable tremor of dread shot through her and she lowered her head. She could have sworn Laurence Rockford stiffened with shock. His head jerked towards her as if trying to see past the rim of her bonnet, but she was absolutely besieged with cowardice and kept her head down.

Nathan glanced at Laurence. 'I suppose I should inform my brother that you are here.'

'Your brother,' said a biting voice from near at hand, 'is aware of that.'

Hearing the scathing tones, a wave of shock and tension seemed to scream through Victoria's veins. She raised her head and looked directly at him, and her dreams of seeing him again collapsed the instant she saw his face—it was as hard and forbidding as a granite sculpture. His eyes were dark with hostility and a kind of savage rage she would never have thought him capable of. She saw his entire body stiffen, saw his gaze snap to her face, his blue eyes turning an icy, paler blue.

Until then Victoria had thought she remembered exactly what he looked like, but she hadn't. His bottle-green jacket clung to shoulders that were broader and more muscular than she remembered. His face was one of arrogant handsomeness and she noticed the

cynicism in those deep-blue eyes and the ruth-
less set of his jaw. Everything about him ex-
uded brute strength, power and an unshakeable
confidence, and that in turn made her feel even
more helpless as she searched his features for
some sign of softness in this aloof, forbidding
stranger. He was still every bit as handsome—
the perfect gentleman. But she didn't want to
admit it. She didn't want to feel anything for
him—that part of her life was over. He hadn't
replied to her letter and that fact was still painful for her.

Her mind ranged through the evocative
memories left over from the days they had
spent together in Yorkshire. Though sorely
lacking experience in the realm of desire, instinct assured her the wanton yearnings gnawing at the pit of her being were nothing less
than cravings that Laurence had elicited with
his lustful courtship. The fact that those feelings were just as potent today completely frus-
trated her efforts to thrust him from her mind.

Neither of them was aware of the moment
when Nathan turned from them and mumbled,
'If you will excuse me. I have things to do.' He
headed for the stairs, his eyes troubled with bewildering emotions of his own. His meeting
with Victoria Lewis had affected him in ways
that surprised him, ways he had not thought

possible, and for the first time in his life he began to acknowledge the fact that he had a sister.

Shaking beneath the blast of Laurence's gaze, Victoria's hands tightened on her reticule. She tried to think how to begin and, because she was so overwhelmed with emotions and explanations, said the first thing that came into her head.

'Are you well, Laurence?'

She saw his shoulders stiffen at the sound of her voice and could almost feel the effort he was exerting to keep his rage under control. 'As you see, I have survived.'

In silent, helpless protest Victoria shook her head and started slowly across the floor, dimly aware that this was worse, much worse than anything she had done in her life.

'If you are wise,' he warned in a soft, blood-chilling voice as he loomed over her, 'you will not come any closer. You will avoid me very carefully while you are in London. And when you leave, you will only communicate with me through Mrs Fenwick.'

She stopped cold, her mind registering the threat in his voice, refusing to believe it, her gaze searching his granite features. She felt sick. What she was being blamed for wasn't even her fault. If Laurence had been honest with her, none of this would have happened. But it had happened. She had shamed and humiliated him, and now he wanted nothing more to do with her.

'Laurence,' she began, looking at him in mute appeal, then lowering her gaze when her beseeching look got nothing from him but a blast of contempt from his eyes. 'I realise,' she began again, her voice trembling with emotion while she tried to think how to begin to diffuse his wrath, 'that you must despise me for what I've done.'

'Correct. Have you come here to apologise? Although you must possess the instincts of a bloodhound to track me here.'

'I had no idea you would be here—I came to the hotel on another matter. But what am I to apologise for?' she asked with infuriating calm.

Laurence cocked a mocking brow. 'You want me to spell it out?'

'If you are expecting me to apologise for not turning up at the church, then I will not. Why did you not reply to my letter?' she continued bravely. 'I—hoped you would at least acknowledge it—that you would—'

'I couldn't care less about the letter or what was in it,' he interrupted in a murderous voice.

For a moment she stared at him in appalled silence, then she said through a constriction in her throat, 'You didn't read it, did you?' Victoria felt destroyed. Her mind couldn't seem to absorb it. All these weeks she had been waiting for him to respond, hoping he would understand and comprehend the pain his deception had inflicted on her, and all the time he hadn't even bothered to read it. 'You might at least have had the decency to do that. I tried to explain—'

'And why would you want to do that, when you couldn't even be bothered to turn up for your own wedding? What was it you told your maid to tell me—that you couldn't go through with it—that it was a mistake! Well, you were right—it was. I don't want to hear your explanations. As far as I'm concerned it was over the minute you decided you couldn't stand beside me in that church and vow to love me unto death.'

Nameless fright quaked down Victoria's spine at his tone. 'You really should have read it, Laurence. You should have read my letter.'

His eyes glittered down at her from a face that was white with rage. 'No, I damn well shouldn't. When I left that church I wanted nothing more to do with you. I will stand by the promise I made to your mother and see that you are taken care of financially—but I do not want you in my house. If you think I'm so desperate for you that I'll come crawling back, you're mistaken.'

Her eyes dark with pain and disillusionment, Victoria began to quake in genuine terror, because he meant that—she could see that he did. At that moment she would have said or done anything to reach him. She could not believe or comprehend that the passionate man who had loved and teased her could turn his back on her without listening to reason, without even giving her a chance to explain.

Laurence stared at her in insolent silence, unable to believe this alluring, impulsive girl he would have married had become this coolly aloof, self-possessed young woman. Now she was out of mourning and attired in a long, high-waisted lavender pelisse and fetching purple bonnet, Victoria Lewis was still strikingly beautiful, but she'd changed so much that— except for the eyes—he scarcely recognised her. One thing hadn't changed—she was still the woman who had rejected him.

'As far as I'm concerned you are out of my life. It is over. Come near me one more time and I will make the devil look like a saint,' he gritted viciously. He stepped back from her as if he couldn't bear to be near her and, turning on his heel, strode toward the stairs.

After a few moments in which she tried to

pull herself together, angry, bewildered and guilty, Victoria started slowly toward the door on legs that felt wooden. There was no sign of him as she climbed into Lady Elsworthy's waiting carriage. So Laurence wanted nothing more to do with her, she thought as the driver urged the horses on.

What was the matter with her letting him turn his back on her like this! It wasn't the time to be frightened and intimidated, but she was. With a shiver of terror she remembered the raging fury in his expression, the wrath in every carefully enunciated word he'd said to her. But most of all she remembered the threat—*Come near me one more time and I will make the devil seem like a saint!* In that moment he'd looked enraged enough to do it.

If he really loved her, he would not have said that. His reaction to what she had done to him was because his pride had taken a battering and not for one moment had he stopped to consider why she had done it. It was one sided, all about him. She was in the wrong. She bit her lip desperately, wanting to go to him and explain, to *make* him listen to her, but he would not. He had nothing but contempt for her now. But then she remembered the pain of the events that had sparked this whole sorry thing off and her courage returned. She lifted her head. Laurence *had* been hurt, but so had she.

All these thoughts marched through Victoria's tormented mind as the carriage sped on. As she went over the scene she wanted to remember it every moment of her life so that she would never, ever, soften in her thoughts of him. She welcomed the icy numbness that was sweeping away her tender feelings for him. The sooner she found employment and he was out of her life the better it would be—or would it?

As Laurence made his way to Nathan's suite of rooms, he wondered what Victoria had been doing at the hotel. Mrs Fenwick had notified him that they would be coming to London and he'd raised no objections to that. Victoria could do as she very well pleased as long as she kept out of his way. But he was curious as to her presence at the Pulteney. Maybe she'd come to see Diana—but then why would she, knowing she would encounter Nathan's wrath?

In furious disgust Laurence raked his hand through his hair. As much as he wanted Victoria Lewis out of his sight and out of his life, he was unable to get her out of his head.

There was great excitement when Victoria received a letter from Mr and Mrs Levinson informing her that she had been successful in her application and they were pleased to offer her the position as governess to their daughters. They were to leave for New York in two weeks.

Amelia was happy for her, but not sure she was doing the right thing. America was such a long way away.

'I know,' Victoria said, trying hard to hide her apprehension. She realised she was about to change her future for ever, a future without Laurence. 'But that's what I want. After everything that's happened, it will be for the best.'

On the day of the Coronation, Lord and Lady Pendleton were to give a celebratory ball. They lived on the other side of the river at Pendleton House in Richmond. Lady Elsworthy and Lady Pendleton had been close friends since they were girls. Because of the distance between their homes, Lady Elsworthy and her family had been invited to stay the night.

It was to be their first big society event since coming to London and Amelia was so rapt with excitement over her first society ball she couldn't sit still.

'The Pendleton ball, Victoria!' she stressed, as if trying to inspire enthusiasm in her friend. 'Invitations to their parties are as coveted as jewels. You have to go. There's no point arguing about it, because Grandmama has already set wheels in motion and she absolutely refuses to be gainsaid.'

'I don't think I can face it, Amelia. I seem to be on everyone's blacklist.'

Amelia sighed when she saw her friend's crestfallen face. 'You won't be alone, Victoria. We'll all stand by you and support you. Besides, the ball will be a complete crush, which I am sure will be to our advantage, and no one will dare give you the cut directly in front of Grandmama.'

Victoria would prefer not to go, but Mrs Fenwick wouldn't hear of it. It certainly didn't elevate Victoria's mood knowing Lord Rockford and his family had also been invited. But then, she would have to face Laurence to tell him she had acquired a position as a governess at some time. After the bitterness of their last encounter, she had no doubt he would be happy to see the back of her. Knowing he would be paying for it, she refused to be fitted for a new gown. Amelia gave her one of hers, but not as slender as Victoria, it had to be altered.

Before that, the family travelled to Westminster to see the grand Coronation procession. The whole of London was caught up in the celebrations. Following the ceremony in Westminster Abbey, the procession—King George wearing his crown and Coronation robes, peers of the realm and foreign dignitaries, the bishops in their capes of gold and heralds with their gorgeous many-coloured vestments—wended its way for the magnificent banquet at Westminster Hall on a raised and canopied processional way. It was a scene of grandeur, a pageant of colour. There was great excitement. People threw their caps in the air and there were shouts of "God Save the King and God bless the King!" The splendid Coronation was a new experience for the vast majority of his subjects, many not having seen the like since the Coronation of George III sixty years before. Crowds lined the streets to watch the parade pass. Soldiers both on foot and mounted lined the route.

Victoria was awestruck by the whole spectacle and felt privileged and proud to have witnessed it. It was a once-in-a-lifetime event and she would never see the like again.

Chapter Nine

~~~

By the time they got back to the house, it was time to get ready for the evening's entertainment. The two shiny black travelling chaises set off for Richmond. Ablaze with lights, Pendleton House, a stately Georgian mansion set in several acres of parkland, was extravagantly beautiful. A long line of lamplit carriages stretched round the curved drive, dropping their resplendent passengers at the front of the house. Footmen carrying torches met each vehicle and escorted the guests inside. Lord and Lady Pendleton welcomed them warmly.

Victoria and Amelia proceeded up the carpeted staircase. Exotic blooms on marble pedestals adorned the balcony. Victoria paused to gaze down on the scene in the brilliant ballroom with reluctant pleasure. Hundreds of glittering candles lit the soaring space while delightful music lightened the drone of conversation. Her first London ball, she thought, and if she was successful in obtaining the position of governess, it would be her last.

A familiar couple swirling around the floor caught her eye. It was Nathan and Diana. Her heart ached on seeing her handsome brother. If only things were different between them, she thought sadly, how much different her life would be. Wearing a gown of rose-pink silk, with soft ringlets that fell to either side of her face and a clutch of dark pink rosebuds in the chignon on top, Diana really did look lovely— little wonder Nathan couldn't keep his eyes off her. Looking up, Diana caught her eye and smiled in recognition. It wasn't long before she found her way to the room that had been allotted to Victoria.

'I can't tell you how much I have missed you,' Diana said, hugging her close. 'I'm so sorry about what happened. You must have had good reason not to appear for your wedding.'

Victoria gave a tight, evasive shrug. 'I did. I saw your husband at the hotel last week, Diana. Did he tell you?'

'Yes, and for what it's worth, he's sorry he was so angry. Of late he's been doing a lot of soul searching. Your break-up with Laurence has affected him in a way I would not have believed possible. He can also see the effect your break-up from Laurence is having on him. Laurence looks more haggard and grim each time they meet, so being apart is not doing either of you any good. I think Nathan feels it's time to perhaps readjust his attitude toward you. Personally, I think you should have been told that you and Nathan are related from the beginning.'

'You knew all along, didn't you?'

'Yes, but it was not my place to tell you. Nathan hasn't told Laurence that you know he is your brother. He will, when he no longer finds the whole situation difficult to deal with.'

'Half-brother,' Victoria was quick to correct. 'Nathan is my half-brother.'

'Yes. But that aside, your leaving like that hit Laurence very badly.'

'I sent him a letter explaining everything. At the time I found it hard to accept his deception. Unfortunately he—he didn't read it.'

'So he doesn't know?' Victoria shook her head. 'Why did you agree to marry him?'

With as much dignity as she could muster, she replied evasively, 'For the usual reasons.'

'What are they? Money, social position?' Diana summarised flatly. This unprovoked attack, which was so unlike Diana, was too much for Victoria to bear. Tears of indignation sprang to her eyes.

'I am neither mercenary enough nor selfish to marry any man for those reasons, so I would be obliged if you would not accuse me of such.'

'Then what am I to think?' Diana sighed and gave her a sideways glance. 'Victoria, I know it went deeper than that.'

'I agreed to marry him because I thought he needed me—and—and I wanted him so much,' Victoria said quietly.

'Laurence tries to give the impression that he doesn't need anyone. He has learned to deal with tragedy and adversity—he cannot, however, cope with a runaway bride. You can't have known him well when he asked you to marry him, yet you still thought he needed you.'

Victoria nodded. 'Clearly, I was fanciful to think that, but there were times when I would look at him and have this queer feeling that he was as lonely as I was. But I was wrong. Had he wanted me, he would not have deceived me.'

'Does it matter terribly to know that you have a brother?'

'Half-brother, and, yes, it does. What matters most is that it was kept from me. Not even my mother told me.'

'You're wrong about Laurence not wanting

you, Victoria. He needs a woman like you. He needs you to heal wounds that are deep, to teach him how to love and be loved in return. If you knew more about him, you would understand why.'

'Will you tell me? Unless you feel you would be betraying a trust…'

'I wouldn't be doing that. It's no secret what happened. Are you aware that in the past he was engaged to be married?'

Victoria felt her stomach clench at the mention of the woman he'd been involved with and at the same time she was helpless to control her curiosity. 'Yes—I remember there was something—some gossip. People talked, but I didn't listen. Laurence was just a name to me then. What was she like?'

'Beautiful—and ambitious. She was called Melissa Piggott. Melissa and her family were social climbers. Her father was a government official—Laurence seemed like a good proposition—incredibly wealthy, with good connections. She agreed to marry him for what he could give her. Unfortunately—or perhaps I should say fortunately as things have turned out because she would have made his life a misery—she met a man of higher rank, a duke, and she would no longer countenance marriage to a mere lord. She ran off with him the day she was to have married Laurence. He was devastated. And then when the duke changed his mind she begged Laurence to take her back. But she was already dead to him. It took a concentrated effort to eradicate her from his heart and mind, but he did it. Perhaps now you will understand why he reacted so badly when you failed to appear for your wedding.'

Victoria stared at her. She felt as if she were in the midst of a nightmare. 'I didn't know, truly I didn't. I know how proud he is—and how much his pride must have been mangled when I failed to appear at the church.'

'He wouldn't believe you wouldn't arrive. Even when Nathan tried telling him you had changed your mind he wouldn't believe him.'

Victoria thought her heart would break, and that was before Diana said, 'He kept the vicar waiting for over an hour for you to come and explain. Does that sound like a man who doesn't love you, a man who doesn't want you?' She paused, watching Victoria's expressive face—tentative, fragile. 'I'm afraid when you didn't come he hardened his heart against you.'

Victoria's eyes glazed with tears. She felt devastated at what she had put him through, what she had lost. In his own way Laurence had isolated himself from the world because it had destroyed his hopes of marriage to a woman he thought had cared for him, and because his parents—albeit unintentionally—had a preference for his younger brother.

'I didn't know—I never thought… Never imagined… Your sister came to see me when I was about to leave for the church. She—she said some terrible things. I was upset…angry—provoked beyond reason—but before that I confess I had had my doubts about the marriage. Your sister's terrible revelations that day made me realise it would be a mistake to go through with it.'

'What doubts did you have, Victoria?'

'Laurence was a lord. I was a schoolmaster's daughter. My mother had been a servant to his mother—which I was not comfortable with when I remembered…' She paused, having no wish to open that particular wound. 'Men of his class make mistresses of women like me—but they don't marry them. His friends—society—I would never be accepted. He would be ostracised himself.'

'Did you really believe that would matter to Laurence?'

'It should.'

'But you still agreed to marry him.'

'He—Laurence can be very persuasive.'

Diana smiled, noting the embarrassed blush that mantled Victoria's cheeks. 'I'm sure he can, Victoria, and that you found him hard to resist. I'm sorry Clara imposed herself on you that day. I know my sister better than anyone. All her life she has been pampered, admired, cosseted and spoilt by doting parents, and if Clara didn't get what she wanted a very noisy balloon went up. She was enchantment itself if she got her own way—if she didn't, then demons paled beside what she became. So you see, I know what she is capable of.'

'What can I do to set things right?'

'The burden of that is on your shoulders, Victoria. At this moment Laurence doesn't want to see you. He will not even allow anyone to mention your name in his presence.'

'So he—he hates me. I cannot say that I blame him. How can I hope to put things right if he refuses to see me?'

'He will have to be persuaded.' Her voice became gentle. 'Victoria, your leaving affected him very badly. I—believe he was in love with you.'

'Please don't say that!' Victoria said in a suffocated voice. 'He never told me he loved me. He never pretended to love me—never even bothered to lie to me when he asked me to marry him.'

'Maybe he didn't acknowledge the feeling even to himself—perhaps he still does not, but he has not been the same man since you left. You're nothing like Melissa. I've seen the way he looks at you. He's in love with you—though I doubt he wants to be. I don't think he wants to love any woman.'

'I can't blame him. I can't imagine how he's survived the humiliation of being jilted twice at the altar.'

'He's strong. Let yourself love him, Victoria—and teach him how to love you. Someone has to save him from himself, to soften his heart and to fill up the empty spaces in his life. Most men love easily and often, but not Laurence. First he'll have to learn to trust you. Once he can do that, he will give you the world.'

When Diana had gone, Victoria's mind was on Laurence. Her heart filled with tenderness for the man who had given her a home when her mother had become ill, comforted her when she had died, laughed with her and teased her, and ultimately asked her to marry him. True, he was frequently moody, distant and unapproachable, but the more she contemplated the matter, the more convinced she became that Diana was right—Laurence must care for her, or he'd never have risked another marriage.

The sound of the party drifted upstairs and

filtered into Victoria's room where she sat alone. The ball was in progress, yet she had delayed joining the guests as she brooded on the moment when she would come face to face with Laurence. He was late—Diana had told her important business matters kept him.

Knowing she could not hide away in her room all night and deciding it was time to join the festivities, taking her courage in both hands, she went to the top of the stairs, the bright lights, the chatter and the music making her pause.

Telling herself to calm down and compose herself, that these society people eager for scandal must be shown a regal young lady, not a rushing silly girl tripping over her own skirts, with her head held high and her slender hand lightly skimming the ornate balustrade, she made the descent of the stairs. Her eyes followed the undulating rhythm of her gown, which flowed in shimmering, glistening waves about her long legs. Nothing of what she saw penetrated her thoughts, for her mind moved like a disembodied wraith through the quandary she faced on seeing Laurence again.

Stepping off the last step, she halted abruptly. Diverted by her appearance, every eager male and jealous female eye in sight turned to look at her, but she was oblivious to them. Laurence was there, his presence a certainty beyond proof of sight. She turned automatically to where she knew he stood, her eyes drawn to him of their own volition. In black-and-white formal attire, his waistcoat gleaming pristine white, he was so handsome he took her breath away.

Laurence knew she was looking at him. The sure knowledge of her presence to the side of him interrupted the conversation he was having with Sir John Gibson, a stout and extremely wealthy industrialist from the Midlands. Sir John, an old friend, was saying something important, but Laurence heard not a word. He turned automatically, his muscles taught by some unconscious force, meeting the gaze of the young woman at the bottom of the staircase.

She was beautiful, even more beautiful than she had looked when they had met at the Pulteney Hotel—a radiant sunburst in a city choked with darkness. She was innocence and purity, and worth far and above all the others pressing around him. He inclined his head to her in deference to her beauty, but her rejection of him still burned in his heart.

Laurence knew she was in London, but his decision to ignore her existence became harder and harder to adhere to since he had seen her at

the hotel. The shock of seeing her had fortified
him since that encounter, but now he no longer
had the advantage of that barrier. Looking at
her now, he couldn't seem to stifle the memories of their time together at Stonegrave Hall,
which paraded across his mind.

Victoria bit her lip apprehensively, her pale
face reflecting her mounting tension. There
was so much she wanted to say to him, so much
to explain. Suddenly her face went cold and any
explanations she'd decided to make flew clean
out of her head. She felt her heart turn as bitter
as acid, for from behind Laurence's muscular
shoulders Clara Ellingham's eyes burned towards her. Victoria steeled herself against any
display of surprise, any indication of agitation.
Instead she forced herself to look nonchalantly
away from them and continued on towards the
dining room and Amelia as if nothing had happened.

Laurence disengaged himself from Clara
and Sir John, and intercepted Victoria before
she could disappear. When he stepped in front
of her she feigned surprise and with false bra-
vado said,

'Why, Laurence. I am surprised to see you. I
am sure Lady Pendleton is delighted you were
able to join the festivities, even if tardily.'

'I have apologised to her for being late,' he

answered curtly. He lifted a questioning brow. 'And you, Victoria? Are you not delighted to see me here? You look beautiful by the way. That gown suits you. Expensive.'

She raised her eyebrows and stared at him in mild amusement. 'I believe it was, but don't worry. You haven't paid for it.'

'I haven't?'

'No. It's one of Amelia's hand-me-downs. After a little alteration, as you will observe, it made a perfect fit.'

Laurence's jaw tensed and, taking her arm he drew her into an alcove which offered more privacy. 'Damn it, Victoria!' The curse was sudden and sharp, startling her. 'You have enough money at your disposal to purchase the finest gowns in London. I'll not have you dressing in borrowed clothes like the meanest serving girl. I assure you that while you remain my charge you will dress yourself with more dignity than you seem concerned about.'

'You can prattle on about pride and dignity all you like,' she retorted loftily. 'Expensive ball gowns have been luxuries I can ill afford of late. Beggarish though what I am wearing might be, it is not borrowed. It was given and it is mine to wear.'

Laurence stepped close and Victoria almost retreated from those suddenly fierce eyes. But she steeled herself and held her ground before his glare.

'You may enjoy what luxury *I* can afford.' He straightened, squaring his wide shoulders, but his eyes still held hers in bondage. 'I suggest you put aside this ridiculous silly notion you have about the allowance I send Mrs Fenwick and accept it.'

Victoria's eyes narrowed and Laurence could almost feel the sparks hurtling out of them. 'I can no more ignore that than everything else you have paid for. I *know* that it was your money that paid for my education.' Her smile was bitter. 'And there I was, simpleton that I am, thinking the money was what my father left my mother. Have you any idea how humiliated I felt when I found out? How ashamed? I do not wish to be kept by you—or any other man. I want to be self-sufficient—my own mistress. Not some kept woman. I prefer it that way.'

Before Laurence could respond to her harsh words, Clara appeared at the entrance to the alcove and re-attached herself possessively to his arm. Victoria was watching her hand, the long tapered fingers against the dark cloth of Laurence's coat. Laurence saw the direction of Victoria's eyes and tried tactfully to disengage himself, but Clara held on. He appeared irritated—almost sorry she was there—yet obligated to put a good face on the situation.

'You remember Miss Lewis, Clara?'

'Of course,' Clara replied with a frosty smile. 'How could I possibly forget? Are you staying long in London, Miss Lewis?'

'No longer than necessary, Miss Ellingham.' Something was dreadfully wrong. The world was rushing at her too fast, surrounding her in a confusing welter beyond comprehension. Her head spun giddily and she felt faint, but she had to make the effort. 'I find it far too busy, with people rushing about all over the place.'

'Don't tell me you prefer Yorkshire, with little to do save grow another day older. I always find it rather tiresome.'

'I feel I must disagree with you, Miss Ellingham,' Victoria said, looking pointedly at Laurence. 'I always found lots of stimulating things to do. I was certainly never bored. One manages to amuse oneself if one tries hard enough—is that not so, Laurence?'

Clara's face, bright and with a slight sheen of perspiration, was smiling in a hideous parody of courtesy and friendliness. 'Since Laurence spends most of his time here in London, I think that speaks for itself,' she said tightly.

'I think what you mean,' Victoria said smoothly, functioning on instinct, 'is that he prefers business to pleasure. Am I not right, Laurence?'

'Not always,' he replied.

Victoria would have gone on but found she couldn't. Suddenly the entire exercise seemed petty and paltry, unimportant in the extreme. But why were his eyes so blue? To mimic the cool sweet depths of a hidden pool where lovers were want to meet?

'I'm sorry, but you'll have to excuse me,' she managed to say in a breaking voice. She turned and walked away, skirts swirling in a flurry of green and gold, with a slight show of a lace petticoat. The garden lay only yards away through the French doors. There she would find much-needed fresh air, air she could breathe without choking, without crying out in rage.

Laurence watched her disappear among the guests filling the entire downstairs and spilling out on to the terrace and the garden, where liveried footmen offered confections and flutes of champagne on silver trays. As the conversation between Clara and Victoria had flowed around him he had understood little, so intent had he been on watching Victoria. That the two women had been hurling barbs at each other he had no doubt. But neither did he really care. He was more concerned with what he felt.

Clara led him into the ballroom just as the

orchestra broke into a waltz. Several couples took to the floor. Clara was immediately approached by a couple of young dandies and Sir John Gibson who vied for her attention. She smiled flirtatiously and countered their ribald remarks with more of her own. Laurence backed off a few paces and watched Sir John sweep her on to the floor, before dodging a number of swaying, spinning dancers, crossing the dance floor and stepping out onto the terrace in search of Victoria, only to see her being led into the dance by young Lord Falconbridge.

Frustration had him heading for the garden, where he remained for the next half an hour, so he did not see Nathan leave Diana's side and head for Victoria.

When Victoria saw Nathan making his way towards her, she paused on her way to find Amelia, wondering if he would acknowledge her. What he did was totally unexpected.

When he was close and she averted her face from him, thinking there must be some mistake and he had come upon her accidentally, he said, 'Will you dance with me?' When she made a small movement with her head, he said quietly, 'How can I convince you that I mean you no harm?' He held out his hand. 'Please,

Victoria. Is it so unusual for a brother to ask his sister to dance with him?'

Victoria's head was slow in turning. Her lips were apart, her eyes wide. 'I'm sorry. I—I thought... Forgive me if I appear surprised,' she said, struggling to keep her voice welcoming rather than ironic.

He smiled. 'We haven't treated you kindly, have we?'

'Why are you doing this?'

'Isn't that obvious? I wish to make reparation to you for behaving so badly towards you.'

Victoria stared at him and she saw him for the first time, not as an angry stranger, but as a young man of pleasing appearance, with an expression that was serious. His eyes were soft and kindly, and she couldn't associate him with the other being.

Placing her hand in his, she smiled. 'In that case, I would be happy to dance with you.'

He waltzed her to a quiet part of the dance floor before he spoke. 'I know you've had a horrible time of it lately—Diana put me in the picture,' he explained when she looked at him warily. 'I thought you might like to talk about it?'

'What? Here?'

'No. You can come to the hotel if you like,

and I promise you the reception will be more welcoming than the last.'

'You mean you—you want to talk about our mother?'

'I'm going to have to—some time. It isn't going to go away. Ever since I was told that the woman I believed was my mother wasn't, I've expended a lot of effort on putting it out of my mind. My real mother was dead to me and that was the end of it as far as I was concerned.'

'Only it wasn't, was it, because then you found out about me.' Her eyes were suddenly dark and brilliant with tears. 'It was quite horrible for me, too. You've had years to get used to it. I didn't find out who you were until I was about to leave for the church to marry Laurence.'

'I know and, for what it's worth, I curse Clara for doing that to you.'

'I don't. At least she told me the truth. It explained why you were so hostile and resentful towards me when we first met. It should not have been kept from me.'

'I'm sorry. You're right, of course. Your mother should have told you.' The look he gave her was one of regret. 'It's a nightmare, isn't it?'

'Yes,' said Victoria, 'yes, I'm afraid it is. For both of us, in different ways. But it is beginning to get better.' Suddenly she smiled at him when he twirled her round and their steps matched perfectly. 'I'm glad you asked me to dance.'

'Me, too,' he said, returning her smile.

Laurence entered the ballroom through the French doors and then he saw her. She was with Amelia, both of them very much the centre of attention with a group of young fops clad in an absurd array of bright colours. It would appear that the fact that she had jilted him had given her a certain notoriety. Laurence did not acknowledge her presence. He stepped into the shadows, his cold eyes sweeping over her. The mere sight of her talking and laughing as though she had not a care in the world was crucifying him. How could he behave as if nothing had happened between them and pretend that she was merely a pretty girl who had once caught his eye? How could he do that when he was rigid with shock?

He wanted her. In fact, he had never stopped wanting her, he thought with bitter disgust. He had begun wanting her the moment he had seen her on the moor and he wanted her no less badly now. Clad in her beautiful gown and with her hair curled high and threaded through with a gold ribbon, she made his body harden with lust.

He wanted to stride across to young Falconbridge, who was leaning close to her ear and had his hand on her arm, and fling him away from her. How dared he put his hand on what was—what should be—his. Dear Lord, what was wrong with him? How could he let a woman affect him as this one did?

Looking beyond the circle of admirers, Victoria saw him. Excusing herself, she paused a moment to steady her rioting nerves. Laurence was leaning against the balustrade, staring at the dancers through the open French doors. His profile was so bitter and desolate that her chest filled with remorse. She gazed at the dark, austere beauty of his face, the power and virility stamped in every line of his long body, and her pulse raced with a mixture of excitement and trepidation.

She took several steps toward him, throwing a shadow in front of him. He stared through her, his stark blue eyes piercing through her as though he wasn't really seeing her at all.

'Laurence,' she whispered.

At the sound of her voice, his eyes found hers.

His granite features were an impenetrable mask and Victoria was too nervous to notice anything about his mood except that he was tense.

It was the way she was looking at him that

melted him—the softness in her liquid amber eyes, imploring him to soften, to smile at her—which obliterated the dehumanising effects of her rejection. He wanted to crush her in his arms, to lose himself in her sweetness, to wrap her around him like a blanket and bury himself in her.

'Shall we dance?' he asked as the orchestra began playing a waltz.

'I'd love to, although I hope Lord Falconbridge doesn't see us.'

'And why not?'

'Because he picked an argument with the last gentleman I danced with. When the gentleman refused to leave the floor, Lord Falconbridge asked him to go outside where they would settle the matter.'

Despite the absurdity of it, something vaguely vexing roiled within Laurence. It was a feeling he had never experienced before, but this time he recognised it for what it was. It was the first sharp twinge of jealousy he had experienced in his adult life.

'Do you find yourself attracted to Lord Falconbridge, Victoria?'

She chuckled at his dark scowl. 'No. He's the jealous type, that's all.'

'Witch!' he chided her, taking her hand and drawing her close. 'It's apparent Falconbridge has incredibly good taste, especially in women, and at this present time I know exactly how the wretched fellow must feel.'

She rolled her eyes. 'You don't really expect me to believe that you are jealous?'

Laurence's eyes fixed greedily on her lips. 'Half an hour ago,' he murmured, 'I would have said I was incapable of such a lowering emotion.'

'And now?'

'I'm not certain.'

'What do you mean, you aren't certain?'

'Where you are concerned, I haven't been certain of anything since you ran away, and the uncertainty is getting worse by the moment.'

'Oh? But why should you be jealous? I was under the impression that for a man to experience jealousy he must consider himself in danger of losing a cherished love to a rival. After what happened between us it is understandable that you don't care a whit about me, so why would you be envious of another man?'

'You could be mistaken.' A meagre smile was the best he could manage. 'In fact, I think we'd better reach some sort of clear understanding about what is going on between us and what we *want* to go on between us.' At the back of his mind, Laurence knew he was being completely irrational, but the emotional round-

about she'd had him on for the past weeks all
combined to play havoc with his temper, his
emotions, and his judgement. 'Do you agree?'

'Yes—I think so.'

'Then come and dance with me and we'll
see where it takes us.'

Victoria let herself be drawn up the steps to
the terrace and hesitated. 'This is a mistake.
Everyone will be watching us and think that
we're back together—'

'Let them. They can gossip and speculate all
they like. It won't make one iota of difference
to what happens in the end.'

'But you don't understand. Their contempt
and condemnation is no better than I deserve.'

In a teasing voice he said, 'I think you're
underrating my gift for strategy and subtlety.
When they see us dancing together, they'll be
so confused they won't know what to think.'

Victoria allowed him to guide her through
the French doors.

Despite his confidence, moments after they
entered the ballroom Laurence cast a surrepti-
tious glance about and realised that what Victoria had said was true. A rippling wave of
excitement was making its way through the elderly matrons. Glancing at Victoria, he slid an
arm behind her waist and captured her slender
hand within his. In a low voice he said, 'Raise

your head in the air and either cut me dead or flirt with me, but don't you dare look humble and meek, because all these people watching us will interpret it as guilt.'

Victoria, who'd been gazing at his chest, tipped her head back and looked at him in bewilderment, then his warning about looking meek and humble hit home, and she began to understand what he wanted her to do.

'Young Falconbridge is in fine fettle tonight, but where on earth did he obtain those yellow pantaloons?'

'Why,' she said, drawing a shaky breath and managing to smile up at him, 'do you like them? If so, you will have to ask him the name of his tailor.'

'I doubt he'd oblige,' Laurence replied on a teasing note in an attempt to put her at her ease. 'If looks could kill, I'd be a dead man. He's clearly resentful of me partnering you. I'm glad I asked you to dance with me just to frustrate the young whelp.'

'Oh dear,' Victoria said, glancing at the irate Lord Falconbridge scowling at them from the perimeter of the dance floor, 'he does look rather angry.'

'Indeed. I swear, as piercing as his glare is, I'm sure it's going to bore a hole right through us. He looks like an adder waiting to strike.'

Victoria chanced a glance toward Lord Falconbridge and shivered. 'Dear me. What did we do to deserve those icy daggers? I think he's about to demand the ballroom to be cleared so he can have the requisite twenty paces.' She laughed, capturing Laurence's eyes. 'Would you like me to be your second?'

Laurence's heart turned over when the chandeliers overhead revealed softness in her beautiful amber eyes. 'Believe me, Victoria, you'll never be that—not even when you abandoned me at the altar on our wedding day.'

'Thank you. I do not deserve your consideration,' she responded, exaggerating her gratitude.

His eyes gleamed into hers as she chanced another glance. In spite of her humble reply, his smile remained undiminished, his hand on her back unrelenting as they danced. He hardly led her—they seemed instinctively to do the same thing. 'You're welcome, but it took no mean mental feat on my part to relent towards you.'

'You mean you forgive me?' she asked, the hope that he would shining from her eyes.

His smiled lessened. 'I didn't say that. You have a lot of making up to do—but I would be satisfied if you would smile merely for my pleasure.'

'What can you expect from me?' she murmured. 'After our meeting at the hotel, you made it quite plain that you wanted nothing more to do with me. Tonight, not knowing why you are being so nice to me, I find myself in a bit of a quandary. I can only wonder why you're even talking to me. When I didn't turn up for our wedding, I gave you the chance to dispense with the whole thing—not only the marriage bit, but the courtship as well. I know how much you must value your freedom after what happened between us.'

For a lengthy moment, his dark-blue eyes probed the amber depths of hers. Did he indeed want his freedom more than he wanted her? That had been the question haunting him in recent weeks, yet even now he was reluctant to dismiss his enthralment with Victoria. But as far as he was concerned, like she said, he had dispensed with the courtship and the marriage bit.

He had once told her that love had no place in marriage, that in his world marriages were arranged for profit and gain. He admitted that where she was concerned he had weakened and thrown caution to the wind, but on reflection, remembering how she had left him to wait for her like a besotted, gullible idiot with a vicar standing by, he realised how true his words had been. And now he could see no reason why he shouldn't have both Victoria and his freedom.

'Perhaps if you were to let me explain why I acted as I did that day...'

'Later,' he said, spinning her in a heady circle. 'Diana told me you and your party are to stay the night.'

'Yes...' She bit her lip, averting her eyes as the music slowed, desperately wanting the night to never end. The light shifted, its beam seeming to single out Laurence, like the light through a stained-glass window in a dark chapel. It was as if her world had changed in that moment, giving Victoria the view she had longed for.

Laurence bent his head so that his mouth was close to her ear and said, 'Would you like to see me later, Victoria?'

Victoria knew that, in that moment, a thousand handsome men could not compare to Laurence. He was the one who owned her heart and he had not deserved to be treated so badly. She swallowed, her eyes drawn back to his by some magnetic force. The powerful volley of sensual persuasiveness that Laurence Rockford was capable of launching against her womanly being could reap devastating results. When his eyes delved into the depths of hers, he all but turned her heart inside out and nibbled at its tender core. Were he to continue such delectable assaults on her senses, it might well mean the collapse of her resistance and her ultimate doom.

Without thinking, she whispered, 'Yes', as the last strains of the waltz were dying away. 'I would like that.'

As Laurence guided Victoria off the dance floor, he turned and slanted the polished fop a meaningful look, staking his claim. Perhaps Falconbridge sensed the murderous anger behind his stare, for he turned on his heel. Sending Laurence one last scornful glance over his shoulder, he strode off.

By the end of the evening a majority of the guests at the Pendleton ball had drawn the conclusion that whatever it was that had made Victoria Lewis rebuff Lord Rockford on their wedding day had been resolved.

Victoria had retired to her room as the last of the carriages drove away from the house. Having removed her finery and excused one of the maids who had waited up to assist her, she unpinned her hair. She had started brushing it out when there was a soft tapping on her door. Believing it to be Amelia, she called out for her to enter.

The door was pushed open. She did not move or speak, but gazed at the figure leaning in the door frame as if it was a ghost. Then quite suddenly she recollected herself. She recognised Laurence's powerful frame in the candlelight staring at her. Her heart began to beat in deep, fierce thuds of joy. When he had told her he would see her later, she had believed he meant he would meet up with her before she retired, not that he would seek her out in her bedchamber. There was a moment's silence as she watched him close the door and stride forwards. The room jumped to life about him as his presence filled it, infusing it with his own energy and vigour.

Removing his jacket and loosening his neckcloth, he sat on the sofa, the image of relaxed elegance with arms spread out across the back of it, his foot propped casually atop the opposite knee. He was watching her—relaxed, indulgent. She'd been brushing her hair when he entered and he watched her go to the dressing table and place the brush on its surface. Her movements were graceful and uncertain, like a frightened doe.

Candlelight gleamed on her rich, dark-brown hair as it spilled forward over her shoulders. It glowed warmly on her soft skin. Her long, sooty lashes cast fan-shaped shadows on her smooth cheeks. As he looked at her now, he marvelled anew at the strange aura of innocence about her, then he suppressed a puzzled smile at the realisation that, for some reason, she was assiduously avoiding his eyes. Her behaviour on their wedding day had opposed, defied and challenged him, yet for all her courage she was amazingly shy, now that the hostilities between them were subdued. Based on that sweet, pleading look she'd given him earlier, she was apparently hoping he'd be as stupidly susceptible to her appeal as he'd been before.

'Well,' he said in the lazy, sensual drawl that always made her heart melt, 'this is cosy.'

Cosy! The word swirled around in Victoria's brain. By his definition, she knew perfectly well that cosy meant—more conducive to intimacy. She knew it, just as clearly as she knew that the situation between them had altered irreversibly from the moment she told him she would like to see him. He knew it, too. She could see the evidence—there was a new softness in his eyes when he looked at her and it was utterly shattering to her self-control. She shook her head at her foolish, futile attempt to deceive herself. There was nothing left of her self-control, no more arguments that mattered, nowhere she could go to hide from the truth. The truth was that she wanted him. And he wanted her. They both knew it.

But something was holding her back. He was

casual, too casual, and her whirling thoughts registered that he was treating their meeting with a cool nonchalance that seemed inappropriate.

'We—we have to talk, Laurence. We cannot keep skirting round the issue. I have to explain—there are things I have to tell you.'

'I haven't come here for conversation, Victoria,' he said, getting to his feet and moving towards her. 'When you told me you would like to see me, I had the distinct impression you were offering me more than talk. Was I mistaken?'

'No—only, I—I didn't realise you intended coming to my bedchamber. I—I have never had a man in my room before.'

'I already know,' he said, taking her face between his hands, shoving his fingers through the sides of her hair and turning it up to his. 'But you are not a stranger to kissing, Victoria, which is making me wonder if you're ever going to kiss me the way you once did—before you invite me into your bed.'

Victoria burned at his implication, knowing she had neither the desire nor the inclination to send him away. 'Of course I will—only—I was hoping you would kiss me first.'

Laurence captured her eyes. He knew her and understood her, and he was more confused than ever by what he was doing to her. When they had planned their marriage and he had offered her respectability and a future, she had withheld her virginity. He had not objected to that for he would have it no other way. Tonight, however, she was willing to surrender her virtue unconditionally. Laurence's conscience chose that moment to reassert itself for the first time in years by reminding him that if he had any scruples, any decency whatsoever, he'd keep his hands off her.

But the feeble protest of his conscience wasn't enough to deter him. He wanted her and he was going to have her. Victoria had deprived him of his dignity and any future they might have had together as man and wife. Neither his conscience nor anything else was going to deprive him from having her.

Laurence lowered his head and his lips captured hers, moving to her throat, her chin, the corner of her mouth, her cheek, her brow. With strong and surprisingly gentle hands he stroked her hair and lifted it with his hands to savour its weight and silky texture, and all the while she was trembling inside, a weak, hollow feeling in the backs of her knees, the pit of her stomach, warmth glowing and spreading throughout her body as he tilted her head back and finally covered her lips with his once again, kissing her tenderly, holding her tight.

Sliding her hands up his chest and around his neck, holding him close, Victoria kissed him back with a strange combination of naïve expertise and instinctive sensuality. Laurence felt the burgeoning pleasure and astonished joy that was almost beyond bearing. Dragging his lips from hers, he brushed a kiss along her jaw and cheek and temple, then he sought her mouth again, rubbing his lips over their soft contours. Tracing a line between her lips with his tongue, he urged them to part, insisting, and when they did he drove into her mouth like a starving man helplessly trying to satisfy his hunger. The woman in his arms was a willing student, melting against him, crushing her mouth to his, welcoming his kisses, the deep amber pools of her eyes pulling him inexorably into their depths.

What seemed to be an eternity later, tearing his lips from hers, he stood back and quickly removed his shirt, and before Victoria could blink, his hand had slid down her arm and into her palm and her own arms went up around his neck and their mouths met once more. While they kissed, somehow he managed to loosen the strands of her robe and slip it off her shoulders. Her nightdress quickly followed suit.

There was almost no time to speak or murmur a faint protest—she wanted him as badly as he seemed to want her.

She buried her hand in the fine, silky black hair that covered his chest, narrowing to a single line just below the belt of his trousers. He made a sound deep in his throat, a guttural moan, and then he slung his free arm around her back and held her tighter still, swinging her in his arms as his lips continued to caress and then crushed, his need aroused, tenderness turning to torment he must assuage. She wound her arms around his neck and hid her face in the curve of his shoulder as he carried her to the bed and set her down on the covers. They were so soft, smelling so sweet and welcoming, and she sank into their softness and looked up at the man who stood beside the bed. Hooking his thumbs under the waistband of his trousers, he tugged and they slid down and his manhood sprang free, ready to rend and ravish. Victoria was limp, she had no will, no strength, and seemed to have melted.

And then he was there, hovering over her, hard and brutal. He kissed her throat and murmured soft words. She held on to his shoulders as her senses reeled, as so many dreams suddenly materialised into a shattering reality. It was real, he was real, he was here, his strong arms holding her to him, his lips tenderly, urgently devouring her own, his warmth, his smell, his lean, sinewy body real, hers, no dream to disappear.

She seemed to soar into a void of violent pleasure. The delirium mounted moment by moment until nothing existed but this man, this magic. His mouth was warm, like his hands moving up the skin of her stomach to hold her breasts—this wasn't the gentle caress he had given her before. This was hungry, explosive, urgent. Pleasure, she thought wildly, as she savoured the moment, erotic pleasure was what this would bring.

They met each other as equals, perfectly matched…and in it, she found a surprising freedom. He took as much from her as he gave and she was only too willing to take. Soon he became a part of her and she experienced pain and she thought she was going to die, but then she felt something new, something incredible as he moved and beauty came, shimmering, shattering beauty, and they moved together, every sinuous stroke of his body lighting fires in her blood. She curled her hands passionately around his shoulders, then raked her fingers down his back. His low groan of pleasure at her touch emboldened her. She kissed him more urgently, caressing his muscled chest, savouring his strength and power as he pinioned her beneath him, her body arching to meet his. She was like a kitten clawing, purring as the beauty became unbearable and she was lost, soaring into oblivion that loomed just ahead, waiting with shuddering intensity.

Closer it came, and he filled her fully and she clasped him and caressed him, expressing her feelings with her heart and all her soul and her body. Their loving drew them closer still, making them one. And then he pulled back and almost left her and she cried out as he filled her yet again, their bodies moulded together, straining to become closer still.

The glory grew and he was hers and she was his and neither of them would be alone again as they moved to the music of love. She knew she couldn't possibly endure it, not one moment more. He shuddered and as the pale rays of moonlight streamed into the room, she felt the life jetting out of him and she was torn into a million shimmering shreds and cast into the abyss of ecstasy.

Chapter Ten

With sleep hanging over her like a thick haze, after letting her mind float aimlessly, Victoria opened her eyes and looked about the unfamiliar flock wallpapered room. As the grey dawn light filtered through the cracks in the curtains, she was surprised to see the candles were still lit. Her waking thoughts were fragmented and confused. Finding her body completely naked beneath the covers, Victoria suddenly felt her mind begin to clear.

'Laurence?' she whispered, as details of the night came back to her in all their intense and exotic clarity. She sensed rather than saw that the bed next to her was empty. Dragging herself up on to the mound of feather pillows she shoved her heavy hair from her face.

Seated in a chair, Laurence was fully dressed, as if he had just come from the ball and nothing had happened in between. He was studying her with a different interest to the interest he had shown in her when he had taken her to bed. And then he smiled—that sleepy, sensual smile of his which had the power to melt her heart. But there was a distance between them, not just a physical distance. A feeling of unease crept into her. Flushing softly and covering her nakedness with the sheet, she met his look with a little frown, her body taut, every muscle stretched against the invisible pull between them.

'Good morning,' he said, his eyes running over the voluptuous lines of her figure below the sheet.

'Good morning,' she answered somewhat shyly. 'You're up early—although I suppose it's sensible that you leave before anyone is about. I should hate you to be seen leaving my room.'

'Quite,' he replied.

'We—still haven't talked, Laurence. I think we should.'

'So do I, but first I want to make you an offer.'

Victoria's heart throbbed with hope and happiness. 'What kind of offer?'

'When you've had time to consider it, I'm

sure you will agree it will be sensible for us both. Do you want to continue what we've started, Victoria?'

'Are you giving me a choice?' As soon as she said it, she saw the imperceptible tightening of his jaw and had the strange feeling that she hadn't given him the sort of answer he wanted.

He looked at her with that straight, disconcerting gaze of his, a glint in his eyes. 'Yes,' he said, after a long pause. 'You can either walk away or stay with me?'

The rush of familiar excitement caused her to become tongue-tied, affected strongly as she was by the force of his presence and the memory of the past night. Emotions swept over her and two spots of high colour touched her cheeks as she remembered the intense passion they had shared.

A tentative smile curved her lips. 'You are willing to marry me after all I have—'

'No. Surely you cannot be that naïve or that foolish? Marriage is no longer on the agenda.' A muscle twitched in his cheek. He eyed her blandly. 'There has been enough deceit and misunderstanding between us. I am speaking plainly, Victoria, because I should hate to think you have misled yourself. I am asking you to be my mistress. It's obvious that despite what has happened between us, we share one common interest. We are compatible in bed.'

Flinching from the sting of his tone and the shock of his words, Victoria controlled a tremor of anxiety as he rose from the chair and his tall, powerful frame moved to the fireplace, where he turned and stood, one hand resting on the mantelpiece, watching her with a clinical calm. He was also treating her as if there had been nothing between them, as if they had never shared the intense passion between a man and a woman. It was incredible to her that those firm lips had kissed her, that those hands had caressed and fondled her and given her such delight. It was this incredulity rather than resentment which held her silent for the moment.

Now, in broad daylight, she was sadly aware that the man who had made love to her with such violent tenderness and need, who had made her cry out and feel as if she were the only woman he'd ever made love to, had also made love to countless women, and she was finding it far more difficult to cling to the illusion that it meant more to her than it did to him.

When she didn't reply he went on, 'My offer will not make you a lady, but it will give you more of a luxurious life than you can possibly expect on your own. You will find that I can be generous. You will have your own house here in London, with servants, your own carriage and gowns that will make you the envy of every woman in town. You will also have as much freedom as you require, providing you share my bed when I am in London and give to no other man what I am paying for.'

The red stains on Victoria's cheeks faded. Laurence caught her eye and the silence between them was again charged with tension. Fire sprang into her eyes. She clenched her hands tightly. Her thoughts now were in disarray, desire and reasoning conflicting. 'Why, you—you arrogant, overbearing—' she choked back the tears that were cutting off her voice '—you want me to be your mistress?' Behind her words lay the shadow of a struggle. Her objective had one minute looked close within her reach and the next as remote as ever.

Having seen the hurt cloud her eyes when he had made the proposition, Laurence sensed her disappointment, but that was for her to deal with. 'Think about it,' he said, turning from her to the door. 'I'll contact you in a couple of days.'

Victoria glanced at the floor, her eyes alighting on her robe which had been so easily discarded. 'Wait. Will you pass me my robe?' she asked with a forced calm.

Striding back from the door, he did as she

bade and, shrugging her arms into the sleeves, she slipped out of bed and wrapped it tightly about her slender form, careful not to expose the tender flesh that had given him such pleasure—although why she should guard against her sensibilities now after all the shocking things he had done to her earlier was beyond her. Feeling less vulnerable now, she could stand and face him. Walking to within an arm's reach of him, she controlled a small shiver of irritation and hurt pride as she struggled to calm her mounting rage.

Drawing a deep breath, she steeled herself against him. She wanted him, as simply and fiercely as she had ever wanted anything in her whole life, but not at the price of her self-respect.

Meeting his gaze head on, managing to keep her fury and humiliation out of her voice, she said, 'I can give you your answer now.' She tossed back her head, her hair falling heavily down her spine. 'So, I am to understand that I am no longer a woman worthy enough—no longer a woman to whom you will offer marriage. Well, for your information, when I allowed you into my bed I did not know what to expect from you.' Her lips twisted with sarcasm. 'I am sure you will understand when I tell you that when I became completely carried away by your amorous attentions, marriage did not enter my head. And now you have decided we are compatible sexually, I see that you have no use for me at all except my body. I am not supposed to think or feel, I am just supposed to amuse you when you are bored and let you into my bed when you are in the mood. What you want from me is some tainted liaison in exchange for my virtue.'

'Which you have already lost,' he reminded her in biting tones.

The belief that he might love her after all evaporated. In a blinding flash of sick humiliation, Victoria understood that he had done this to degrade her—his monstrous pride had demanded this unspeakable revenge for her crime on their wedding day. Bile rose in her throat as she realised she had submitted to him without a struggle. He hadn't deceived her, she realised with shame and self-loathing, she had deceived herself. He hadn't stolen her virtue, she had given it of her own free will.

'Of course. How foolish of me to forget,' she bit back, blinded with wrath and humiliation, her hands clenched into fists at her sides. 'I've just realised what a monster and a heartless blackguard you really are, Lord Rockford. I am not accepting your offer,' she clarified. The freezing look on his face as he watched her saunter away from him was nothing compared to her own fury. 'When I failed to turn up at the church on our wedding day—for which I have apologised—I was unaware that the same thing had happened to you once before—'

'Would it have made any difference?'

'No. After learning what I did that day, I have to say it would not. I was saying—when you were so stuffed up with your own battered pride and the knock to the inflated opinion you have of yourself, did you stop to consider for one second *why* I had run away?'

'No,' he snapped.

'And so you have judged me ever since without a hearing,' Victoria taunted, too furious to quail before the murderous look tightening his face.

'Very well,' he conceded, eyeing her carefully, curious as to what it was she had learned that had driven her away. 'I am listening now.'

'Now it is too late. It no longer matters. You can go and jump in the river for all I care.'

Laurence stared at her in silence, unable to believe the coolly aloof, self-possessed young woman had become this furious vixen, her eyes sparking with wrath.

Victoria instantly noticed the altering of his expression. He was watching her, his face inscrutable. Suddenly her determination wavered.

She wanted to throw herself across his chest, lock her arms around his neck and plead with him. She wanted to ask for another chance. Perhaps if they went back to Yorkshire… She turned away and pressed her knuckles hard against her lips. It was no use. He had decided, and even if she begged him to take her back as his wife and not his mistress and he agreed, there would always be this thing between them. Driven by the whip of her pride she pushed away a strand of her hair and faced him, trying to hide the pain in her heart, to forget what lay between them.

'I want nothing from you, Laurence. Not now, not ever. Forget the contract you made with my mother. As far as I am concerned you no longer have any say in what I do. You have no rights over me whatsoever.'

'Try telling that to a court of law.'

Victoria's emotions veered crazily from fury to mirth as the absurdity of the bizarre tableau suddenly struck her. She laughed harshly, unable to believe he would go to such lengths to keep her with him. 'I would like to see you try,' she scoffed. 'If, after all this unpleasantness, you wish to continue as my guardian out of some obligation you still feel to my mother—although I shudder to think what she would make of you seducing her daughter last night—

then take me to court by all means. What you did to the girl you were supposed to be *guarding* should make an interesting—and most hilarious—court case, which would do your reputation as a respected and upstanding man of the community and in the world of business no good whatsoever. In short, you would become a laughingstock.'

Laurence's eyes narrowed dangerously. 'Let's just get one thing straight, Victoria. I did not seduce you. As I remember, you were a willing partner.'

She shrugged nonchalantly. 'Whatever. One thing you should know is that I'm going away. I was going to tell you. I didn't want to simply disappear as I did the last time. I've managed to obtain a position as governess to a respectable family—an American family. We are leaving for Liverpool next week, where we are to board a ship bound for New York. Now go away and leave me alone. I never want to see you again.'

Taken completely off guard by her announcement, Laurence hesitated for a moment and then walked out, closing the door quietly behind him. He never raised his voice or slammed doors as Victoria would have done. He lost his temper in an icily controlled way. She found it disturbing. She would have preferred shouting and slams.

Damn you, Laurence Rockford, she thought in helpless rage. She never wanted to think of him again. But she knew that she would be unable to stop thinking about him. She had no power over him or her thoughts. Everything had all been disastrously snatched away from her. She was trapped by her own nature, when all hope was gone, and her vitality ebbed away. Tears came to her eyes, beading on her thick lashes, and trembled without falling.

Over the following days, Laurence tried to purge Victoria from his mind and tear her from his heart with decreasing success. He knew he was losing the battle, just as he knew he had been losing when he'd walked into the Pulteney Hotel and seen her for the first time after she'd jilted him.

Travelling to the docks, he gazed out of the window of the coach, trying to concentrate on the meeting he was going to have with some business acquaintances that day. But it was Victoria he saw in his mind, not ships and profit and loss—Victoria riding beside him—Victoria sitting with her feet in the water on the day he had proposed to her—Victoria looking up at him when he held her in his arms.

She had told him she was leaving—going to America. When she had told him he had thought he didn't care. But he did care. Very much. Wearily he rested his head against the upholstery and closed his eyes, but he couldn't banish her from his mind. Where was she? What was she doing? Was she preparing to leave—never to return?

Whatever thoughts of revenge had driven him to her bed, they were forgotten the moment he'd taken her in his arms and her soft, glorious body had yielded to his. From the moment their lips had met, what had followed had been the most wildly erotic and sexual experience of his life. He wasn't proud of himself for having ruined her and there was the possibility that she might be pregnant as a result of his irresponsibility. With this in mind, unable to bear the thought of spending the rest of his life without her, he refused to allow her to disappear from his life so completely.

The letter! Why hadn't he read her letter? He'd known she was apprehensive about marrying him, but he'd thought she'd got over it. If he hadn't felt so furious and betrayed that day, he'd have gone after her and demanded to know why she'd run away. And then when she'd tried to explain her actions in a letter, he hadn't even had the courtesy to read it, but tossed it unopened into the fire.

Now his anger had diminished enough, he

felt the only reason she could have had for marrying him was because she loved him. Both his heart and his intellect told him that. Halfway to his destination he knocked on the carriage roof and instructed the driver to go to the Pulteney Hotel instead.

Diana watched Laurence stride into the room. A worried shadow darkened her eyes as she patted her elegantly coiffed hair into place and thought about Laurence's unexpected visit. His visits were infrequent and usually disappointingly brief—it seemed odd somehow that when he spent every hour working, he had decided to call on them today.

Laurence stepped swiftly across the carpet and, ignoring her outstretched hands, he caught her in a brief embrace and pressed an affectionate kiss on her smooth forehead. 'You look lovely as always, Diana.'

Diana leaned back, anxiously studying the deeply etched lines of strain and fatigue at his eyes and mouth. 'We're delighted to see you, Laurence. Is there a reason for your visit?'

'No. I was just passing.'

He flopped into one of the chairs and Nathan poured a liberal glass of whisky for him from a decanter that was waiting on the bureau. He smiled his thanks and, feeling the need of the strong liquor to revive his spirits, he took a big gulp at the glass, wishing it would blot out his thoughts, his memory, as it did everything else when he drank too much.

'Have you seen anything of Victoria?' Diana was brave enough to ask—Laurence had told them that if anyone brought up Victoria's name to him again, he could not guarantee not to lose his temper, but Diana would not be threatened.

He took another long swallow of his drink to dull the ache that came with just her name. 'You know very well, Diana, that I saw her at the Pendleton ball and that I danced with her.' He dragged his thoughts away from that night. He preferred the more refined torture of thinking about the joy of her—the tender way she had looked at him when she had been in his arms—how she had melted against him—her kiss—how soft and yielding her body had felt before he had stolen her innocence. 'Why do you ask?'

'I was wondering if you had made things right between the two of you—that now you've heard her explanation—'

His eyes shot to hers. 'Explanation! What explanation?'

'Do you mean she hasn't?'

'No. Why?'

'Because unlike you, I feel a responsibility

for the part I played that day—in fact, we were all responsible.'

'What are you talking about?'

'How much do you know of what happened, Laurence?' Diana asked.

'As much as you do, I expect.'

'You would have learned a good deal more had you read the letter Victoria wrote you,' Diana admonished gently.

'What are you saying?'

'Diana spoke to Victoria at the ball—before you arrived,' Nathan provided. 'After hearing what my wife had to say, it's my opinion that Victoria was justified in doing what she did when she ran away.'

Laurence's eyes snapped to his brother. 'I can't believe you are saying this, Nathan. I have gone through hell keeping the truth about your birth from her. You're the one who didn't want Victoria at the Hall, don't forget. You couldn't wait to see the back of her.'

'I don't deny it, but after giving the matter some *rational* thought and reminding myself that she is, after all, my sister, I would like to do right by her. She does not deserve antagonism from me. None of this is her fault. Victoria knows, Laurence. She knows I'm her brother.'

Laurence stared at him in stunned surprise.

'And how on earth would she know that? How did she find out?'

'When she was about to leave for the church, Clara paid her a visit. She told her everything— about Nathan and how her mother had given him up at birth. She also told her how her education was paid for. There was nothing she didn't spare her.'

'Oh, Victoria!' he gasped softly, the full horror of what Victoria must have experienced registering in his mind. 'No wonder she ran away.'

'Precisely. Not only was she devastated, she felt betrayed—by you—by me, but most of all by her mother. All in all, we have treated her very badly. I'm sorry I made things difficult for you,' Nathan apologised softly. 'I don't think I realised how much you loved her.'

Laurence drained the rest of the glass at a swallow.

'I am right aren't I, Laurence? You do love her, don't you?' Nathan asked.

Laurence answered him sharply. 'I asked her to be my wife.'

'But it's not only that,' Nathan went on recklessly, knowing his brother's anger was just below the surface.

'Yes, I love her. I'm just learning how much I love her as I'll never be able to love again.' He stared at his empty glass, his face grey and his eyes dark with misery. 'Love,' he said. 'Love,' mouthing the word, weighing it. 'How many definitions are there to that one word? When I want to say I love Victoria, it doesn't sound like what I mean.' He banged the glass on the table so hard it cracked. Laurence dropped his voice to a fierce whisper. 'I love her so much it twists my gut. I love her so much that to think of losing her now is like thinking of dying.'

'Then go to her,' Diana said, 'before it's too late.'

He clenched his fists and got to his feet. 'I'll not lose her now, not again . I'll go to her and when I find her I'll tell her this.' He stopped and frowned. 'I don't think I've ever told her I love her. I've said marry me and you're adorable, but I've never told her I love her.'

'Perhaps that's part of the reason she left you, Laurence. Perhaps because you never said it she thought you never felt it.' Nathan was watching him with a strange expression of understanding.

'I'll find her,' said Laurence, 'and this time I'll tell her… If it's not too late.'

Laurence tracked Victoria down to Hyde Park, where she was strolling with Amelia and Mrs Fenwick. The day was fine and sunny and the park was beginning to fill up with Quality.

Being the fashionable hour, in no hurry to return home, Mrs Fenwick was content to sit on a bench close to the Ring and pass the time of day with two ladies of her acquaintance while Amelia and Victoria continued to promenade.

Hyde Park was a source of wonder and delight for Victoria, drawing all classes of a pleasure-seeking society. It was the time and place when every woman was seen as a challenge to the predatory amorist. There was an open and tantalising mingling of the sexes and endless opportunity for intrigue.

Dressed in their finest, the two girls attracted many admiring glances. A gleaming red phaeton driven by Sir John Gibson flashed by, a smug Clara Ellingham seated beside him. She gave Victoria no more than a cursory glance before slipping her arm through her escort's. A group of fashionable dandies astride prime leggy mounts paused to admire and gather round, among them the fastidious Lord Falconbridge. With their high spirits and droll sarcasm and harmless fun, they took it upon themselves to flatter and tease, and Victoria and Amelia took it all in good humour.

Lord Falconbridge nudged his horse close to Victoria. 'Don't look now, Miss Lewis,' he drawled, smirking as he cast a supercilious glance behind her, 'but I believe I see Lord

Rockford bearing down on you. He's certainly persistent, I'll say that for him. But don't be alarmed. I'll protect you,' he said drolly.

Victoria turned around to see a gentleman, wearing an exquisitely cut, dark-brown coat and fawn breeches, with black riding boots polished to a dazzling sheen, mounted on a grey thoroughbred riding towards her, a groom out of his stable close behind. Seeing him again made Victoria's heart quicken its pace. He was almost upon them, his hard stare fixed on her. Her feet rooted to the ground, her heart began to hammer in nervous anticipation and more than a little dread. Then a firestorm of humiliated fury erupted inside her. Not wishing to make a fool of herself, she stood her ground.

Laurence's gaze locked with that of the arrogant Lord Falconbridge. After having been consumed with the need to see and speak to Victoria for the past twenty-four hours, he had been taken aback to find her surrounded by the dandyish fops, but managed to keep his temper in check. Her expression was clearly hostile as she watched him approach, telling him she did not wish to speak to him. This possibility was intolerable to his pride. After all, he had matters of importance to speak to her about and he was not about to be turned away by her or her foppish friends.

He drew rein. After a curt nod in the direction of the dandies, he looked at Victoria. 'Good afternoon, ladies.'

Knowing full well how this unexpected encounter would be affecting Victoria, but choosing to ignore it, for Amelia thought Lord Rockford the most handsome of men and the right choice of husband for her friend, despite their past differences, she beamed up at him.

'Why, Lord Rockford, how nice to see you,' she greeted him with warmth. 'Isn't that so, Victoria?' she enthused.

Victoria was quietly seething. How dare he approach her here? He left her no choice but to speak to him. She stared at him coldly, as though she did not know him—as if he did not exist—then looked away, dealing him a rapier-like snub.

The direct cut stopped him in his tracks, fury searing its way through every vein and artery.

Lord Falconbridge picked up on it immediately. 'I don't think the lady wishes to speak to you, Rockford. I would go on my way if I were you.'

'You're not,' he bit back, wanting to kill him.

Victoria's chest constricted at the surprise and anger she saw in Laurence's face, but she refused to feel guilt. It was the least he deserved for the way he had treated her after the Pendleton ball, but from the corner of her eye, she saw the astonishing speed with which his expression of anger turned into cold disgust.

A small piece of her heart died in that moment. She could not bear to look at him. She was aware of him urging his horse closer and him dismounting. Lord Falconbridge was staring at him through narrowed eyes, as though Laurence were the first fox of the season.

'Miss Lewis appears to have an aversion to you, Rockford. Why do you persist?'

Laurence ignored him. 'I have matters I wish to talk over with you, Victoria. I know you are leaving shortly and there are a few affairs that need to be settled before you leave.'

'If we have anything left to talk about, it can be discussed at the house.'

'I have called at the house, but you're never at home. I would be grateful if you would take a short stroll with me and listen to what I have to say.'

'You must, Victoria,' Amelia said, hoping that what Lord Rockford had to say to Victoria would clear the air between them and stop her leaving for America, which, in her opinion, would be a huge mistake.

Victoria stared at him for a long, indecisive moment. In contrast to all the colourful dandies hovering about her like tropical butterflies, Laurence Rockford was like a dark, forbidding force. Just when she had thought that she would not be affected by his presence ever again, he appeared, and all her carefully tended illusions were cruelly sundered. Why hadn't he stayed away and left her to be reconciled to leaving? Why did he have to prolong her misery?

'Very well,' she said reluctantly.

'I'll go back to Mama,' Amelia said, already tripping away from them. 'We'll wait for you.'

Smiling farewell to her admirers and the glowering Lord Falconbridge, after Laurence handed his mount to his groom, Victoria fell into step beside him, walking over the grass.

'I do hope your intentions are honourable, Laurence.' She tried to sound flippant. 'I seem to be at your mercy and you appear quite determined to compromise my reputation.'

'I think,' he said quietly, with an underlying humour, 'we should go back to my house and talk. On the other hand, I might be tempted to kill you, so perhaps it's as well to be somewhere more public.'

'I know you're loathe to find me here with the detestable Lord Falconbridge, but I beg you to pause to consider if killing me is worth hanging for.'

'Don't tempt me,' he said and his face and

voice were both distorted, made harsh with anger. He caught her just as she was about to turn away from him and pulled her back around, his hands clamped on her arms. 'Come. Let us walk where it's less public.'

'As you wish,' she said, and her own voice was suddenly sad and full of pain. 'But if you hate me that much and you want to kill me, then I'd rather you did.'

Laurence looked at her and she could see that she had pierced his rage, touched a more tender nerve. Quietly, he said, 'Don't be ridiculous. I don't hate you. Quite the opposite, in fact. But you did hurt me when you rejected me.'

'Don't talk to me about hurting. I can be hurt, like I was hurt when my mother died. I can be hurt, learning all those terrible things about her, and I can be hurt trying to unravel what really happened, what was behind it. And then I could be hurt again, by you deceiving me, keeping from me the one thing I really needed to know. It was callous and amoral and it shocks me. How could you, Laurence, how could you? You of all people. You who were supposed to be my friend—almost my husband. I know I ruined that when I left you, and if you weren't so angry with me you'd be able to understand—because—because—' She stopped suddenly, unable to go on—to tell him that she loved him—her voice, dying, smothered by pain and tears.

Laurence's face had quite changed—it was tender and shocked. He put out his hand and touched her face, traced the gentle curve of her cheek and, for a moment, just a moment, she thought he was going to take her in his arms, but she stood there, staring at him, hardly daring to hope, to think.

'I'm sorry I hurt you. Will you listen to what I have to say?'

She nodded. He released her and she spun round to leave. He recaptured her arms. With a pained look in his eyes, he said, 'Don't walk away from me, Victoria.'

'Can you blame me?' she flared, trying, ineffectually, to twist free. 'When I think of what you asked of me—the proposition you put to me—you—you despicable, loathsome wretch.'

Drawing her behind some well-positioned shrubbery, for which he was grateful at that moment, he then released her. 'I have another proposition to put to you.'

'Really? Well, I am not interested in any more of your propositions!' she raged. 'I am still hurting from the last one. You have insulted me once, I will not allow you to do so again.'

He winced at the reminder of his last offer, but he refused to be deterred. 'Victoria, I am asking you to marry me, to be my wife.'

She stared at him with incredulity. 'Your wife? You asked me to be your wife once before, as I recall. You've already used me like a—a whore. I am so ashamed. It was sordid.'

'Don't say that.'

'Why? Because it's the truth? Or are you suffering from an attack of guilt?'

'Guilt?' He gave a harsh, embittered laugh. 'The only guilt I've felt where you were concerned was wanting you for myself the moment I set eyes on you. There was nothing sordid about what we did. We were lovers before that—from the moment your lips touched mine. Why won't you listen, Victoria? Can't you see I am telling the truth?'

Victoria blinked back the tears that threatened. 'I don't know and I no longer care. Stay away from me, Laurence. I'm going to America. It's what I want.'

'I don't believe you—to be at someone else's beck and call. Marry me, Victoria. Be my wife.'

'Aren't you afraid I might not turn up for the wedding again?'

'I'm prepared to risk that.' She was clearly angry and upset and they couldn't very well begin again until the past was dealt with. 'I know what happened—what made you run away. Diana told me that Clara paid you a visit when you were about to leave for the church. I was an idiot. When you didn't arrive, all I could think of was myself. I should have realised it would have taken something drastic to make you turn your back on me.'

Victoria bit back a teary smile, lowering her eyes. 'Yes, it did.'

'Look at me,' Laurence said, tipping her chin up, and this time her glorious eyes looked into his. 'I have several reasons for wanting to marry you. When I close my eyes, all I ever see is your face. There is no place, no time without you. Where I am doesn't matter when we're apart. All I want is you. There are so many things I want to say to you.'

Happiness began to spread through Victoria until it was so intense she ached from it. 'Please don't say that if you don't mean it. I don't think I could bear it.'

'From the very beginning I wanted to tell you there was no woman I had wanted to pursue, except one—you—and you were out of bounds. I did not often regard a woman as out of bounds and I knew why I felt it so strongly about you. I have, in my time with the most efficient ruthlessness, disturbed love affairs—come between friends. But I was not prepared to take you on. I spent long hours wrestling with the reasons why you were so special, why I wanted to be with you, and I was forced to admit it was because you roused feelings I had never felt for any other woman—not even Melissa. These newly awakened feelings did the impossible and made me careful, considerate and unselfish. But I could not pursue you, unless I had my brother's blessing.'

'And in the end you did.'

'Yes.'

'I cannot believe that we are related. You should have told me. It was cruel to let me find out the way I did. I was devastated.'

'I know, and for what it's worth I am sorry about that. Nathan didn't want you told. He hadn't counted on Clara.'

'She couldn't wait to tell me. Her visit at that time had the desired effect. I saw her just now—being driven in a striking red phaeton with a rather handsome gentleman.'

'Sir John Gibson. He's from the north— Newcastle, to be precise—and a widower. He's also a business acquaintance of mine. I introduced him to Clara at the Pendleton ball. Since then the two of them have become inseparable.'

'Long may it continue. Hopefully they will become enamoured of each other and Clara will move to Newcastle.'

'That may well happen. She isn't getting any younger and she's afraid of being left on the shelf. And I know for a fact that Sir John is looking for a wife and mother for his three children.'

'I shudder to think what kind of stepmother she would make. I feel heartily sorry for the children. I find it rather odd that your brother and Diana are staying at Pulteney's when you have a house in London.'

'As a rule they do stay at my house, but when Clara said she would accompany them, aware of her persistence to ensnare me, they considered it prudent to stay at the hotel.'

'I see.' And Victoria did see. The first time she had seen them together on the moor she'd sensed Laurence wasn't attracted to Clara Ellingham in the romantic sense. 'Before she died, my mother said there was something important she had to tell me. I think she wanted to tell me about Nathan.'

'Perhaps you're right. Nathan was the product of my father's dalliance with your mother. She couldn't keep him on her own and, knowing how much my mother yearned for another child, she arranged for her and my father to have him, to raise him at Stonegrave Hall. To your mother it made sense of it all—my father having his son—whom he had wanted desperately—and taking care of him. When she handed him over the day of his birth, that was the last time she saw him.'

'Was—was my mother recompensed in any way?'

'There was no deal made—no money changed hands if that's what you mean. But the understanding was that she would always be taken care of.'

'I think if she had told me, I might have found it easier to cope with. Discovering there was someone else she loved, that she had loved before my father, was difficult to accept, but to find out that they had had a baby was devastating for me. I imagine the child you lose is always the most important. It made me realise she must love him and that was why she never really loved me.'

'Victoria, you are being absurd. Of course she loved you.'

'No, she didn't,' said Victoria flatly. 'She tolerated me, that's the nearest she came to love. I had love, from my father. I can tell the difference.'

'Nathan meant nothing to her—he was either at the Hall or away at school and then university. There was no contact between them in the whole of their lives.'

'But I think she would have liked there to

have been. It—it would have brought him—your father—back as well. If she'd loved him as much as she said she did, she must have thought about him all the time.'

'Maybe she did,' he said, taking her hand and drawing her close. 'We will never know. I have told you that your mother and I were as close as two people could be, coming from different classes and backgrounds, and she worked for my mother. When I needed a friend—which I did from time to time since I was never close to either of my parents—she tried to be that friend. My isolation was complete when Nathan arrived and Betty left the Hall.'

'Was your father hard on you?'

'I have thin experience of the affection that is meant to exist between father and son. He demanded a great deal from me, being the only son and next in line to inherit. When I was twelve years old he insisted I learn all there was to learn about running the estate.'

'But you were only a boy.'

'I was old for my age. By the time he died when I was eighteen, I had already been running things for two years.'

Victoria put her arms about his waist and rested her head on his chest. On the day she should have married him, she had foolishly thought she knew what a broken heart was

like. How wrong she had been, for it was only
now that it was breaking, breaking for the man
she loved, who as a boy had been treated with
indifference by his parents, having to watch
them dote on his brother while he had been
made to realise his responsibilities. She knew
it had been hard to reveal himself, but she understood. Like no one else, she understood. 'We
have much in common, you and I.'

'We have?'

'We both felt unloved by our parents—at
least that's how my mother felt about me. But
I always loved her. Very much.'

'I know.'

She stood back and looked into his face.
'How old were you when Nathan was born?'

'I was six years old when the long-awaited
second son was born. I had no idea how he'd
come into the world then. I watched as my parents doted on him—I was no less smitten—Nathan was an adorable child and hard to resist.
But I learned not to count on my parents' affection and let the hurt and disappointment wash
over me like the river that pours through Ashcomb to the sea. As a youth I was aware of all
I had missed, but, done with pining for my parents' affection, I learned to use my emotions
to fuel my ambitions.'

'And you were successful. Were you resentful of Nathan?'

'Not in the least. He was my brother and I
loved him as a brother. I learned how to fend
off sadness and quell despair by staying busy,
hoping this life lesson, learned the hard way,
would carry me through.'

'When did you find out he was not your
mother's child?'

'When I was fifteen. Nathan was nine.
Giving birth to me had been difficult, leaving my mother incapable of having more children. Apparently she was devastated. When
your mother became with child, they went to
Bath for an extended stay. When they returned
Nathan had been born and it was assumed by
friends and neighbours he was my mother's
son. But servants aren't stupid. It was no secret what was going on between Betty and my
father and that he hadn't shared my mother's
bed since I was born. It generated much talk in
the servants' hall and Father thought the truth
should come from him before we heard it from
someone else.'

'Truth and honesty are always the best way,
Laurence. I wish someone had told me the
truth. It might have shaped my life in a different way, but it would have been kinder to tell
me about Nathan.'

'I knew you were entitled to know all this when I proposed marriage the first time, but forgive me, Victoria, I could not tell you without Nathan's permission. And now,' he said, turning from her so he didn't have to look into her accusing eyes, 'if you really feel you cannot be my wife and would prefer to make your life in America, then I will not pursue you any longer. All I ask is that if…if there is a child after what we did, you let me do my duty in that, at least.'

She stared at his broad back, tears pricking her eyes. 'You have just made me a proposition, Laurence—although I think the position of housekeeper might be more appropriate. I had my doubts about being Lady of Stonegrave Hall the first time. I'm hardly cut out to give house parties and entertain dignitaries and try to look down my nose at everyone else and convince them I am far better than they are. I might have difficulty with that.'

Laurence stiffened and did not speak for a long moment. Then he drew a deep breath and let it out slowly. He turned around. 'You can learn. Although you might have to learn to treat the servants with all your diplomatic kindness, smoothing over any feathers ruffled by the irate lord, who is known to be impatient and not always thoughtful of the feelings of those who work for him.'

'Not to mention difficult to satisfy,' she said quietly, a puckish smile twitching her lips. 'Oh dear, I really do think I might be better cut out to be the housekeeper after all.'

'The position of housekeeper is already taken. However, I do have a vacancy for a wife. But I have several things to ask of you before you consider accepting that position.'

'And what are they?'

'That you give me children—boys and girls in whatever combination you prefer. I will be grateful for any child you may give me. I would like the girls to have your beauty and the boys your courage. I ask that you love them unconditionally and, when you're not lavishing attention on your husband, you lavish on them all the attention and care that was lacking in our own parents.'

Happiness began to spread through Victoria until it was so intense she ached from it. 'Is that all?'

'Not quite.' Cupping her face in his hands, he tilted it to his. 'I want you to be called Rockford,' he said with a tender smile, 'so there is no doubt in anyone's mind that you belong to me. From the day we speak our vows I want us to be together always. I want to share your bed every night and make love to you until dawn and for you to wake in my arms. I love you, Victoria, and I want to hear you say you love me.'

Her heart almost bursting with love and a soft tear coursing down her cheek, Victoria turned her face, kissed the palm of his hand and smiled. 'I do love you, Laurence. So very much.'

Her words filled Laurence with love and pride and he melted beneath the radiant heat of that smile. 'Thank you. From this day on there will be honesty and truth between us always—no more recriminations, no denials or pretence.'

So saying, he bent his head and placed his mouth on hers, parting her lips with his. She crushed herself against him, answering his passion with the same wild, exquisitely provocative ardour that had haunted his dreams since the night of the ball. He dragged his mouth from hers.

'Let us go and find Mrs Fenwick and ask for you to be excused. I want to show you my house,' he said in a thickened voice he hardly recognised. He really meant to show her his bedchamber.

She nodded, knowing exactly what he meant,

and she led him from behind the shrubs and in the direction of an expectant Mrs Fenwick and Amelia.

Mr and Mrs Levinson were disappointed when Victoria told them she could not accept the position as governess to their children, but they wished her well on her forthcoming marriage and said not to worry. The young lady who had been their second choice would be pleased to accept the position.

Nathan came to see her. It had taken almost twenty years, but the first, tentative steps towards something approaching friendship had been taken.

They exchanged many things, putting together things they had been told and had found out for themselves, pieces of fact, half-formed stories—and then they stared at each other in amazement that they should have come so close in so short a time, and they both smiled, and relaxed, sitting back on the sofa together and talking, talking about their mother, who was less of a stranger to Nathan now as they proffered reasons, theories, explanation as to why and how she had behaved as she did, and they felt the first tender, cautious roots of friendship beginning to form between them. At the end of it, Victoria understood at least something of what Nathan had endured and felt the seeds of sympathy for him, since he was the one who had grown up not knowing his birth mother.

Four weeks later, Laurence and Victoria were married at Laurence's house in a private ceremony with no more than thirty guests. Situated in the heart of Mayfair, it was a splendid house. From the basement to the attics, every room had fine furniture and an air of comfort.

The drawing room was aglow with sunlight and perfumed with lavish urns of orchids and white lilies. Wearing a simple cream silk-and-lace gown, Victoria was so happy her heart almost took flight as a proud Nathan walked her down the makeshift aisle on the Aubusson carpet strewn with rose petals. Amelia, beautiful, smiling and serene, her only bridesmaid, walked behind her.

Victoria was acutely aware of what would be passing through Laurence's mind and her heart ached with remorse at what she had put him through the first time. Sensing the moment when she entered the drawing room, he whirled around so violently he almost knocked the prayer book out of the vicar's hand. To save his pride, Victoria summoned up a bright smile and walked to his side.

His eyes blazed with relief. Sensing the absolute rightness of what was about to happen, when they said their vows, there was a reverence in him he had not felt before, a sense of quiet joy, as he slipped the gold band on Victoria's finger.

Epilogue

After the wedding they had returned to Stone-grave Hall. Much to Victoria's relief, the reception had been warm and welcoming from staff, friends and neighbours alike, although no matter how often Laurence told her to the contrary, she could not believe that anyone with the least instinct for class differences could tell she was not a born lady. However, she played the part so well—and possessed the little subtleties of behaviour, the grace-notes of social superiority, that all came naturally to her—and she was so charming that no one would not believe she was anything else.

Laurence and Victoria had eaten breakfast in the privacy of their quarters. The day was overcast and it had just started to rain. Laurence had a busy day ahead of him. He had to go over the ledgers with his steward and he wanted to inspect some farm land. Although he had a very efficient bailiff and a number of able assistants, Laurence liked to keep abreast of things on the estate when he wasn't occupied with his other business affairs.

He stood up now, tall and superbly built, wearing breeches and a tan jacket. Dark hair curling about his head, his handsome features thoughtful as he contemplated the day's duties, he stood for a moment beside the table, and Victoria looked up at him with admiration, telling herself once again how very fortunate she was.

Six weeks had passed since their marriage—six weeks of heavenly peace, yet with a speed that equalled the degree of its pleasure. Victoria had no cause to regret the decision she had made. Catching her looking at him, Laurence smiled.

'Don't forget to take your coat,' she said. 'It is raining and I should hate you to catch cold.'

'You would?'

'Of course. I want you strong and healthy.'

A smile curled his lips, lifting them slightly at one corner, his eyelids drooping seductively over his deep-blue eyes. Although she hadn't meant it to sound provocative, Laurence interpreted it that way, recalling, no doubt, the private times when his being strong and healthy was definitely an asset. In the bedroom he was a potentially sensual male, superlatively aggressive and masterful.

She came to know every aspect of him—his face, the way his lips twitched or the corners dipped when he was about some inanity. Though his eyes twinkled slightly when a mediocrity smote his fancy, he could just as easily give uproarious vent to rich appreciation when she failed to see the cause for mirth. His moods were like the changing character of the seasons, sometimes infinitely gentle, at other times curt and angry because of some injustice or offence. She had learned to read the tensing muscles in his face and the lowering of the brows as forewarnings of a storm and was thankful that his anger was never carelessly applied or anything but just—which was in complete variance to what she had once believed.

She had come to know there was a baseness to him, too, when his kisses could be fierce and demanding, his passion all-consuming. His amorous zeal left her breathless, but thoroughly content in the warm security of his embrace. That aspect of their marriage could not possibly be improved.

Standing behind her, he leaned down and

circled her with his arms, resting his cheek against her head.

'Have I told you recently how extremely lovely you are?'

'About thirty minutes ago.'

'And captivating?'

'You just want to sleep with me,' she accused.

'You're right about that. Come back to bed,' he murmured, his lips nuzzling her ear.

'You're extremely persuasive, but there's no time. You have far too much to do.'

'It could wait.'

She laughed softly. 'You really are incorrigible.'

He caught her earlobe between his teeth and bit it gently. 'And you look absolutely delectable in your lavender robe. Are you wearing anything underneath it?'

'Behave yourself, Laurence. Sally will be back any minute.'

'Sally is the soul of tact. She'd go right back out again. We could make love right here. It would be quite a novelty.'

'You're outrageous.'

'Utterly.'

'The answer is no, definitely not. I think you have married me under false pretences,' she said, feeling her body beginning to respond to his persistent mouth against her ear and the warmth of his breath on her flesh. 'I thought I was marrying a gentleman, not a savage.'

'Are you complaining?' he enquired.

'Go away. I would like to finish my breakfast in peace.'

Laughing softly, Laurence kissed her cheek and stood up straight. She turned her head and gazed up at him, taking his hand in hers and placing a kiss on the back of it.

'Are you happy, Victoria?' he asked, his eyes caressing her upturned face.

'Extremely.'

'No regrets?'

She shook her head. 'No. How could I? I have a passionate husband, a wonderful house to live in here in Yorkshire and one in London, with loyal servants and everything I could possibly want. I am a very fortunate woman.'

'I'm the fortunate one,' he murmured on a more serious note. 'You're my life, Victoria. I cannot bear to think that because of my stupidity I almost lost you.'

'Then the next time I write you a letter, make sure you read it. If you had read it, you would have understood. It cannot happen again, Laurence.'

He grinned. 'Don't tell me you're going to

be the kind of wife who will come after me with a broom.'

'It won't be a broom—nothing so delicate. It will be a shovel.' Hearing him chuckle softly as he turned from her and strode to the door, she said, 'Laurence.' Pausing, he looked back. 'Are *you* happy?'

Walking back to where she sat, he raised her out of the chair and held her tight. 'I couldn't be happier.'

Victoria fell under the spell of his heavy-lidded eyes and slid her arms round his neck, holding him close. 'I'll make you even happier. I swear I will.'

Placing his lips on hers and feeling her body melt against his, Laurence felt joy within his heart that he could not describe, filling him up in a way he had never thought possible.

It was instant, and would last for the rest of his life.

* * * * *

A sneaky peek at next month...

HISTORICAL

IGNITE YOUR IMAGINATION, STEP INTO THE PAST...

My wish list for next month's titles...

In stores from 1st November 2013:

- ☐ Rumours that Ruined a Lady – Marguerite Kaye
- ☐ The Major's Guarded Heart – Isabelle Goddard
- ☐ Highland Heiress – Margaret Moore
- ☐ Paying the Viking's Price – Michelle Styles
- ☐ The Highlander's Dangerous Temptation – Terri Brisbin
- ☐ Rebel with a Heart – Carol Arens

Available at WHSmith, Tesco, Asda, Eason, Amazon and Apple

Just can't wait?

Special Offers

very month we put together collections and
nger reads written by your favourite authors.

ere are some of next month's highlights—
nd don't miss our fabulous discount online!

n sale 1st November   On sale 1st November   On sale 18th October

Save 20%
on all Special Releases

Find out more at
www.millsandboon.co.uk/specialreleases

*Visit us
Online*

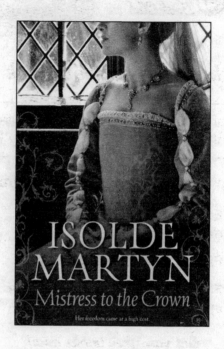

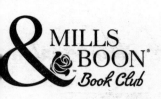

Join the Mills & Boon Book Club

Want to read more **Historical** books?
We're offering you **2 more** absolutely **FREE!**

We'll also treat you to these fabulous extras:

- 🌹 **Exclusive offers and much more!**

- 🌹 **FREE home delivery**

- 🌹 **FREE books and gifts with our special rewards scheme**

Get your free books now!

visit www.millsandboon.co.uk/bookclub
or call Customer Relations on 020 8288 2888

S/ONLINE/H1